THE WAY OUT

Judith Mehl

PENNYSTONE PRESS

Also by Judith Mehl...
The Kat Everitt Handwriting Analysis Mysteries

FORMULA FOR MURDER
GAME, SET, MURDER
MURDER MOST FLORAL

The Lizzie Ort Herbal Sleuth Mysteries
FOUNTAIN OF DEATH

Learn more at www.judymehl.com

This is a work of fiction. Names, character, most places and incidents are the products of the author's imagination or are used fictitiously and are not to be construed as real. Any resemblance to actual events, locales, organizations, or persons, living or dead, is entirely coincidental.

Pennystone Press
ISBN-13: 978-0-9862766-7-5
ISBN-10: 0-9862766-7-7

Printed in the United States of America.

THE WAY OUT

The Way Out is dedicated to the tireless individuals
who work to aid victims of substance abuse, and ease
the fallout of addiction on the lives around them.

This book is a mystery with witty, fun characters weaving their way
through a serious problem. *The Way Out* follows the inimitable Lizzie
Ort tackling crime. Yet, it's bigger than the characters. It's a plea to
open our eyes and delve into recovery solutions for, and prevention of,
opioid drug addiction before the epidemic worsens. And it's a warning
to hurry—time is running out in the hourglass.

CHAPTER 1

Lizzie's powerful fingers strangled the steering wheel. It was a test of will. Of control. To stay on the right side of God she'd have to contain her frustration and let the steering wheel live. If only to avoid crashing the car. She breathed deep, slowing her rhythm, then loosened her bunched fingers. If a run up a mountain couldn't affect Lizzie's breathing, she sure wouldn't let that implacable obstructionist do it.

Stonewalled by a bureaucrat. At a meeting to help teens, no less. Why won't those nitwits recognize the harm teens suffer from opioid drug addiction? Their own, their parents, their friends. A teen center could abate the dangers from all three. Instead the weasel of a principal and his cohorts whitewashed the problem.

Driving home from the meeting, Lizzie wondered how deep their heads dug into the sand. She'd only asked for their backing of a teen center concept, not their gold fillings. Punching her front door in with the flat of her hand, she shoved and grumbled. She hated meetings. And to have no success in her plea transmitted acid into her cast iron stomach.

At home now, the day was on an upswing. Time with Delia, her cheerful and loyal sister, would calm her down. The promise of tranquility through commingling with herbs in the garden would cool her anger. Herbs don't mouth insensitive, shortsighted inanities.

Then she found Delia, just sitting there. Tears jerked her body. Unlike her own wrinkled appearance, Delia's usually unlined face belied her elder status by eleven months at age eighty-three. Now, her face looked ravaged. She sat on the antique sofa, one hand resting on the curlicued wooden arm, polished to a rich gleam. The other held her slumped forehead.

Lizzie knelt next to her. "Delia, my dear, what happened? I haven't seen you cry since you were five and your bike sat mangled in the road."

More composed, Delia raised her head and sniffed. "You forget, I also had a broken leg."

"But I do remember the one thing you moaned, "My bike, my bike. That stupid car ruined my bike.""

Delia stood up swiftly and rammed her hands down at her side. "This time it's not a bike. It's a human being. It's little Tyler."

"Little Tyler? Isn't he in his teens?"

"Okay, so he's fourteen." Delia said, then sniffled again. "Somehow I let the friendship fade away and hadn't realized what a horrible situation Tyler's mom, Emily, lived in. Maybe I could have helped and Tyler would still be at home."

Lizzie took her hand, opened her fingers, then gently pulled her to the kitchen table. "I'm fixing tea, then I'll get the full picture and work from there."

Delia succumbed. Not her usual response. Normally, Delia would fix tea for her. The kettle shrieked. Lizzie raced around the sunny kitchen, preparing the weakest, and thus, fastest, tea possible.

Fresh picked herbs sat in a glass of water on the oak table, ready for snipping—a typical Delia move. Over the years, Lizzie had learned most of the herbs and their uses. Her sister's expertise drew many seeking help, but there was such a thing as osmosis of knowledge. These were parsley, oregano, and basil—a sure bet for soup, though the lunch hour passed long ago.

What could have made her sister so frazzled? Delia never forgot meals. They both worked in the garden now that Lizzie was retired, but Delia tenaciously clung to her role as chef. Thank heavens. Lizzie didn't mind dirt on her hands. She'd lived with that a long time. But cooking? She might poison them the first day out.

Tea she could handle. Delia had dried and labeled the herbs. Her own knowledge led to historical usage. Which herbs decorated the mummies for help in the afterlife. Dried and dead. That she could expound on. But even Lizzie knew that chamomile calmed.

The timer rang. Two minutes would have to do. She slid her sister's favorite mug, delicately adorned with spring flowers, into Delia's cold hands. The warmth would help, though the taste might not meet Delia's standards. Sitting down, she yanked her own chair closer, and leaned forward, elbows on the table.

Not a coddler by nature, she instinctively took charge, and spoke with firmness. "What's with Tyler?"

Delia drank her tea and swallowed loudly.

"Okay Delia. Tell me now. What happened to him?"

"I don't know. He's missing. Emily's an old friend, though she's been distant in past years. That jerk of a husband deserted her eons ago. She raised Tyler on her own."

"And?"

Delia looked straight at Lizzie and didn't flinch or hold back. "Emily's afraid he's gone. She confessed she thinks he's been on some drugs. In with the wrong crowd." She sipped more tea.

Lizzie saw that Delia was more collected now, but before she could question her, Delia lifted her head and said, "She's frightened, panicky. He's been gone three weeks and barely stayed at home before that. He's only fourteen. His mom called everyone she could think of from the school phone. They'd disconnected her home phone long ago. But she doesn't know his, you know, his druggie friends."

Lizzie arched her back. Drugs she knew. Kids she didn't. She tried to remember Emily, picture a shape, a blurred image. Nothing came. But Delia had a myriad of friends.

"Did Emily contact the police?"

Delia sniffed again, most of the tears gone now as she bucked up and attempted to address the problem with her usual stoic calm. "She feared calling them. What if they found him with drugs? With little Heather at home, four years old, she didn't know what she'd do if they arrested him. Or her."

"But what if he's in danger?"

Delia sipped the last of the tea. "I tried to tell her that, but she burst into tears again and wouldn't listen." Delia stood to study the newest emerging plants through the large window. Most people didn't have picture windows in their kitchen looking onto a vegetable garden, but Delia and Lizzie defied the norm in many ways. Outside that window new growth spurted from the ground everywhere, portending spring, a bright and enlightening time of year.

Delia turned to Lizzie. "She left a few minutes ago, sobbing, hugging Heather so tight she cried." Her tormented sister's eyes pleaded, "Could you help me find Tyler? I wouldn't know where to begin. But you would."

Lizzie appreciated the confidence in her abilities, but felt it necessary to point out, "I might, if he was lost in some hovel in a foreign country. But here, in safe ole Mountain View?"

Her sister went limp and plopped back into the chair. "Please?" She leaned forward. "They live around those old shacks at the edge of the woods. Nowheres near the big town in stature."

Lizzie barely remembered that area. Maybe it wasn't this nasty back when she explored as a teenager. She didn't have time to reconnect with old haunts since she moved back home.

"Of course I'll help. Did Emily give you any leads? Names of friends we could talk to?"

Delia's frown lines converged. "His mother said there were few. He acted embarrassed to bring them home. She kept the bungalow spotless, as best she could in that bad part of town."

Lizzie sat and bounced her knee in frustration. "There must have been somebody."

"She did mention a friend, Ethan, but she hasn't seen him in weeks."

"Okay. First, I'll nosy around the school. They know me. The principal attended the meeting this morning. Didn't give me any support for the teen center I advocated. Maybe he'll feel guilty and answer my questions."

This time Delia laughed. Quiet, but a distinctive laugh. Warm. Delightful to hear.

Delia said, "Fat chance. That Matthew wouldn't bend if a hurricane blew through. And I'm sorry he didn't support the teen activity center. Still, I can't believe he bashed your biggest foray into helping out the local community."

Occupied with leafing through her book of phone numbers, Lizzie raised her eyes to Delia's sympathetic ones and pursed her lips, appreciating her concern. She paused. "Some bread would be good."

"Wonderful idea." Delia's tall, slim body slid smoothly into action. For her, if it wasn't digging with a trowel and planting outdoors, then cooking took over. She tied on her apron. "Making bread relaxes me. You're right about Matthew though. I hope he helps with Tyler."

Lizzie perused the phone book, a small one, since in her former life, phone numbers were locked in her brain, not written down. She took a minute to respond. "It was a long shot. I don't know teens well enough. Or this community. What I do know is that this area, all of Pennsylvania, is ripe for drug dealers and the forging of new gangs, and worse, victims. These things I know. I can't let our community go the way of the drug-drenched foreign countries where the innocent traveled in fear. Not to mention the filth and shredded shirts and torn pants that flagged the worst of circumstances."

Delia frowned. "We'll get these young lads the help they need. May take a little time." Then she dredged the counter with flour and dug in.

Lizzie sensed bread on the horizon, and imagined the delicious scent of a new loaf in her head before Delia began. She took that as her cue to look for the principal's number, again. Ahh, there it was. Next time she'd know not to write it under 'D' for dimwit. She called his secretary first. Direct lines were handy, but she'd followed the circuitous route many a time to the answer she needed. Since old Matthew hadn't taken kindly to her forceful overtures this morning, she'd try a maneuver.

Before she dialed, Delia interrupted, shaking flour from her hands before she fiddled with her fingers, and spoke. Slowly. "Umm, tone down the interrogations when doing this. I know you're not used to dealing with normal humans, what with all your years in the CIA."

"You mean, like, just ask them soft questions in a kind manner?"

Delia rolled her eyes at the sarcasm and went back to bread making.

Lizzie debated checking with Tyler's mom first, but Emily seemed the type to need a cooling off period. And Lizzie didn't harbor patience for tearful women. Unkind in some ways, but often necessary. This time, she'd find out more from an unbiased source, before she tackled the mom.

Lizzie grabbed the cordless phone and wound around Delia through the kitchen into the living room. She watched Delia snip numerous fresh herbs, then glide back to the dough, like a ghost, as if her thoughts were mired in more than flour. The pungent scent of oregano, one of her own favorite herbs, followed her. She gave it credit for much of her strong constitution throughout life. Delia's use of it today convinced her that she was sealing a point, thanking her for her assistance. Lizzie saw no need to disturb her. To see her sister, who always radiated enthusiasm and hope, so bothered by this missing child, broke Lizzie's heart.

Finding people was Lizzie's bailiwick. She hoped when it mattered to Delia she wouldn't fall short. All those years serving her country, patriotic. Not helping her sister, unforgivable.

She stood near the front window, inhaled the sweet scent of lavender that reigned in the living room most of her life. She chose a tone of voice and sequence of words to entice Matthew's personal assistant, Elizabeth, into aiding her search for Tyler by finding his friend.

Lizzie moved to the garden to walk around the culinary beds, where green shoots raised their heads through the soil, interspersed with plants already reaching their prime. Swiss chard stood tall, waving in the breeze, ready to pick. What a vegetable. It contained a whole alphabet of vitamins and minerals. The stroll provided time for focus, to compose her words, and begin with chitchat between herself and Elizabeth, easing slowly into her request for restricted information about Ethan.

She said, "Elizabeth dear, I'm glad the new reading program that we set up a few months ago is well underway. I feared we would have to wait until the fall. Great job." Humming in silence while the woman chattered effusively, Lizzie's blunt nature forced her to interrupt, as much as she knew the value of conversation in communication. "Thank you. Good to see it helping. I donated anonymously, remember. I could, however, use your help in an urgent matter."

Upon her request for Ethan's address and information on his whereabouts, the woman reverted to the stalwart guardian of student information. Lizzie prevailed. She asserted, elevated the urgency, wheedled. And finally got what little there was. An address, and a worry that no one had heard from him.

Whispering into the phone, Elizabeth said. "Even Tyler's mother came here asking if Ethan had come to classes. I checked around myself. None of the kids that knew him had seen him."

Armed with the unsaid nuances, and the meager information she imparted, Lizzie thanked her and sat down to plan an attack. Tulip buds popped out on short lime green stems in the last few days, adding spikes of color to the emerging landscape. Deep red buds stood firm and strong, tightly woven and waiting for the kiss of the sun to open wide and smile for the lucky few who strolled by. In the many years Lizzie came home for a respite from the dank horrors of her job, she'd never been here when the early flowers bloomed. She snuggled down onto the time worn oak slats in the garden bench, raised her head and sniffed spring.

A huge contrast to the offal of the streets she'd wandered in Calcutta. She'd been to many sad places, with destitute people. Bucharest, Mali, Macedonia. Of course, her job always took her to the nastier avenues of countries, not the new and gleaming high rises.

This time there'd be no enemy, at least she hoped not. If Tyler'd become addicted to drugs, then these were the immediate danger. How did you fight a pill? Lizzie could fight a person. Once she'd determined where to find the solution if it became necessary, she settled on the more urgent need, how to find a young lad.

Not her normal course of events. Time to change her methods with retirement, and God, her new guide, at her side. Somewhat changing. Finding was finding, after all. She lingered briefly, analyzing the flower beds instead of her usual, how to plot murder. Delia had nothing to worry about. She'd already morphed back into a normal human being.

The concept of stillness without purpose was alien to her. Rising, straight and tall, she surged forward. Had Tyler chosen to hide, or worse, no longer controlled the decision?

She must ferret him out.

CHAPTER 2

Taking the lead on the visit to Tyler's mom, Delia parked their nondescript Ford sedan at the edge of the street, which lacked a curb and true definition. What pretended to be a lawn marked the boundary between public and private property. She walked slow, looking around at the summer cottages up and down the street masquerading as homes, with shingles falling off and cardboard over windows. Probably the one attempt at protection. Delia was appalled at the lack of safety and warmth those in poverty endured.

Emily waved her and Lizzie into the kitchen, "Come sit. We've got the window open. It's warm for an early spring day."

Delia took note of the mystified expression on her friend's face. She understood. Though friends with Delia for years, they'd always met elsewhere. Delia now suspected Emily felt shame in her shabby home despite the attempts to hide the decaying walls. She smiled and thanked her, ever congenial, and introduced Lizzie. She held back the flattery, but her face radiated pride. "My sister recently retired from the CIA. I admire her abilities, and am delighted she's come home to stay."

Wanting Emily at ease, she swiveled to look out the window over the sink for a moment to think, and found a way—praise. "What a heavenly scent. Is that rosemary growing there?"

"Yes, one of the few herbs I can grow indoors. The light is perfect for it here, I guess."

Touching the tender leaves, Delia looked at Emily with new regard. "That's an extremely difficult plant to sustain indoors. You stand out in a crowd of many who have tried and failed. The Lord has blessed you."

She nodded her thanks, though the praise didn't seem to alter her despair. The grooves in her face never lifted into the resemblance of a smile, though her eyes held a glint of hopefulness at their arrival. She asked no questions. Maybe she feared the answer, and patience appeared her norm.

As they sat in the cracked vinyl chairs, Delia suggested her sister might be able to help locate Tyler. Emily straightened quickly, with renewed vigor. Her long wavy brown, hair hung clean and becoming, despite the scraggly ends. As did the child's. She wondered what had brought them to this.

Delia had briefed Lizzie on Emily's story, at least the parts she knew. The school provided minimal information, and certainly nothing personal about Tyler's parents. Delia talked her inimitable brand of heartwarming chatter, giving Lizzie time to observe and absorb, something she did well. As Emily talked, Delia noticed little hints of poverty, and fewer indications of financial stability. No desk holding bills, no pillows on the hand-patched sofa, no TV. She knew that Lizzie saw this and more. The perceptive ability came with her sister's past and had become ingrained. Delia envied it, but kept on track.

"Please have some tea with me," their hostess said, busying herself at the stove while the sisters eyed her attempts at keeping the squalor at bay. Delia sighed. So near to Grandham in miles and yet distant in culture, these streets had no formal town name, but a resemblance to inner city streets of the poor worldwide.

Gracious as a queen, Emily presented tea in chipped cups with a little bowl of sugar. Delia wondered, could it be the last in the house? Both sisters declined the sweetener. No need to tighten Emily's struggle for the family's food.

Her daughter, Heather, sat tucked in a tiny niche of the room set off as a play area. She scrambled around the floor, visible but out of hearing range, if they remembered to curtail their voices. She played with a few raggedy but clean characters resembling dolls, holding one in each hand and whispering admonitions to both of them as to behavior.

Next to the child sat a funny creature. Like a monkey in a blue sweatsuit. It leaned on her, neglected at the moment.

Her mother's hard-edged face softened around the jaw as she watched her daughter. But otherwise that face mapped a rough existence in past years. Only her eyes portrayed a lightness of spirit yet to be squelched. In the end, her missing son might dim them forever. Delia hoped to prevent that final blow to her humanity. She knew Lizzie would help.

With time as the enemy, Lizzie coaxed answers from Emily while Delia kept the tea flowing, and offered some, masking a good dose of milk, to the child. Lizzie couldn't help but hear her as she wheedled, "Would you enjoy some of our oolong tea? We don't often give it to children, but you are such a well-behaved sweetie I thought you could have a cup."

Even at four, the child mustered a sweet smile and recognized a compliment, not realizing that Delia hoped to provide her as much nutrition as possible in the transaction. Heather reached with slow movements for the cup, cradling it as the prize it was. Her bright eyes peered up behind long bangs. "Can Lily and Marcus have a sip? I be verrrrry careful."

Lizzie watched as Heather first cuddled the monkey, and with a gentle firmness, held his head to give him a fake sip. With a wide grin, she said. "Marcus loves tea, and he never spills."

Heather picked up her doll, Lily, next. Delia winked at Lizzie, and stayed with the charming child—her clue to Lizzie to focus on the mother while the child stayed occupied.

Delia eavesdropped while playing with Heather, and pretended to steal Marcus to make the child laugh. Lizzie and Emily's voices floated in. She listened as her sister established background and nuance.

Lizzie said, "Tell me about Tyler."

And Emily did. "Such a divine baby, and smart."

She hung her head. "His dad didn't marry me after all, and left me with Tyler when he was two years old. Barely a toddler. I never saw that man again."

Lizzie asked, "How did you manage with a small child and no financial support?"

Delia held in her smile. Lizzie knew no social byplay.

Emily lowered her head. "God was with me. We had this house, and right after that man left, the landlord disappeared. No one came to collect rent."

Lizzie continued. tipping her head gently, "And for food?"

"I stood in line at the food pantries. We walked to the bus, Tyler and me, and people at the pantry also offered me clothes. They insisted." Her head and voice drifted lower. "I felt humbled, but grateful."

What a life Emily had lived. Thank God Lizzie didn't push any further. Delia clutched Marcus and waved her finger at him. "You be a good monkey. No sassing." Delia shifted slightly to better see her friend's face. She saw her flick her eyes one way, then the other, maybe in undeserved shame.

Lizzie finally prompted, "And what about Tyler?"

Emily smiled. "A mother's delight. Acted mature most of the time. I guess he sensed the situation. I took pride in seeing him start school. He got all A's. And praise, till lately."

Her hands rested on the table while she spoke of her son. "The name, Tyler, means sensitive and affectionate, you know. And that he has an imagination."

Lizzie added, "They also say those with that name are spiritual, and help others."

Emily's voice wavered in uncertainty and her hands brushed across tearless eyes. "Do you think he's doing that now. Helping others?"

Lizzie didn't answer.

Delia listened to Heather chatter, while hoping to overhear more from Emily.

"I married, and my new husband, John, never minded having him around. But John was gone all the time. No idea what he did. He wouldn't speak of a job or tell me where he was going."

"Is John around now?"

"No, he left shortly after Heather was born. I cried constantly at first."

"You couldn't get a job?"

"I had one. But I fell and fractured my back. Lost my job. I wore a brace for months. But I still have terrible pain."

Extending her hand, patting Emily's, Lizzie said, "My heart aches for you. Do you have anything for the pain?"

"A prescription. It helped. But it costs a lot. There's not much left."

Lizzie squinted. "What kind? Maybe we can get you more."

Emily rose to find the bottle. She returned, saying, "Here. It's oxycodone. But there's only three left. I thought I had at least a few more than that. I haven't been taking them every day. I can't afford to."

Delia saw Lizzie swallow her suspicions. She joined them at the table. No need to scare Tyler's mom. In preparation for the teen center, they both researched opioid prescription drugs and avenues of access. Delia hoped Tyler wasn't involved in the frightening opioid epidemic happening among the young in their rural area.

Delia sensed Lizzie's concern and moved into the conversation. "You're no longer able to work then?"

"Nothing that will pay for day care," she muttered.

Lizzie spoke with sharp words. "Tyler's not a child anymore. He may be fourteen, but more mature in some ways than others his age. We need to find him."

Would that curtail Emily's despair? Delia waited to see. The mother cleared her throat and expressed her gratitude.

Delia looked to Lizzie for confirmation, then plunged to their conclusion. "If he helped you in the past, he probably wouldn't disappear and leave you alone. We must find him quickly. He may need us this time."

"Yes, yes. What can I do?"

Lizzie resumed the lead in questions while Delia leaned forward, anxious now to be out there, searching.

"Name his friends. Tell us whatever you know," Lizzie said.

"No friends come over here. Well, Ethan did a few times. Tyler talked about him the most. How Ethan protected him at school. They always went away to play those video games." Her brow wrinkled. "Um, he said nothing but good about Ethan, mind you, but after

Tyler disappeared I looked for Ethan. I heard people talk." Her head jerked up. "Not about Ethan. About his dad. They called him a drug dealer. Maybe that's why the family took off in the night."

"Lizzie can look into that. But for now, let's see what else we can learn about Tyler that might help. What kind of games did he play?"

"You know, like I said, computer games."

"Where? What kind?"

His mother winced. "I don't know. When he was young, he told me everything. Nothing since he became a teenager. I'd ask, but I got shrugs."

Delia patted her hand. "It's okay, dear. You've been a good mother in difficult circumstances. He is acting like most teenagers, but then, he is one."

Lizzie smiled. "It sure sounds normal. Any idea what kind of games he plays? Maybe it would provide us a clue to where he is."

Emily started. Then hesitated. "I think it had to do with mines. I heard Tyler and Ethan mumbling about it once or twice. They seemed happy, enthusiastic."

"Hmm. Enthusiastic about mines. That's a new twist."

Delia jumped up. "Wait a second. I know a game. It's Minecraft. I helped at day care for a while." Then she fell back into her chair, holding her head in her hands. "But it's similar to Legos. I don't think your son and his friend have been playing Legos at their age. We'll check."

Delia knew it was a lead. She bit her lip in surprise when Lizzie asked instead, "Can you describe more about how Tyler acted in the last couple of months?"

Emily lifted her chin and hesitated. "His grades dropped. Hungry all the time. But that's normal for a teenager, isn't it? And . . ." She paused. Her voice fell. "We didn't have much food some days. I did the best I could."

Delia's eyes, glassy with tears, looked to her sister. This family will never go hungry again. Not with her plentiful garden. There wasn't much growing right now, but she'd been out to prepare the beds. She'd spouted endlessly to Lizzie on what seeds would go where, what plants she would buy from the organic growers, what soil needed a touch of fertilizer. Each year they grew more than needed—on purpose. She shared.

Neither sister said anything now, but understood each others' thinking.

Lizzie interrupted the silence. Delia tilted her head, recognizing the sidetrack from immediate concerns. "Boys develop slowly over their teen years. First, they can control coordination which is why many prefer physical activity. They also crave excitement, but things that require low effort. Video games work. That's normal."

She opted not to add that many reach age twenty-five before they learn good emotional control and reasoning. She gave Emily a minute to recover, then switched gears and asked again. "Any other concerns you had?"

"He seemed tired despite being in bed all night. I thought maybe it was because he played those computer games with the other kids. When I asked, he'd hedge. Wouldn't talk. There's no place for teens to hang out around here. I heard about centers in other towns."

Emily scrunched her shoulders in defeat. "Maybe they played at the bar a few streets down?"

"Have you ever seen him there?" Lizzie asked.

"No, I would never take Heather to such a smutty place. We took a walk that way once, but there were two large men on the corner. Smoking. Cursing."

She looked over at her daughter. Seemed relieved she still slept. "I turned her right around and we marched home. We walk the other way. Safer. Now that she's older we can make it to the park sometimes."

Delia knew the area. "That's a long walk."

Emily cringed. "I know. And she's heavy if I have to carry her back home. What else can I do?"

"When does she start school?"

"Next fall. Then the bus will come here. They have to. But not the same one as Tyler. I hope she'll be safe."

The sisters left with a photo of Tyler to plan. His disarming smile held no secrets and also, no distinguishing features. But it might help. Though they had no game plan, they left an aura of hope behind.

CHAPTER 3

Lizzie awoke in the early hours after midnight, dressed in her dirtiest gardening pants, and left without making a sound. Though she'd professed to leave her old ways behind, some had melded into her, and she couldn't change. Movement without breaking the silence, a maneuver from her covert days in the field, aided her exit.

Anyone out there could hear the slight snick of her shoes as they hit the sidewalk, until she shifted to the packed surface of scruffy lawns. She sped to her reconnaissance mission. Furtiveness didn't bother her. A good attribute, stealth saved her life many a time. She chose a starting point. Tonight she wanted to check around the corner bar by Tyler's home. She tucked her hair under an old ratty watch cap that had served her purposes time and again in the past. One of the few items she'd brought home with her.

She jogged the few miles to the area Emily had mentioned, the travel method another action from her past. Her muscles grumbled, then remembered the rhythm. Some of the areas she'd visited in her work with the CIA didn't lend themselves to modern conveniences, like cars. You blended. Until it was time to strike. Tonight she would commingle and search.

Would the bar compare to the ratholes in Mali where cocaine tamped down men's sorrows until they turned into needy non-human creatures with no ethics or rules? She couldn't envision that, in what used to be a quaint country area of kind farmers and milkmaids. Okay, they have milking machines now. But this ex-farm reeked of more than sour dairy.

She scrunched up to the side of the brick building. Despite its grime, it offered safe cover in dark shadows. She scampered sideways to avoid a grey-black mass tucked next to the wall. It moved, but she skittered further out to avoid stepping on it. A drunk, under a scruffy cloak. Hmm, great disguise to get her inside. She would borrow it and return it unharmed—hopefully. Her stealth training came to the fore and she confiscated the cloak with a light twitch that flicked it off the body, the man unaware he'd been denuded of the holey warmth.

Scuzzy it was, but she'd seen similar before. Maybe not ever worn it, but she could delouse later. Right now she wanted to check inside. She doubted that Tyler and his friend ever frequented here, and was sure his mother, Emily, had never been inside. Certainly not in the bar at night. The pale light of morning sometimes camouflaged buildings into seemingly innocent brick and mortar.

As she approached the door she heard men mumbling. Despite the distance, she caught a few pieces of it. The lean guy with a shoulder twitch spoke loudest, saying, "That's what they call it?" He laughed enough to shake his whole back.

Hmm. Laughter. Maybe he didn't have anything wrong with his shoulder; she'd have to look out for him. Couldn't deal with too many surprises right now, and he moved smooth when not laughing. Drunk, but walking *into* the bar. How bad could he be? The other guy may have had a beer belly years ago, but in the intervening time it had become a beer body, muscle replaced by liquor over time.

Liquor drunk she could handle, and hoped that's all she would find here.

Beer body swayed and crushed her shoulder for an instant. "Whyn't you watchin' where your going?" he muttered.

Loud curses followed. Words that didn't include an apology. She'd heard enough, though, to notice no beer breath. Maybe there was more than beer in the guy.

She knew that a pill abuse epidemic in Staten Island took barely half a decade to morph into a heroin crisis, where overdose deaths grew rapidly into the hundreds in the city. And the crisis spread west, into Pennsylvania. Her days in New York City rivaled her years in the desert, only the death of choice changed.

Her thoughts had reached back a little too far and she moved into what she might find today. Somehow she doubted that it would be a brightly lit game room with a small bar on the side for family drinks. Time to know for sure.

Shuffling to the bar she dragged the right leg a little. She knew how to mislead. The ratty cloak, lowered head, hunched shoulders, bum leg equaled weak—not a threat.

A slight injury to her vocal cords caused a permanent raspiness to her voice, convenient when she needed to portray a coarse male image. A long bout with laryngitis irritated her at the time while in the field, and seeking the man who'd punched her in the throat. The second reason to find him.

Mission accomplished, she'd skipped the medical attention and moved on. Her throat healed eventually, and the new voice suited her cover. Doing covert work for the government in foreign lands caused enough problems for women without her sounding breathy and little girlish.

Her voice crackled perfectly when she dropped her arm to the bar, nodded to the bartender, and gasped, "Give me a beer." The huge sign on the wall carried a smudged over name, 'Jumpin' Lizard' and made sure she knew how much it would take to feed her soul—one shot at a time.

"Waddya want?"

"Your cheapest beer."

"Show me the dough."

Delving into her jacket pocket beneath the cloak, she fished out a crumpled single. Her other hand scrounged around her pocket hoping to convert the lint into another dollar. Finally she pulled out the correct change. So what if one of the coins looked faded and bent as if it'd been through the war. It probably had. But the dirty coins had come in handy. Thank heavens they were American.

She knew not to bring lots of money on these little trips but forgot to come prepared. Looks like her comfy work jacket never made it through the wash before she came home, or after. It'd hung in the back of her closet since. Who needed that kind of jacket at a nice resort in Florida? She started her retirement in earnest there, in a trip with her sister right after she returned from her final job in Bucharest. St. Pete Beach registered high on great relaxation. Until they found the dead body. Retirement wasn't going too smoothly as yet.

She chuckled to herself. That's for sure. Look where she was at the moment? She turned her head back as the bartender slipped the glass in front of her. Years of sensing movement around her timed it perfectly.

The beer added to her cover. An essential prop. She took a swig. "Gak!" The next miniscule swallow barely touched her throat. Too dainty for her role, but the swill was tough to take. She hated the stuff. The drinks in Istanbul were rot gut but seemed smooth compared to this.

Then she felt sorry for those who couldn't afford anything else. Of course, maybe they should be spending their money on getting a leg up in the world. Open mind, Lizzie. Open mind. She didn't dare beseech God here, though he'd hang out in the strangest places. His mind must be more open than hers.

She swiveled around enough to see half the room. Nothing spoke kid-friendly here. Studied everything in a quick glance, then shuffled her feet the other way, kept her head down, and picked out discrepancies she could contemplate later. These weren't locals. Look at those shoes. She muffled the whistle. Not appropriate here, she realized in time. The shiny shoes were one item of note.

The left side of the room catered to elegant drunks, while a scan of the right side of the room revealed shoes worn and ready for boot heaven. More appropriately, hell, since these men looked to be drinking their way to a quick end.

Her hearing still better than most, she eavesdropped shamelessly. Voices clamored everywhere. She tuned up her mental filter and zeroed in on a few words here and there. Nothing that would help. How on earth could this crowd lead her to Tyler?

The light was too dim inside to see her reflection in those fancy shoes to her left. It would take a touch of sun to use them as a mirror. As she took a slug of the watered down beer, she overheard one of the fancy shoe crowd say, "This place." Nose raised high, he swiveled his head from one corner to the other. "Looks kinda sketchy to me.

These guys ain't got the money for heroin."

She hid her smile as she heard his partner's gravelly response. "You want your dope cheap but not the surroundings?"

The first guy growled. "I'm running short this week. Heard to try this bar."

"There ain't nobody here lookin' rich enough to sell drugs. Ya know what I mean?"

These two could be a lead, but she'd still check out the rest of the place. Not much talking going on. The mumblings she heard were nondescript. She listened in the other direction, barely moving her head and keeping her eyes forward.

She heard, "Stop the local yokel imitation. You're a geek. You can't pull off anything but geek. I'll look around. Listen. Be right back."

The geek giggled. "Yeah. I'd check out the chicks, but there ain't none here. It's mostly men."

"At least it looks that way in the dark. Keep out of trouble."

No intellectual ferment going on in here. Focus, Lizzie.

She moved her head in slow notches, figuring the odds at about eight to two on the gender ratio. And those few women didn't resemble church ladies. Another flick of her chin toward one corner and she realized the place was a throwback to the pioneer days. The walls could have been that old. The lights were electrical in nature, though the wiring looked primitive and too visible for safety.

There, beyond the lighting, a furtive movement near that table seating a lone man, head hung over a beer bottle. The head snapped up as two men inched closer. Whispering. She couldn't hear a word. Ahh. A vacant table. She snagged her drink and moved over to it faster than the buxom broad and her guy who were ready to grab it.

She lowered her voice, "Gotta sit." She didn't want a scene. Might look suspicious if she decked two people at once. She wanted to hear. Too bad she missed most of it already.

"What do ya mean you don't have any?" The lean guy with the grey goatee snarled at the man hunched over the table.

His less polite partner slapped beefy hands down on the tiny table, rocking it on the uneven legs. "We heard you were the man.

Why hide it from us?"

The goatee wobbled. "Yeah, our money's good."

The gungy man at the table cringed. "Keep it down! Ya gonna get us busted." He'd settled too far into the dark for her to see any features, but he couldn't hide the tremors that rattled his body intermittently.

The beefy hands guy had the same problem all of a sudden. "You going to sell to us or not?" He stuck his shaking hands in his pocket.

Goatee man had lowered his voice. She could barely hear. She knew they weren't bartering peanuts. But was it oxycodone or heroin? Did it matter at this point? Maybe if she found one she'd find the other. But nothing changed hands. That much she *could* see. So, more than one man came here seeking drugs. Maybe Emily knew more than she said.

Leaning as far forward as her table would allow, she heard directions, about Roan Street to the old warehouse. Terrific. The town was rife with old warehouses. The economy had lurched downhill in recent years. Businesses shut down. Some abandoned. How would she find the right one? Should she try to follow these guys? They looked half-way between new shoes and the down-and-out bums. Probably had a car.

She wiped her chin with her shirt sleeve, afraid to touch the borrowed cloak more than necessary. Time to leave. It bordered on two in the morning but nobody else headed out the door. The bar must have a sliding closing time here—when everyone left, they closed.

Despite the lack of cover, she slid out the door without notice, right behind the addicts. She flung the cloak in the direction of the wall drunk. She strode across the road along the trunks of the trees. There. She could see which way they headed at least. She made note of the car when it pulled out of the gravel lot, if you could call it that. But the car wouldn't be hard to find. How many BMW's drove around this part of town?

She'd never heard of Roan Street, though. Maybe over Stroudsburg way. Not a chance she could run that far and still keep up with the rapidly disappearing sports car. She'd race home and ask

Delia where it was. That ought to be fun. Asking Delia anything before seven in the morning was generally useless.

She'd have to persist.

CHAPTER 4

Lizzie raced their old Ford toward Roan Street. Dense woods populated either side of the road, unhampered by street lights. Good ole Delia knew exactly where this particular warehouse stood, hidden in the weeds. Said to look for the faded Wanton Industries sign.

Delia had given directions, then rolled over and gone back to sleep. Lizzie wondered if her sister would remember the conversation. She stepped on the gas, hoping cops were far and few between at three in the morning. What if the men had already left the warehouse? Was she mistaken they would be buying drugs there? I can't be late. Too many days have dragged on with that child lost. I need information. Now.

"Ahh! That defunct building by the train tracks must be it," she spoke aloud to the trusty car, an old, though infrequent, friend for many years. A sign. Too dark amidst the trees to read. She inched closer and made out the capital W and an N and a T.

Sheesh, no wonder the place went under. The guy should have changed his name.

She drove past the sign and turned the corner where she found a break in the trees to hide the blue sedan off the road. What the night didn't hide, the dense stand of oak trees and laurels did.

Thank God for this dark car. It may be faded some, and need a few parts to rev it up, but inconspicuous fit perfectly.

Delia identified it as a barrel hoop manufacturing plant in the 1800s. It made sense. How many barrels need hoops these days? The building adapted through numerous incarnations before it produced other parts. She also mumbled that the operation died around 1950.

Lizzie walked around the entire building. The brick walls, cemented over, had crumbled in places over the years. Broken pipe pieces covered with enough filth of history to cause a sneeze. And the open spots revealed rotting lath that served as peepholes for the curious. That included her.

Not a soul in sight. And certainly not that spiffy BMW. Was that good, or bad?

The plant stood abandoned, disused for many years. At least for its original purpose. She crept inside. The manufacturing area loomed dark and empty, and every step echoed. She lightened her tread. No cars didn't necessarily mean no people, though the blight and mold would keep most of them away. Graffiti covered the walls, but a few nooks and crannies held cardboard cartons and moth-eaten blankets. Who were their owners? Where were they?

This type of place would attract many trespassers over the years, and maybe the needy and homeless found it a haven. At least it offered dryness and a wind buffer, especially in an inner room minus the broken windows. Not much manufacturing equipment remained, except rusty metal pipe pieces, broken into bits, and huge screws the size of her fist, blackened with mold.

After exploring a few of these rooms, she stumbled past a shape in a dark corner. Almost. Her instincts jumped in. Inching closer, she recognized it as human from the white face partially covered with a grimy blanket. She moved with discreet steps towards the head.

Oh no! A young boy. *Please God, don't let it be Tyler.*

She unwrapped the child and realized the fetal position had camouflaged his height. This boy could be the fourteen-year-old Tyler. Black hair. Scraggly. Looked to be home cut. A gaunt face, sharp cheekbones. The smile from the photo, long gone.

He didn't move, but she felt breath when she held her hand in front of his nose. A quick examination by touch showed no visible broken bones or injuries. She couldn't tell more in the dark.

Still, the boy didn't stir. She'd have to risk taking him outside for light. By now the partial moon might reveal his condition. She squatted and slid her arms under his shoulders and knees. His eyes flickered. If he'd used drugs, he could be in real danger. She needed to get help immediately.

Uncaring of who else may be around by then, she raced through the two rooms she'd traveled this far into the building. She wondered if he'd been further inside and had tried to work his way toward the entrance near the plant door.

Funny how your mind didn't quiet down even when your body pumped full out.

His body hung limp, and scared her limbs into optimum strength as she exited the building and tore through the shrubbery in the most direct route she could find to her car. Stealth had slipped away with the need for speed.

Hearing a sound in the underbrush, she swiveled her head for a second, and squinted to see in the dusky dawn. Shadows, but the little light coming through the trees flickered too much to identify anything. Her foot snagged on a root.

She recovered in time to jostle the boy back up, averting a fall. His body did not respond to the shaking. Fear fought with her concentration. Why didn't she park closer? Jerking open the passenger door with a hand still under his knees she knelt in the gravel and slipped him inside. He beat out a rag doll for limp, and hadn't made a sound or a motion since she found him. She strapped him in and ran around to the drivers side.

Preferring to travel light, she'd left everything in the car, including the cell phone, hoping the car wouldn't draw attention while there. Grabbing it now, she called 911 and started the engine.

Driving one-handed, she screeched down the street, remembering where she'd find the nearest hospital and navigating as best as possible in that direction. Thank God her car could fly when she needed it to.

And thank you, God, for still providing me dexterity and speed when I need it.

She shouted to the emergency operator who responded to her call. "I have an unconscious teenager and I'm heading toward Mountain View Hospital. I'm on Roan Street. Passed Sterling a minute ago."

As the calming voice came through the line, she softened her tone and added, "Can you give me the quickest directions to the hospital? He may be drugged. Needs help immediately."

The operator gave her the directions she requested without question. But then she followed protocol and asked for identification and more details.

Lizzie saw no harm in providing truthful answers. "I'm Lizzie Ort, and I found the boy at the old Wanton Industries warehouse."

Listening for a minute she said, "No, I'm not sure who he is."

From Tyler's photo she thought it was him, but left that bit out for the moment. She swerved onto the hospital street and announced, "I'm here. I'm hanging up."

"I called ahead. Drive to the emergency entrance. They're waiting for you."

Lizzie took her first deep breathe since she'd found the boy. "Thank you."

She simultaneously put the phone away and shut off the engine as two men reached the car. Seeing the boy, they ran to the passenger side, gently extracted him and placed him on a gurney.

Lizzie followed behind, through the doors that said 'No Admittance,' and flashed her old CIA badge to the nurse guarding the gate. Thank heavens they didn't notice the altered date. She couldn't leave the boy now.

Standing back out of the way, she realized that by calling the emergency number and saying the word "drugs" there would be repercussions. But now, the boy's immediate needs prevailed. She watched as they efficiently diagnosed his condition.

"Do you know what caused the overdose?" One nurse snapped out with an abrupt glance at Lizzie.

She answered a couple questions—where she found him, and if she knew what he had taken. Explaining quickly about the possible oxycodone use, she admitted the fear he'd overdosed. "I have no proof." No time to reveal her background with the agency, and her life near the criminal element where drugs reigned daily.

The nurse raised her eyebrows, but made no comment, turning back to respond to the doctor's request to remove the dirty jeans.

The lean, elderly doctor, who looked two days away from

starvation, moved in a whirlwind.

Without glancing from the boy, he asked, "How long has he been this way?"

Knowing he must be talking to her, Lizzie shrugged. "I found him fifteen minutes ago."

They stabilized him immediately, with an IV tube running lifeblood into his arm. She wasn't a medical provider and with no experience, she opted to remain quiet and not draw any conclusions. She surmised an overdose based on the situation, but he could be severely undernourished instead.

She watched the doctor.

He looked up. "Good. Good. His body is responding already. Maybe he wasn't away from us too long."

He nodded twice as he studied Tyler's face, then added, "He will need to be admitted, of course."

His features softened when he spoke of Tyler's chances. While they waited for the boy to return to consciousness it might be a good time to call his mother. Noticing the time on the big wall clock, she winced. Barely four in the morning.

"I might know who he is. I have to call someone. She'll know. She'll be relieved we found him. He's been gone a few weeks."

She didn't have Emily's number, and wondered if she had a phone. Delia must know. Besides, her sister would have to drive Emily here.

"I'll be back in a few minutes." She nodded with a firm thrust of her chin. No way they could keep her out, and she hoped the brisk attitude would forestall a deeper interrogation as to her identity.

Delia would understand about the time, if the continual ringing would wake her up. Her foggy voice came over the wire. "People only call about death and babies at this hour. And probably not babies. So it must be Lizzie. What's up?"

"Glad you're awake." She heard the snort over the phone but ignored it. "I have good news. I found Tyler. Could you drive over to Emily's and tell her. Then bring her here to the hospital?"

Delia perked up. "I'd be delighted. But you have the car."

"Ugh, this can't go on. I have to buy my own. For now can you beg one off of our neighbor, Julia. Her sons have several."

"Good idea. I'll get moving, but it will take a while. I doubt if Emily and Heather are up yet, either."

The next couple of hours grew mentally into days as Lizzie sat there. Tyler gained consciousness in a rush, but comprehension followed slow behind.

The nurse who'd waited with her, held the boy's hand as he stumbled around meaningless words. Thank heavens her demeanor and identification badge placed her light years away from Nurse Ratched, from the old movie, *One Flew Over the Cuckoo's Nest*. The name tag read Suzie Joy and her smile outperformed a sunbeam. Lizzie stayed to the side. Tyler would need as much warmth as he could get.

She heard his voice fumble over the word, bully, and the name Benji, and a mine. Lizzie stepped forward when he pulled loose from the nurse's hand and thrashed, mumbling Zombie. Anxiety clutched every muscle, yet she didn't know how to help.

Nurse Joy smiled at her. "He's talking about a Minecraft game. Lots of kids play them on the computer."

Lizzie breathed deep and uncoiled her springs. "He sounds terrified."

"Some of the creatures are horrendous. Zombies are hostile. He appears tangled in the game, not able to distinguish from it and real life."

Lizzie plopped into the visitor's chair. This had been her life through the years, but at eighty-two, it didn't fit as easily. Even her skin felt tired. Though she'd seen the havoc drugs had on the human body, she listened to Nurse Joy explain.

"In reality, if this Zombie was his drug dealer, he may have gotten caught up in the dangerous and scary lifestyle that he couldn't leave because of his addiction. It depends on what happened with this young lad."

A few minutes later the nurse raised the head of his bed a little to change his position. It startled him into a wide-eyed glare that slid past her smiling face and zeroed in on Lizzie in the chair.

She stood.

He squawked, "Who are you?"

Nurse Joy's smiling face altered into a frown of epic earthquake ridges as she pinned her gaze on this new threat to her charge.

Lizzie'd been on the spot before. But not since she left the ravages of war-torn countries and her field work with the agency. A bit rusty, but instincts came to the fore, and she said, "It's okay. He's never met me."

Nurse Ratched came back to mind as the furrows deepened. Nurse Joy was a disguise?

Maybe it wasn't okay.

Emily rushed in the door, with Delia seconds behind.

She burst into tears. "Oh Tyler, thank God you're alive."

After hugging him, she stepped back for a better look. "You worried me sick."

Tyler grinned at her. "Zis okay, mom."

Emily saw Lizzie and raced over, practically standing on tiptoe to squash her with a frantic hug. "Thank you. Thank you for finding him."

Nurse Ratched faded back into Joy.

CHAPTER 5

Sergeant John Torkless shouted, "You did what?"

Lizzie barked back. "I just said, I put him in the car and sped to the hospital."

"Don't you know you're not supposed to move an unconscious person? What about injuries?"

"Of course. I examined him first. No injuries. No signs of beating. I made an educated guess as to his condition, and got him medical help the fastest way."

Torkless seemed to have marshaled his wits because he lowered his voice and slowed his speech. She looked closer. Okay, maybe it was the grinding of his teeth that slowed him down.

He said, "Let's start over. Tell me again from the beginning why you are here."

"His mother hired me to search for him since he'd been gone for days."

He leveled his shoulders. "Why didn't she report him missing to the police?"

Lizzie straightened her spine, raising her two inches higher than the sergeant. "Not my place to ask. My mission was to find him. I did."

He nodded for her to continue.

"I found him at that Wanton Industry warehouse."

The young cop said, "Vandals and homeless, and drug dealers hang out in that dump. What was he doing there?"

"I don't know. He wasn't clear on that yet."

She sucked in a deep breath and exhaled a few slow puffs, trying to loosen her clenched jaw. "He was unconscious when I found him. As I *said*, I assessed his condition and got him into the car and raced to the hospital lickety-split."

Seeing his youth shine from his clear eyes and his starched new uniform, she realized he was probably too young to have heard that old fashioned term. Ugh. I have to watch everything I say and do to I fit in this part of the century.

She reiterated. "I put him in the car and sped to the hospital."

He looked at her, up, then down. "How did you get him to the car?"

She tired of the elderly implications and stated in a clear, crisp voice. "I carried him from the building and ran with him to the car. I knew he was alive, but didn't know for how long."

His skepticism marred his flawless skin with wrinkles as he frowned at her.

She'd had little sleep and didn't wait for him to make any cracks. "You want to arm wrestle?"

The frown disappeared, replaced with a smirk. His lips twitched to disguise a smile. A tiny one, with duty warring with the youthful reaction to a challenge. The smug look widened—convinced he could win.

Her age allowed her to hide her reaction. She knew nothing in life was a sure thing.

His youth won the struggle. He planted his elbow on the counter and raised his hand. Lizzie complied.

Within seconds it was over. His startled eyes and slumped shoulders recognized the defeat but he couldn't grasp it. "How old are you?"

"Eighty-two. How old are you?"

He mumbled a twenty-seven before he picked up the phone and said, "I'll ask Detective Fury to come out."

As soon as he called, he sat at the desk and ignored her. When the detective arrived, Sergeant Torkless gathered his demeanor into a semblance of politeness and introduced her with a brief explanation of what she wanted.

The detective ushered her into his office and motioned for her to sit. "I'm sorry. What was your name again?"

She glanced around as she answered, "Elizabeth Ort. Nice digs."

He ignored her comment, but at least smiled before he got down to business. "And your concern today?"

"I reported possible drug use when I brought Tyler Hopson into the hospital in case it might help in his treatment. I don't know if they report that to you or not." She hesitated, seeking a response. Detective Fury remained silent.

Allowing him points on that one, she continued, "But I did want to make sure the police were aware of that Wanton Industries hellhole and will deal with it."

Fury nodded his head and added, "Okay."

She noticed the distinct question mark in his voice as he wobbled out the word with hesitation. He also didn't rush her to continue. But she didn't want to waste time, either.

She raised her voice, gesticulating. "Anyone and everyone can find easy access to the place. There's rips in the fence; the metal siding, what's left of it, is torn and bent; and the doors, the ones that exist, aren't locked."

She'd never seen a calmer cop. He smiled. And kept smiling. His clean cut look reminded her of her friend, Detective William Milano, in Florida, yet this guy lacked crispness, looked ready to melt soon.

She wondered, was it due to the sleepy little town, or did his demeanor hide a keen mind? Time would tell.

When Fury puckered his lips to speak and squinted his eyes, it didn't detain her, at least he reacted. She continued her rant.

"It's obvious people take beer back there. Looks as if someone spilled buckets of multicolored paint everywhere."

"Paintballers," he mumbled.

Lizzie shoved her hands on her hips. "So you know all about the place."

"Druggies are always hangin' in the alley. We roust them out and throw them in a cell till they look and act better. But no drugs on them? We can't do much about it."

She never got huffy in her life. This time she chose it over the slow burn inside. She harrumphed her way out the door. She'd save her explosion for another day. She needed to return to Tyler.

As soon as he gained coherency the next day, Delia watched Heather while Lizzie drove Emily to the hospital for a visit. The rapport between mother and son revealed a depth of love. Tyler reassured his mom constantly that he would be home soon to help out again. After Lizzie stepped away to give them some privacy, she saw him sneak his mom two oranges from the fruit bowl they'd given him as a gift, and drop an apple in the open pocket of her purse.

He would be there a while to get stabilized. He was not on the drug oxycodone long enough to cause serious damage. Thin to begin with, he was malnourished from being away from most food for months and not eating.

After his mom went home, Lizzie came back. Tyler turned from Lizzie and scrubbed away a few tears. When she raised her eyebrows he said, "I miss Heather." He moaned, "Why did I start taking those pills!"

Lizzie made it into a question. "Do you know why?"

And Tyler finally talked about how he came to be in such a state. "I stole oxycodone pills, one at a time from mom. I think they were for the pain in her back. "I couldn't sneak out too many. She needed them. I felt awful taking them from her."

Tyler sat in the corner chair and tried to explain to Lizzie how he started. He confessed he'd been eating only a little for a while. The three guys who hassle me about my name shoved me all the time. The big guy—Ben—kept stealing my lunch food. He and the two puny ones were like griefers."

Thank heavens she followed up on the nurse's tip about Minecraft. She'd read everything she could find last night—still tough to distinguish between griefers and wolves but she tried.

Tyler dropped his head and dangled his arms down to the floor. "My fault, Miss Ort. I didn't fight them. One beating was enough. I learned to let it go."

Lizzie winced inside and held a surface expression that would fool anyone into thinking she had no reaction.

Tyler added. "They kept after me. And when the teachers backs were turned, they dragged me to a corner of the playground. They would have beaten me to a pulp but one of the teachers walked by. When they faked doing nothing, I crept away."

Lizzie stared him down, waiting for the rest. ". . . And?"

"Okay. I also slipped lots of my food onto mom and Heather's plates at supper. They weren't eating enough."

Lizzie raised her eyebrows.

"And I lied. I told mom sometimes I ate at Ethan's so she would have more food."

Settling deeper into the chair, she asked, "Did you eat at Ethan's?"

"No. we didn't go there much. His dad went into screaming fits. Or slept all the time."

"I knew I couldn't steal any more. But Hector, the kid on the corner at school, had spread the word. 'Need drugs. See me.' "

She interrupted. "Did you ever get drugs from Ethan's dad?"

"No way. Ethan was clean. Never took drugs. Why do you think his dad had drugs?"

"Rumors. I'm glad your friend stayed away from drugs."

She studied her fingernails. "What is his dad's name?"

"Verge. Verge Innis. Same as Ethan."

She nodded to encourage him to continue.

"I went to Hector. He was nice. Acted friendly. He'd seen those jerks jabbing me. I hurt from the punching. But mostly, I think, I hurt inside. It's no fun being the one picked on." He hung his head.

Lizzie clenched a hand but hid it behind her skirt. She would love to deal with these kids. But they were kids. How to handle a fourteen year old who wasn't holding an Uzi didn't fit into her normal realm of events. She managed a smile for Tyler. Acting as if this was a normal chat between friends.

Tyler said, "I took the money from my piggy bank. I wanted my own computer some day."

Lizzie sparked up, back straight. "You had enough for a computer?"

He grumbled, "No way. It was a dumb dream."

He shrugged. "So I took some of my savings and got one pill. A few days later. Hector gave me another one at half off. And again. And again."

She didn't have to ask any more questions. He kept talking. More than she'd heard any teen talk. He mumbled, almost to himself, trying to get it straight in his mind, maybe.

He continued, "But cops came to the school. Hector, the kid on the corner disappeared."

She sat, and waited. This she needed to hear.

"I heard you could buy some at that old warehouse. I had missed school days by then. Afraid to go back. But I was hungry, and scared. So I went to the warehouse. Saw this guy, big, and mean. He spoke kind, but his eyes didn't."

She'd known grown men who were worse, but had hoped her old world would not traipse on home with her. Listening to him, she realized this was why she wanted that teen center. By golly, she'd get it. First she'd let Tyler finish his confession. The dirty, greasy hair and scar he described went right into her memory bank to be pulled out later.

Tyler continued, "It was like Zombie Pigmen and the Wolves attacking me. That's why I started screaming when you picked me up. I thought they were back."

"You didn't make a sound. I thought you were near death."

"I must have been screaming inside. Felt real."

"Had they been in the warehouse with you?"

"No, I don't think so. They were made of Legos. Chunky, one of the attackers from school, is a big guy. Fat. I was afraid he could really hurt me. He didn't have the Zombie Pigman look. I think they were nightmares in my head."

"You don't seem scared now."

He looked up through the hair hanging in his eyes. "No, they're gone. You're here."

"When the others come in the room—nurses and doctors and the kid next door—you kind of shut down. You're quiet, look away, you rarely talk. What happens?"

"I don't know." He looked straight at her, not away.

She frowned. "You appear shy when they are here. Too quiet.

Afraid?"

"Not afraid."

"What then?"

"Don't know," he mumbled. "It's hard to talk with people around."

"You talk to me. Sometimes you sass me."

"I'm sorry."

"No, don't apologize. I think it means you are comfortable. Is that why you talk with me?"

"You're like a Passive Mob creature. You wouldn't hurt me."

A mob creature? That could have been ominous. Maybe this Minecraft for kids isn't such a good idea.

She remembered he'd thrashed side to side and mumbled Zombie Pigmen when he was coming to that first night. One of the nurses who worked with pre-teens knew exactly what he meant and explained details that Nurse Joy hadn't mentioned.

"So you talk to me because you know I wouldn't hurt you?"

"Yeah. And you carried me out of that awful place. You ran. Carrying me. All that way to the car."

"Yes. I did that. But I thought you were unconscious. I feared you might not recover."

"You saved me. Nobody knows anyone like that."

"What do you mean?"

"A woman of uhh, umm, you know, I mean, older. They can't run. And I'm fourteen years old. Heavy."

"That you are. You wore me out. But time was very important. Young people are most susceptible to drugs. Doses are uncertain, the added chemicals more deadly than the drug itself. You are too young to die."

"I'm not dead. Umm, thank you."

"And you will work hard with your mom and me to stay healthy now. Right?"

CHAPTER 6

Later, Delia spotted Lizzie standing still as a stork near the newly emerging sorrel. "Where have you been? I was worried sick."

Lizzie followed the path and met her sister part way, laughing. "You look blooming with health to me."

Delia stalked past her, then reached back to grab her arm as she rushed to the kitchen. "You know what I mean! You promised me you would get some sleep as soon as Tyler improved."

Lizzie did look beat. Delia dropped her anger and bustled around filling the kettle. "I'll make you some soothing tea and then you need to get to bed."

"I'm sorry, dear sister. I'm not used to having someone worry about me. I worked alone for so many years. And I did sleep last night for a few hours. More than I'm used to sometimes. But I'll tell you where I've been. And maybe how you can help."

That clinched it for Delia. Lizzie seldom asked for help. She plonked down dainty flowered china cups in front of their places at the table as if they were tin and less fragile. She wanted to hear how she could finally support her sister.

"Okay. Spill it. What's going on?"

"I went to the police to report that horrid warehouse where I found Tyler. It was ho-hum for them."

"What do you mean?"

"Well, that Detective Fury knew about the vandalism and drug dealers in that place and responded with such infuriating calm."

Delia almost choked on her tea as she laughed.

Lizzie reacted with a stretched neck and scrunched eyes. "What's that about?"

"They could have named molasses after him, for sure. He's the slow and steady part, but that's how he traps them. They're stuck before they know it. It's a great disguise."

"It's all an act?"

"No, no. His demeanor is naturally calm. His mind provides the traps. Works great for him. I find him appealing. You will. too."

Lizzie frowned at the possibility, but moved on to her next concern. "There are no criminal grounds for Tyler to be arrested or of interest to the police."

"That's good, right?"

"True. And when I spoke with the doctor, he said Tyler could be released within a week or two. I need to follow up on his detoxification with a recovery plan."

Looking at her weary sister, Delia said, "Why you?"

Lizzie swallowed the rest of her tea, then studied Delia, seeking the answer in her ethereal face. "I've taken to the kid. Besides, can you see his mom being able to deal with this? I've read up on the holistic approach to full recovery. I think that's the way we should go."

Delia noticed the "we" aspect and nodded.

Lizzie continued, formulating as she went. "We need to reduce his stress and improve his physical well being. I know herbs will help but we need more knowledge on that."

Ahh. Now she understood. "You want me to help devise an herbal treatment plan."

Lizzie peeked out from behind straggling hair. The bun had long ago sunk down her head and left wisps hanging everywhere. "Would you? You know I strongly believe in the benefits of herbs, but this has never been my area."

Picking up empty cups, Delia cleared the table, cleaned counters, and stood arms akimbo next to her sister. "Do you have enough strength left to go see Agatha?"

"You mean at the Bittersweet Herb Shop?"

"You got it. She's the one to help us."

Lizzie straightened. "I've thought of her, but do you think this is the way to go? Reveal his plight to a stranger? I've been fading in and out of my past life attitudes frequently the last few days, I'm not sure what to do. I've been trying to do a complete turn around from my CIA field work, but my skills and take-charge mindset keep acting up."

"Because you act on instinct in certain occasions where it calls for it, doesn't mean you have given up on finding a higher plane. Doesn't this fit in with your new hopes of establishing a local youth center? Wouldn't it help kids akin to Tyler?"

Now Lizzie jumped up, gave Delia a hug, and said. "You are right. Maybe Agatha would be willing to establish a recovery program as part of the youth center. Or better yet, if we set up and help with good eating habits along with a support base before they get to the drugs, maybe the kids will be able to avoid them altogether. Let's go."

Agatha greeted them with hugs, but Delia's dour countenance persuaded her to usher them into her office and close the door.

"What's up, ladies?"

Delia took the lead as Lizzie stepped back, a seamless transition of authority. "We need your help, dear."

Delia and Lizzie had been instrumental in saving Agatha from a demented killer a couple of years back. Agatha hadn't seen Lizzie since. It didn't seem to matter. She quickly responded, "Sure. Anything."

Delia stood near the chair unoccupied with catalogs and herbal wreaths. She inched closer to Agatha and whispered. "We need your help. Can you devise an herbal program to follow after detoxification from opioids?"

Agatha plopped down in her chair behind the desk. She stared at Lizzie. "Oh no. Did that happen in Bucharest, too?"

Lizzie glared at Delia. "How many people know I had trouble in Bucharest? They hospitalized me for a few days because of my broken ankle. Nothing more."

Agatha smiled, the relief settling around her plump form like butterflies on nectar. "I'm glad. But, then who will benefit from the program? We need to know more before I can design a plan."

Lizzie explained about Tyler, without using his name for now. Most people didn't know him and his mother, but privacy was important to her. She provided it for others when she could.

"Wow. Fourteen years old. I've never tried anything for young teens. But it's doable. How soon do you need this plan?"

"Um, three days?" Delia moved the catalogs from one chair, and wreaths and stuff off the other chair and placed them out of the way on the floor. She sat and signaled with a quick motion of her eyes for Lizzie to sit. She stalled, not willing to look at her old friend.

"Sorry. It's kind of an emergency. We need to bring him home from the hospital and continue his rehab there." Delia looked at Lizzie. "Our home, you think? A different environment at first, if his mother agrees?"

Agatha pulled forward a large note pad. Snapping the cap off her pen, she looked at each of them for a second.

"Okay. The where doesn't matter right now. Let's determine what we need. How healthy is the child?"

Lizzie said, "He's malnourished. Barely got enough to eat before this happened and he disappeared from home. He told me he sold his lunches for weeks prior to that to buy the oxycodone, when the bullies didn't steal his lunch."

Making no comments about the situation, Agatha started writing while she spoke. "Users must overcome the compulsion to engage in substance abuse. Rehab stabilizes the methods of doing this, making it second nature."

Both sisters planted their feet simultaneously and leaned forward.

"Nutrition is only one aspect. You need to remove whatever other stresses led him to the drugs. And teach him how to deal with those he can't change."

The sisters shared a look only they understood. They took care of him now. He would learn.

Agatha continued. "First, we can get you two started on grocery shopping. Cut out the processed foods and stick to proteins, vegetables and fruit for a quick return to health. While you're doing that, I will research a list of vitamin and herbal supplements to aid in the recovery."

Delia and Lizzie both knew the value of many herbs but they

both looked quizzically at Agatha for further explanation. "What is the goal here?" Delia asked.

"A group of supplements can work synergistically to rebuild neurotransmitters, refill deficiencies and help support emotional health. If we can get him strong physically, mentally, and emotionally, then he won't feel the urge to solve his problems with the drugs."

Lizzie said, "I heard that having a natural, safe environment can play a role in recovery. Do you know if that is true?"

"It certainly is."

Lizzie and Delia spoke over each other, both making the same point. Lizzie said to Agatha, "Then we should keep him with us for a while."

Delia added, "The garden can do wonders for anyone."

Agatha had been in their garden and commented on how it would be beneficial. But added, "He can come visit the herb farm, and maybe help out there a little. It would give him a source of pride in work done, and the chance to get outdoors in a somewhat natural setting. Plenty of sunshine."

Lizzie knew the farm fed the Bittersweet Herb Shop with many of the herbs and potions sold there. "Tell me more about the farm."

Agatha beamed. "It was owned by Margaret Kinney before she died. The young couple that now own it kept the name, Kinney Herb Farm, and raise their herbs with the same organic methods and quality standards. We have a great relationship. I'm sure they'll love working with your young man."

"Thanks so much," Lizzie said.

Agatha explained that she would research and make a list of vitamins and supplements appropriate for Tyler's age and condition. We'll probably work with the B vitamins, calcium, magnesium, maybe ginseng. Then add a few others depending on his condition."

"Such as?"

"Does he have anxiety, severe withdrawal symptoms, trouble sleeping, or unusual reactions?"

Lizzie closed one eye in thought, then said she would check with his doctor for any symptoms that might apply.

The sisters rose together, smiled effusively at their dear friend and said they would head to the grocery store while Agatha worked on the rest.

***

Lizzie and Delia tiptoed into the hospital room. Delia tilted her head sideways, grinning at Lizzie. Tyler's eyelids fluttered, leaving a slit. She knew he was aware of them, and continued the game. The thought that he tried to trick her, thrilled her. A few days ago, he barely recognized her.

When the first giggle escaped his cracked lips she stopped dead.

Lizzie had spent many hours sitting with him while Delia stayed home to keep up with the herb business. She's the one who responded to the giggle first. "What, you think us hippopotamuses can't tiptoe?"

He rolled over and sat up. Eyes wide. "You're not a hippo!"

Delia settled a small bag at the foot of his bed, while Lizzie answered, "Some think I am because I'm big."

His smile faded. "If you weren't so big you wouldn't be able to carry me all that way to the car."

His forehead creased, too much for a young man, barely a teenager. She waited.

He smiled. "You're not big. You're just tall. They should call you a giraffe. Skinny arms. Just like giraffe legs."

Delia stayed back, delighted to see them both interacting splendidly. Although she known her sister wanted to set up a teen center to help people in similar circumstances to Tyler, this proved to her Lizzie would be able to adjust, and open up enough to pull it off.

She grabbed the bag and carried it toward him, hoping he'd forget about his first awful days in the hospital. "New day, kiddo."

Staring at the bag now, Tyler smiled. She understood. New life —good. Presents—better.

A small bag of jelly beans emerged, and two huge bottles of vitamins. He tipped his head to read them. Calcium and magnesium? "What are they? They look like pills."

"In a way they are, but let's call them your blues blasters. These are your ticket home. They'll help you stay strong and keep you away from those other pills."

"How? Hands up, pretending to be a traffic cop?"

Delia giggled.

"You got it." She handed him the jelly beans and re-bagged the vitamin bottles. The jelly beans will help for now, but no more two an hour with two walnuts. The walnuts will last longer in your stomach, and they won't mess up your blood sugar."

She handed him the small bag. They'd clear the extra food and supplements with the nutritionist when they came.

"Why you takin' the pills back?"

"These go home with you. The nurse will be giving you some until then. A few more days, and one more blood test, and you leave this joint."

Tyler rested back against the pillow, still weak. The sisters studied him. Delia saw the change more than Lizzie, since she hadn't been there for a few days. He'd never resemble last year's photo again. His experience aged his face. But the smile was almost back. Much better looking than that first day.

Intrigued with the jelly beans, he didn't notice her concern.

"Two?"

"Yep."

"Willpower. It's a test."

"Like when they draw my blood to do a test?"

"No, this is my test." Delia said. "Can you follow directions to do what's right for your body when no one is looking? You know how the doc or nurse put that cuff on your arm and check your blood pressure, and your breathing?"

He nodded without speaking.

Lizzie answered this time, "If you kept taking the drugs, and took more to make yourself feel better, you could kill yourself."

His eyes widened. He sputtered, "What would happen?"

Lizzie kept solemn, lips firm, and no smile.

Delia smiled inwardly. She was glad her sister handled this one. No way would she look as stern.

Lizzie said, "Your heart could start thumping out of control, making you think it wanted out of your chest."

His head jerked back to the pillow.

She added the final touch. "And your body would start burning hot, and maybe you'd have seizures." She shook her whole body as she talked. "And then you'd die."

Delia ushered her sister out, but winked at Tyler to make him smile. Maybe Lizzie needed more time to relearn social skills. Delia would help with that.

CHAPTER 7

One problem solved. Emily had agreed to let her son stay with them for the first weeks of rehab after he left the hospital. Lizzie's meeting with her vociferous enemy, Matthew Doren, Tyler's principal, raised other issues.

Matthew protested, as expected, when she spoke of the bullies. "Oh, we might have a few problems at this fine school, but we take care of them."

His bluster diminished when she convinced him dealing with the bullies quietly, without publicity, served his best interests. His hesitancy at tackling a problem didn't come from lack of intelligence. He understood her threat immediately. He sighed. Bad publicity carried a nightmare of horrid repercussions. He buckled. "Go ahead and talk with some of the teachers. We need them on board if we are to register complaints to any parents."

Lizzie approached a few teachers, who lined up to help. The English teacher, Mr. Arsenault, gave her a couple of teacher's names she might want to talk with, and wished her the best. Not exactly a strong supporter of her cause, but helpful.

When Lizzie spoke with the others, their eagerness to help was palpable. Ben, the worst of the bullies for some time, enlisted such fear tactics that no one would lodge formal complaints against him. The math teacher, Mrs. Donegal, and her assistant, agreed that focusing on Ben would stop the other bullies, too.

"Take down the leader and the troops will disperse," Mrs. Donegal urged. She ruffled through her desk drawer, and pulled out a bedraggled complaint form. "I've waited forever for someone to request this form. We can't push them on parents." With a brisk stroke of the pen, she filled out Ben's name, his parents and their address from the file on her desk. "I've talked with them, but they refuse to believe Ben could harm anyone."

The assistant stood nearby, bouncing on her heels and nodding her head up and down in eager agreement. At least one person would be joyed to see Ben taken down. Happy to hear that the characters in Tyler's nightmare were, in fact, monsters in real life, Lizzie reached eagerly for the form and discussed with the teachers what would happen when Tyler returned to school. It was good to know that the bully would be suspended. Once there, he would serve detention, be restrained in his movements, and not allowed near Tyler for the rest of the year.

Tyler would have to gain some confidence and bravery before he entered the school grounds once again. Lizzie discussed it with his mother earlier and she asked to arrange tutoring in some of the classes. Lizzie set that in motion and left to plan what else she could do to help the boy.

As the sun rose the following day, she stepped into Tyler's hospital room. He looked too peaceful to disturb. She knew rest was essential to recovery, and she slipped into the cushioned chair, a recliner with a foot rest. Maybe she should raise it and find sleep herself. The concept was foreign to her. She'd never just taken a nap while she waited. Her past involved hiding in a corner in the dark, alert until someone arrived. Interesting this change of life style. She'd probably get fat and sassy. Some said she sassed too much already. Better to just sit here and wait.

Lizzie's hands held no file folders, no papers that contained information from interviews with drug rehab people she could find, drug addiction treatment centers, and interventionists for addiction. It took root in her head and she knew each step to take. The addiction treatment centers mostly treated adults and were a distance away. Hospital personnel implemented a simple detox program with Tyler. Their attention and progress impressed her.

Tyler listened and helped, and because he hadn't been on the oxycodone too long, he was already on his way to recovery. A few more days and he would be ready to leave. His doctor wanted to introduce more fluids and stabilize his health, more from the nutrition point of view than the withdrawal from the drugs. The doctor agreed with the rehabilitation counselors about the importance of proper food for long term recovery.

The home rehab devised with Agatha's help would hopefully give him a new start. She knew Delia had already begun a plan to include Emily and the family in a healthy eating program. Getting the food to her was easy. Still, they needed to devise an enticing way to ensure she'd accept it.

Lizzie speculated on how this problem of Tyler's fit so perfectly into her mission to start a teen center in town. While recuperating in the hospital in Bucharest she mourned the loss of the life that suited her well for many years. They'd grabbed her right out of college when an elderly friend in the CIA found she had attributes that suited the field work. She never looked back.

But she'd never looked forward, either. Not feeling the need to find something different, something better. Her stay in the hospital at age eighty-one to repair her ankle forced her, and the agency, to accept her retirement. Thank heavens for Delia, who'd tended the home front all those years, and served as the cover for her work while between assignments. And they managed to share the love of herbs, enough that Lizzie used it as a disguise of purpose when she traveled to foreign countries.

Tyler groaned but rolled over in bed and settled into a quiet sleep. Nurse Joy from the emergency room appeared silently at the door. She widened her eyes and jerked her head sideways toward the corridor and stepped back. Lizzie acknowledged the summons and tip-toed from the room. They moved down the hall toward an empty room before Nurse Joy spoke. "I have to confess."

That startled Lizzie. What now?

"I checked on who you were after you brought young Mr. Hopson in. Once I realized you were Delia's sister, I was surprised. As many times as Delia has helped us out here in one way or another, I never knew she had a sister."

Lizzie smiled. If it involved Delia it couldn't be too bad. "Just out of curiosity, how did you check on me?"

"Oh, everyone knows Delia. I just asked a couple of her friends and found out about your career with the CIA. It seemed kind of secretive. One lady, who shall remain nameless, kept looking sideways to check if anyone lurked near by."

Lizzie pictured a tiny old lady hunching low and glancing furtively around while she whispered. She broke out laughing at the thought, and barely caught the sound with her hand in time.

Nurse Joy grinned in return. "I wondered, how did you manage getting in?"

"In here this morning?"

"No, of course not. We were all notified to let you in whenever you want. It's what prompted me to check out who you were. This floor is a lock down area. You need clearance to get in. We're pretty strict about it. I heard the new nurse questioned you before letting you in this morning. But she'd never met you. Once you gave your name and showed your identification, she buzzed you in."

Lizzie winced, knowing she must get a real ID soon to replace her doctored CIA one, but nodded agreement. "No problem."

"I meant how did you get accepted into the agency?"

Those long ago days returned in her memory as if she'd just lived them. The smile vanished. "I endured. Training is harsh. They crush office employees through the gristmill, too."

A dull mask filtered over the nurse's eyes as disappointment registered. "Oh, I should have expected that."

Lizzie wanted to make her feel better but didn't know where this led. She did find it uplifting to be able to talk about her past life. She could share little of it, but this wasn't classified. "They discovered I could quickly assess a situation and develop a plan. Snapped me right up."

Nurse Joy confided. "I have a young daughter. She seems inclined toward serving her country. I am trying to convince her there are many avenues of government work. I hoped maybe an office job, though."

"I couldn't stand working at a desk, but the CIA *is* mostly office work. From its inception it was primarily an intelligence gathering community."

The nurse looked pensive for a moment, then thanked her. Before leaving, she whispered. "I also heard of your efforts to open a teen center in this town. Heard you've had some opposition. Some of us nurses wanted to let you know that we will openly support you on this. Let us know what we can do to help."

She handed Lizzie her business card with her home phone number penciled on the back. Waved. And left without another word.

In Tyler's room, Lizzie pondered her half-planned attempt to establish a place for troubled teens. Delia told her of the horror that drug businesses inflicted on their peaceful, rural area. Lizzie had needed a hobby or work to help ease into retirement. Or a new life plan, depending on who you talked with. Keeping the teens safe became a priority before Tyler went missing.

Footsteps at a fast run past the open door forced her mind to the present and her feet rushed forward without thought as she sensed the emergency. The short, elderly nurse from the front desk followed behind. Lizzie didn't hesitate but took after her, running past her with ease toward the first nurse who just turned into a patient's room down the hall.

Lizzie halted inside the door. Assess.

The child in the bed lay semi-awake but barely able to move. The man, unshaved and ranting, shook the bed violently, yelling, "Wake up, Jimmy." He grabbed the kid's arm and pulled. "Get up, son. They can't make you stay here."

The nurse grasped the man's forearm and tried to free the child, whose eyes widened in alarm as he looked at the man. The boy groaned, unable to move his arm.

The child looked emaciated to Lizzie, but she chose her goal and acted. Disable the man and detain him. A quick palm jab to his chin caused him to loosen his hold on the boy. Within seconds, Lizzie had both his gnarled and toughened arms behind his back and tied with the lamp cord she'd swept off the floor and out of the socket.

If the man moved, he'd be dragging a heavy lamp behind him. He tried it once. It rocked forward and slammed into his shoulder blades. He stopped. Bewildered. Subdued.

The nurse broke out of her surprised stupor, soothed the boy, and tucked him in. He'd already drifted back to sleep. She stifled an obvious attempt to hug Lizzie, and settled for saying thank you.

Lizzie straightened the nurse's name tag that had shifted in the struggle, and said, "Nurse Becky. You are welcome." Lizzie politely asked, "What should we do with this," pointing to the man as if he were a bag of garbage.

The nurse who'd lingered in the hall stepped in. "I've already called security. They will remove him from the floor and make sure he doesn't return."

Nurse Becky scowled at her. "His mother brought Jimmy in and requested this man not be allowed near him. Could we please listen when this happens?"

"But he seemed nice when I saw him the other day."

Two security men asked both nurses to step aside to determine what happened and how to deal with the man, who stood unmoving, head hanging, not looking at the boy he called son.

Lizzie saw the situation was in good hands and slipped out and down the hall, unnoticed. Tyler woke as she walked in.

"I talked with your teacher today."

"What? Who?" Frowns etched his forehead.

Was that fear? Anger? She didn't know how to read kids.

"It was Mrs. Donegal." The furrows smoothed. Good. Maybe what she'd done was all right.

"Why?"

Oops. The furrows were back. *God guide me here. Remember I'm a babe in the woods with kids.* I'll try straight forward. "Because you're missing your school work. Your mother doesn't want you to get behind. Is it okay I spoke with your teacher?"

He rose and plopped down into the chair next to the bed. He made a cocoon there with the extra blanket. Maybe he felt vulnerable in bed. Feet propped onto the front of the seat, knees bent at an angle to fit in his legs, he said, "Mrs. Donegal. Yeah, she's good. But I am *way* behind. What did she say?"

"You're way behind."

He pulled the worn blanket up to his chin. His mouth quirked. Just a little smile, but it showed. "Yeah. Now what?"

"She thinks you need a tutor."

"No. No. No." He peeked out from the blanket. "You can teach me."

Whoa, where did that come from?

"Honey, I know nothing of new math. Two and two. That's my kind of math. At first, Mrs. Donegal thought your close friend, Ethan, could help you."

He interrupted. "He's smart. And good. Though his dad is mean."

"What do you mean?"

"Just seems cruel. I stay away from him."

Lizzie let it go—for now. "Mrs. Donegal checked on Ethan. She hadn't seen him in a while. He left the school about a month ago."

His smile faded. "I wondered. Never even said goodbye."

She vowed to look into that. The dad comment tugged at her. Needn't tell him yet. Tyler waited. Expectant. She grimaced. Now the difficult part. "Your teacher thought Jenny Lyn would be a great tutor for math and English."

"She's a girl."

"I know, but she's a smart girl, and you need that right now. I thought I could bring her by a few days till you get to go home."

His shoulders hunched. He crossed his arms. "Just so no one knows she's coming here."

"I promise. I'll hide her in the trunk."

Finally, the smile came back. Just as long as he didn't hold her to it.

CHAPTER 8

"We need to speak with you, ma'am, before you go in."

Accosted by her two favorite policemen. Great. Yesterday, Lizzie felt a presence when she arrived at the hospital but saw no one. It reminded her of that snapped twig and shadow when carrying Tyler to the car. Proud of her stellar skills at surveillance, she didn't appreciate being the one shadowed. Now this.

Today was ominous, not because they were cops, but because they knew to find her on the way to Tyler's room at six in the morning. Some days work out better than others, though. Today was still rated good. For instance, if Jenny Lyn lay in the trunk, dead or alive, with the cops stopping me outside the hospital, it could have gone the other way. The kind teacher had released Jenny Lyn for later this morning to tutor Tyler. And for sure, if she needed a ride here she'd be in the front seat. Tyler would just have to toughen up about girls.

Julie's car was a godsend. Once locked, she needed to face the police. "What can I help you with, Detective Fury?" It was good he stood nearest. Lizzie decided snickering in Sergeant John Torkless's face before composing herself could be construed as a bad idea. He wasn't such a bad kid, really.

The detective stepped forward with authority, almost arrogant, despite the youthful pelt of tawny hair and a skin resembling the color of the oak trees predominant in the area, though his color probably came from wind and sun.

He motioned Lizzie inside. The kid turned to follow. A slight nip in the air didn't deter this beautiful spring morning. It wouldn't linger once the sun heat its peak. His request seemed reasonable. Didn't want to sound too easy though, and countered with, "How about we sit on this bench and enjoy the gorgeous day?"

Fury sighed, as if she asked him to sit in the rain. "Sure."

Aargh. Considerate and quiescent. What does he want? He waved Torkless over to the other side. "Detective?"

"We need to speak with Tyler Hopson. The nurse at the desk didn't want to share his mother's phone number with us. Suggested we wait for you and you'd be able to help us."

"Of course. Emily doesn't have a phone. We stop in when we want to speak with her."

"So. there's no need to take the nurse in for insubordination? She just didn't have the number?"

Sergeant John Torkless snorted first, giving Lizzie time to cover hers with a harrumph. At least the kid shared the same sense of humor. "Why do you need to talk with Tyler's mom?"

"We don't. We have questions for Tyler. Need her permission. Or his dad's."

"Wise not to ask about the dad. He hasn't been around for a while now. Least ways that's what I heard. What do you want with Tyler?"

Detective Fury winced. Moved his head in a half circle. Maybe taking in the sun striking the blooming pink-tinged tulips, or stretching his neck. Didn't know the guy well enough to tell. Good time to wait him out.

He broke first. Huh. Learned some things from her past job. Like patience.

Fury said, "Give us a break. We've been up all night. Found a guy yesterday in that Wanton warehouse. Dead."

Lizzie jerked her head toward him. Games were over. What did he suspect? Just ask, silly. This is the good ole USA. "And what does this have to do with Tyler?"

"They found him just one room over from where you described finding Tyler. And the coroner suggested he might have been dead for a couple of days."

Lizzie remained forthright, despite the picture of a days-old body forming bile in her throat, no matter how many she'd seen in her lifetime. No wonder Detective Fury had lost his crisp edges. Still, it was time to protect her own. First, she needed more information. Turning to the detective, concern showing in her faint voice, she asked, "How did he die?"

Sergeant Torkless, unable to remain sliced out of this interrogation, reached for her arm and spun her around. Short memory over who had the most strength? No, it appeared to be a spontaneous act, but foolish under the circumstances.

He realized that, but recovered enough to say, "The dead guy was a drug addict. Death hovered nearby. But someone hastened it. They shoved a bag of fentanyl down his throat."

"Fentanyl?" she whispered. "A few grains are lethal. Doesn't that raise some questions?"

"Yeah, it sure does. For instance, where was the young lad, Tyler, at the time?"

Fury stood. "Torkless, that's enough."

The sergeant loosened his hold on Lizzie's arm. "Sorry about the arm. But you did ask how he died."

Fury accepted that the punch line was already delivered. He might as well tell her the rest. "They left oxycodone on the ground around him."

Before she could grasp about the oxycodone, she tried to understand why someone would waste fentanyl. Couldn't have been a drug addict.

"Was it for revenge, do you think?" She looked at Fury, standing right in front of her now, then around to Torkless. She would get her answers from one of them.

Just then, a giggling, curly-haired child raced from the parking lot and squirreled herself between Fury's legs and tried to burrow behind Lizzie's skirt.

Fury bent down, peering under the bench. "What the . . ."

They heard a whispered "Shh. I'm hiding."

All three adult heads swiveled toward the parking lot, where a mother holding a young baby stumbled forward, shuffling her purse and diaper bag and baby, keeping as fast a clip as she could toward the hospital entrance. She looked frantic. Panic in her eyes, darting here, there. Tripping in little steps. Slowing her pace as she clutched the baby tighter. Torn between each child's needs.

Lizzie saw it. Saw the fear. She whispered to the guys, "We have to tell her."

The girl had stopped giggling. She made her plea. "No, she'll make me go in the hospital, again."

Fury obviously knew kids. Or how to hedge. "Okay, we won't tell her."

Meanwhile he faced the mother, made a shushing sign with his finger on his lips, and pointed beneath the bench. He wasn't in uniform, but Torkless was.

The woman stopped her scrambling and settled the slipping purse back on her shoulder. In this area, this town, police meant safety. She nodded and approached the wide front doors. When close, she spoke loudly, "Justina, where are you? Did a monster take you to his home to cook his food?"

The little girl giggled again. "I can't cook." She crept out from behind Lizzie realizing she'd given herself away.

Mom said, "I'm happy you're okay. Did you forget the rule about not leaving my side by the streets or parking lots?"

Justina lowered her head. "Yeah. I didn't want to visit dad again."

"Don't you love him?"

"I love daddy. Sitting still is hard."

Having passed the rack of children's items on each floor, Lizzie stood, pulled out five dollars and knelt in front of the child. She held the money out to her. The child's eyes brightened.

"If it's okay with mom, you can buy a coloring book and crayons inside with this. But you must promise to keep your coloring in the book. And very important, promise you won't run around when cars are nearby."

The girl nodded solemnly, looked to her mom for approval, then reached out for the money.

The mother mouthed, "Thank you," and they walked into the

hospital, crisis averted.

Lizzie's smile converted to a frown as she reverted instantly back to the previous conversation. "So Tyler's a suspect in a murder?"

"Depends on his answers to my questions."

"I'll have his mother here in a few hours. It *is* barely dawn, you know. Delia won't answer the phone this early."

She saw Fury's glance pass over her head to the sergeant, no mean feat considering her height. Apparently neither Fury or Torkless were willing to question why Delia just got involved. Now she'd find out how crass Fury, and the police in general, would be. Small town. Friendly folks. Maybe Tyler would be okay.

She had to ask. "Did you talk to the child at all? Does he know about the dead body?"

Fury bristled. "No. Of course not. We told the head nurse. No one else. Though Tyler Hopson is not a child. He's fourteen years old."

She frowned. Looked at Torkless, then back to Fury. Would they understand?

"The age number doesn't mean much. Parts of Tyler were forced to mature early, to protect his sister and mom. To respond according to adult rules. Other parts slowed down and remained, for example the simple games in a computer world."

Hanging his head, the detective nodded. "I know."

She moved. "He's not going anywhere. I'll call you when they're on the way. But you'll have to hurry. His tutor arrives before noon."

Walking into the building, she resisted turning back to look, but as soon as the extension wall hid her from view, she did peek. She overheard their conversation. Fortunately, she'd already covered her mouth to keep from laughing.

"You gonna let her just tell you what to do?" Sergeant Torkless sputtered.

Fury stood. "Hell yeah."

He shifted his weight and walked away. The sergeant scurried after.

"What!"

Fury stiffened his neck and and waited for the hapless sergeant to catch up. "Don't you know who she is?"

Torkless grasped his arm to hold him still and face him. "Duh, an eighty-two year old lady who just dismissed us."

Before the detective sped away, Lizzie heard him chortle. That was enough for her. He'd unearthed her background. Many people misjudged what she did for the CIA. And some didn't. Detective Fury's response convinced her that he understood completely.

Didn't matter. She needed to plan.

First, talk with the nurse. Then prep Tyler. No way would she let the cops hit him cold about a dead person. She could have used more information.

Lizzie, calm and steadfast in her past work, had masqueraded as the quiet sister here at home. She continued to be fearless after retirement, as strong and cunning as ever, but the big catch, now she was involved with people she knew. She felt the bonds on her fearlessness, the possible side effects on others that matter. Fear didn't creep in, but caution ruled as she moved forward in her home territory. She would protect what she could.

The head nurse staffed the reception desk. Lizzie hadn't met her, but her stance made her titled ID unnecessary. You *knew* she was in charge. She stood, reminiscent of an oak tree, arms akimbo like branches, all in all—a drill sergeant. But as Lizzie approached the desk, she could see the woman's skin glint with perspiration. These days they called it sweat. She would treat her kindly, despite the stalwart stance and the telltale pink flush that rode her cheekbones like eagles wings ready to take flight. It could be anything. Assume nothing.

For now, she needed the woman to have compassion for one of her patients. Tyler.

Nurse Becky breezed in, not catching the tension. She halted when she reached Lizzie.

"Hi, ma'am. I'm glad you're still around, though that man from yesterday shouldn't manage to reach this far again. Security has taken measures."

Lizzie smiled. "I'll be around a couple more days. Then, you'll be on your own, though your security department seems competent."

"Nevertheless, thank you for your help. Have a good day."

Lizzie hoped the pleasant nature of their conversation would bleed into her discussion with the head nurse, who stood in the same place, still frowning.

Gentility was bred in her. She learned it at her mother's knee. But submissiveness had required training. Surprisingly, she'd mastered it. A natural trait of an herbalist who'd unwittingly been pushed into the global world, she needed it. That's what people believed of her. Little did they know of the woman who traipsed through the rain forest following local tribesmen to the illusive healing herb they'd discovered.

Or trailing the enemy.

She approached the desk, still smiling. "I hope you can help me. I'm here with the young boy in Room 410, Tyler Hopson. Your staff has helped remarkably with his recovery. But now, we have another problem." Lizzie waited. Most people would have responded, questioned about the problem. Not this woman. Pursed lips exhibited the only change in her demeanor. Okay, she'd forge ahead. "You see, the police want to interrogate him about a coincidence regarding where I found him. I don't know how to protect Tyler because I don't know exactly what they want. Did they say anything to you?"

The nurse stepped forward and slapped her arms onto the counter, the sound an echo similar to trees felled in the forest.

"Yeah, they told me you were CIA. Are you spying on us?"

Lizzie's widened eyes surprised the woman. Lizzie saw it and settled for honesty. "I did work for the CIA. Do I really look like I still do?" No point in telling her she'd *just* retired.

The woman's expression crumbled. "It did seem strange, with your age and all. But then I heard from Nurse Becky how you subdued that man with just two moves."

"You don't forget the moves. They were drilled into us. For those with desk jobs it came harder. They drilled, plus the office work." Okay, a little misleading. But who will tell her. My work report is all redacted.

"I'm sorry. I overreacted. I just couldn't stand the idea of a spy in our midsts."

Lizzie noticed she didn't smile, but at least the scowling wrinkles readjusted some.

"I understand. You run a great ship here. But honest, I don't even own a pair of sunglasses."

She couldn't believe it. The woman showed no emotional response whatsoever. *Well, humor was never my strong suit.*

A few seconds later the steel-spined woman cracked a killing grin. Lizzie beamed back. *I guess her humor gene is as rusty as mine. Maybe it'll be fine working with her.* She'd try her pitch.

"Who would want interference? But I'm here to help Tyler. Did the police say anything to you about him?"

"Yes. The young cop implied Tyler killed someone."

CHAPTER 9

Lizzie crept down the hospital hallway, its softened lighting in deference to sleeping patients. Beeping machinery from some patient's rooms, troubled groans of sleepers in pain, the swishing of a nurse's pant legs as she rushed to answer a call button, echoed loudly down hollow halls in the quiet night. Daytime sounds would resonate soon enough when the change of shifts wakened the wing.

A silent sentinel in his doorway, she found Tyler out cold in his bed, a the slight breath and rising chest attesting to life. The removal of the IV made her smile at progress. She admired his curly black hair. Her hair hung so blasted straight she resorted to stuffing it in a bun. He would be leaving soon. He might not admire the curls as much. She'd ask. Maybe they would stop at a barber on the way home.

She stayed in the doorway, happy to see him sleeping soundly, but loneliness in the silence of the moment overwhelmed her. Strange. She'd been alone her whole life. A whisper of noise. What was it?

She stepped back to survey the hall for a trace of movement. No more sound to help her identify it, not a swoosh of clothing or a cart of meds. The sound was gone now. She chided herself for making something of shadows. She looked back one more time, puzzled. She knew it wasn't her imagination.

In the past she'd always sensed someone following her, but here, in her home territory, while she monitored a young kid's progress back to life? Didn't make sense. Better regroup. Not enough information. Not enough time. How soon should she call Delia?

Conversations from the nurse's station echoed down the hallway. The nurses were stirring. Must be shift change at seven. She pressed the timer on her watch. She'd call Delia by half past seven.

Her thoughts reverted to Detective Fury. Was he ham-handed? Clueless? Willing to see Tyler's side of things? Would he believe the kid's side of the story? Did he know how to investigate a murder? What evidence did he search for? The whole area had probably been trampled by now. Thoughts jangled, but none fell into sequence.

She needed more facts. Could she finagle information out of Fury? Perhaps Sergeant Torkless? Hah. Not likely. Maybe with others, but she'd put the wrong arm forward earlier. Bad move, though he so asked for it at the time.

Everyone fell under Delia's charm. Her sister could turn Torkless into a congenial human being. Maybe she could get inside evidence details from him.

She called Delia, who answered, barely alert. She kept saying mhmm. She needed to repeat twice the part about stalling the detective when he waited outside for Emily, before she got it right.

Now Lizzie needed to get any information she could from Tyler. Talk with him before the police came. She juggled his shoulder with a slight touch of her fingers. "Tyler, you need to wake up now."

He sat up with a jerk. Eyes opened. She held his shoulder to steady him. He must have realized who it was because his breathing calmed.

"What?"

"The police are coming soon to have a talk with you. I need you to tell me everything you remember about your time in the warehouse."

"Wow, me? Why?"

His face revealed surprise, and not a hint of a frown to show worry, or fear. Good. She expected he wasn't involved, but his initial reaction now convinced her.

Using her soothing voice she said, "They have questions about an incident that happened there." Might as well say it outright. He'd know soon enough. "They found a body in the warehouse. Maybe you can help, depending on what you saw. What happened while you were there?"

"Not much. I remember going. Feeling terrible. They said I could find more pills there. Not that I had much money left."

"You mumbled about a guy with a scar after you came awake in the emergency room. Tell me about him."

"Umm. He was in the warehouse. I found him in a back room. Asked about oxycodone. He took my money. All of it. Then he snickered. I remember I was shaking again. I asked where the pills were. Said I needed some."

Lizzie nodded for him to continue.

"The guy stretched his legs out in front of him on a dirty blanket and pushed the back of his head against the rotting wall. His long, dirty hair blended into the dark wood. He almost disappeared into it. Then he said, 'Come back later. I got a meetin' now. Scat, before he gets here.' He said it like that—meetin.' I especially remember that part, because I was so mad. But I saw a knife stuck in his waist band. I didn't wait around."

Lizzie did wait. She grimaced internally. No sense in scaring him more. But she'd find the guy and he wouldn't be frightening anyone again. She smiled gently and asked, "Then what?"

He groaned. "I don't know."

She patted his chest. "Nothing else?"

"You were carrying me. But I don't know when that was."

"Okay, let's back up. What day did you go to the warehouse?"

"I think a Tuesday or Wednesday. I checked the corner for Hector first but he hadn't shown in days."

"I found you on Friday."

"You never said why were you looking for me?"

"Your mom, of course. She was worried sick but afraid to call the police. She found out Ethan's dad dealt in drugs. Since he was gone, they couldn't ask him if you kids were involved."

He hopped out of bed. "No way. Not Ethan. He hated drugs. He was ready to beat up that kid that hung on the corner. And that was before I bought some stuff from the guy."

He hung his head. "Ethan was gone by then." Then he lifted that head as if it weighed a ton and looked at her. "I should have paid more attention to my friend."

"Some things are easy to say after the fact."

He blinked his eyes—looked to be hiding tears, but she didn't comment. Then he grinned at her. "Ain't that the truth?"

She glanced at her watch. "The policeman's name is Detective Daniel Fury. When he comes, just be honest with him. But short answers. Don't add anything. Oh, and the good news. He needs your mom's permission to talk with you. You'll get to see her for a bit today, too."

"Great!"

"Okay. I'm going outside. Quick, get dressed."

"Are you leaving me?"

"No. I have to make some calls. I'll bring your mom in with the detective when they come."

She saw the tension drain out of him with a big exhalation. Why the kid latched on to her was a mystery, but it felt good. Now to find a way to help him from this sticky mess.

She called Delia with a plan.

"Jeesh Lizzie, I just pulled up in front of their house. But I'm on it."

"Cool it, sister. I need help with a plan."

"More help than getting me up at seven in the morning?"

"Thought you wanted to be my partner in fighting crime?"

"I forgot for a minute. Brain not functioning without my tea. What can I do?"

Lizzie spoke abruptly as she marched outside trying to shake off the stress. She needed to be alert. "I must be there when you introduce Fury to Emily. Prep her about what I'm going to do. I'll be setting up my phone to record what is being said in Tyler's room. Tell his mother to wear clothes with big pockets. When you arrive at the hospital try to divert the detective's attention enough for me to slip the phone into Emily's pocket."

She turned the corner and bumped into the detective, coming up from the parking lot. She'd just replaced her phone into her pocket. *Thank you God. Maybe I'm doing the right thing after all if you're watching over me.* She knew that reacting defensively would sound suspicious. Instead, she coyly asked, "Why detective, what a surprise.

Delia and Emily won't be here for an hour. What brings you this early?"

He struggled with two cups of Starbucks coffee while he jiggled keys into his pocket. "Quick grab the right one. It's yours."

She reached for the coffee and sniffed. "What is it?"

"I gambled that you would be a regular, no expressing, no foaming, no sugar."

She took a deep swallow. "Perfect. But why do I need bribing?"

"Too cheap for a bribe. But I ran my errands in record time and needed the caffeine. Thought I'd come here and relax until young Mr. Hopson's mother arrives. We can sit in his room and chat, no interrogation, I swear. Or sit out here."

She took another sip. Swallowed. Pursed her lips. Maybe getting to know each other, casual like, might be to Tyler's benefit. She kept walking, knowing he would follow. They took the stairs. Lizzie wanted the exercise.

"Too much sitting and I'll get out of shape," she said as they made the third landing and continued up one more floor. The detective kept up with her with no problem. He apparently didn't need the stairs, but it couldn't hurt him.

She formally introduced Tyler to the detective. Fury kept to his best behavior and responded in kind. Tyler shook his hand, but grinned when he did it.

Detective Fury said, "I would have brought you a drink, too, but didn't know what you'd want. Can I get you anything from the hospital cafeteria?"

The grin widened. "Anything?"

"Sure thing."

"What about a chocolate malt and an egg sandwich?" Lizzie shook her head.

"I mean a veggie smoothie and an egg sandwich."

Lizzie smiled. The kid would make it yet.

Fury swallowed the last of his coffee, tossed the cup in the trash, and said, "Right on it."

Balancing the veggie smoothie and the egg sandwich, Fury entered, then pulled the chocolate shake from behind his back. "For later." He set it on the bedside table next to the bowl of fruit.

Tyler grabbed the sandwich, took a big bite. He saw them staring at him, and took smaller bites. They sat having a friendly conversation about the Philadelphia Flyers, Penn State baseball and hospital food.

Lizzie and Fury left the floor and reached the parking lot as Delia's old Ford screeched up to the front door. Delia leapt out while Emily moved with quick steps to the curb. Anxiety marred her forehead. Heather climbed out, moving with hesitation.

Delia bent a slight nod to Lizzie to come closer as she swept Heather up with a laugh, glad the child held her favorite toy, Marcus the monkey. She grinned at the girl and said, "Good morning Marcus. Were you a stow-away in my car?"

Heather giggled. "What's a stoway?"

"Why, someone in hiding who wanted a free ride." Delia converged on the detective at the same time as Emily and her sister. Lizzie smiled at the picture they made, similar to synchronized swimming, or at the very least, a choreographed dance. But it suited her purpose.

Delia introduced her friends. "This is Heather, and her stow-away, Marcus. Say hello."

He wisely played the game and shook hands with Marcus first. "Hello Heather, glad to meet you." Heather wiggled Marcus's hand and laughed. Lizzie dropped her phone unseen into Emily's pocket while the child said, "Silly, that's not Heather. That's Marcus the monkey. I'm Heather."

Detective Fury apologized as he looked up and caught Lizzie's grin. Probably never been called silly in his life, but played a good sport and just winked at her. Maybe he would be fine with Tyler, but she wanted to be sure. Thus the phone on record.

Fury told Emily why he needed to question Tyler. As they walked in, he said, "It would help if you don't interrupt or try to explain things." His whole face smiled as if he sincerely cared. "He'll be fine. We'll be gentle. And if there is more you want to say, we can talk later, okay?"

Tyler raced from the room and hugged his mom in the hall. Lizzie put her finger to her lips to remind him not to disturb the other patients. Once they were all settled inside, the detective began with simple questions that didn't mention opioids.

When Fury asked why he started taking the pills Tyler said, "The kids mocked me. They knew who I was, how poor we were. They said Tyler was a highfalutin name."

Fury nodded. "That's it?"

"One guy threw a brick at me. They knew the holes in my jeans were from wear, not fashion. They hit me. Spit on me. One guy offered me a pill. Said I would feel better. Called it oxycodone." Tyler stopped abruptly.

The detective waited, then said, "It's okay son. You can tell me the rest. I spoke with your doctor. There were no drugs on you when you were brought in."

The kid continued, "I didn't take his pill. But then I saw mom's pills. They looked the same. Said OxyContin. So I took one. I liked feeling good. Sure hadn't been lately. My one friend disappearing. The tough guys picking on me."

Fury just waited in silence. Finally Tyler glanced at his mom, then down. "Mom wanted me to be strong, happy."

He repeated everything he told Lizzie, but added, "I don't remember too much after that. I said I tore off. But I guess I meant I barely got out of there. I'd been sick to my stomach. I hadn't eaten in days. I was dizzy. Maybe made it a couple of rooms over. I tripped. Fell. Lay there. Real cold."

Fury said, "And . . ."

"I guess Miss Ort found me later."

"You said you saw a knife. Describe it?"

"I umm, saw the top of the handle. I guessed it was a knife. It reminded me of my friend's pocket knife, only maybe bigger."

Fury stood and nodded.

Tyler's mother shifted on the small chair they'd brought in for her, but kept quiet.

And then it was over. Emily hugged him, and whispered goodbye.

Lizzie passed the detective as he left the room and thanked him for the coffee. "Are you done with him?"

"For now."

Intercepting Emily as she passed through the doorway, Lizzie lifted her phone from the woman's pocket. Nodded a silent thank you. "Delia is at the front door. She'll take you home."

Then she and Tyler sighed in unison. Both said, "Not bad." and smiled.

Tyler took one last slurp of the chocolate malt, and grinned.

Standing at the window, watching the leaves blow in the wind, Lizzie said. "The worst is over."

Tyler's smile turned into a frown as Jenny Lyn peered in from the hall. "Oh no. The worst is right there."

CHAPTER 10

Jenny Lyn ventured in, bent, and slung her book bag to the floor as if it carried all the woes of the world and she needed a break as caretaker. She managed a shy hello to Tyler and glanced at Lizzie with downcast eyes.

Lizzie took charge. "I'm Lizzie Ort. I arranged with Mrs. Donegal for your tutoring. You can call me Lizzie. I'll be hanging around outside or down the hall as you have your sessions. If you need anything, just look for me."

Jenny Lyn looked flustered, maybe wondering if she should shake her hand, but let it go and dropped her own fluttering hand. "Hello."

"Thank you for coming and if you need rides to and from here, let me know."

Jenny Lyn nodded.

Lizzie gave her money and asked her to go to the cafeteria and purchase her and Tyler a drink. A ruse to give Tyler a moment to regroup. First a cop. Then a girl tutor. A moment was all he'd get today.

Tyler refused to sit on the bed. He straightened his clothes, combed his hair, and using the bed as a desk, spread out his books and papers. He obtained folding chairs from the nurse, one for him, and one for Jenny Lyn. The room became crowded, but Lizzie understood. He'd draped his book bag over the comfortable chair by the bed. His move said, no dallying here. This is business.

He sat and leafed through a book. The port for IV's still taped to Tyler's hand obstructed fluid movement, but at least he could move his hand with the IV tubes removed.

Lizzie saw the shaky confidence hidden beneath. "You okay, Tyler? Not worried about what she'll think, are you?"

He grimaced. "I'm in a hospital room because I was addicted. What will she think?"

"That you're a guy, and for a while you let your school work drift. Put it on the back burner while you tackled other problems."

"Does she know about the dead guy?"

"No way to know unless she speaks about it. You just need to concentrate on a game plan to review your work and catch up."

He took a deep breath and raised his chin up a notch.

Jenny Lyn breezed back in, handed him a drink, opened her book bag, and pulled out a legal pad of paper covered with a list. Her long blond hair, tied up high in a ponytail, swished when she moved. Despite the cool temperature, she'd arrived in skinny jeans and a T-shirt. Lizzie bit her tongue and said nothing.

Jenny Lyn and Tyler chatted about school and classes. They were freshmen in high school, fourteen going on twenty. They quickly settled into a routine as Jenny had Tyler review what he knew of each subject and they agreed on a starting point of covering new information. Tyler smiled a little at one of her remarks.

She said, "Let's tackle the worst first, shall we?" She pulled out her algebra book.

Tyler frowned. Liz backed away a step at a time.

Jenny flipped to a chapter mid book. "Were you in class when we learned exponents and roots?"

"Yeah, that was gross."

"Sure was. Couldn't wait to move to simple equations."

Liz noticed the bonding. It was a good plan after all. At first she feared it would blow up on her. As they discussed exponents and roots, equations and inequalities she realized how intense education must be these days. More to learn than the plain equations she studied. She sighed. Didn't matter. She'd done a job and done it well. Math didn't often factor in, but it had honed a skill for logical thinking. That meticulous planning had saved her skin many a time.

Jenny Lyn's question to Tyler interrupted her memories. "Do you know how polynomials involve different powers of the same variables?"

Wow. Polynomials. What would they think of next? She wondered how that could have helped her in the field. No way of knowing now. She was out of it for good. She'd planned to leave, before her ankle buckled. She'd feared for a while that the orders coming down to kill people weren't backed by true American need for safety and security. Politics had infiltrated worse than the enemy.

Lizzie felt a light touch on her shoulder and managed not to jerk as she turned around. The present beckoned in the form of Nurse Becky, who stood there and motioned her out of the room. Her pursed lips were the suggestion Lizzie needed to suggest they move further down the hallway.

Taking her to the empty room next door, Nurse Becky shook out her hands as if ridding them of dirty water, then prefaced her concern with caveats before she began with her main worry. Nurse Becky said, "I've notified security, but there wasn't much to tell them. Still, I wanted you to know. Not that there's much to know, you know what I mean?"

Lizzie took her hand, stilled it with her warm fingers, and said. "Why don't you start from the beginning?"

"Have you met Nickeisha Clarke? She's the night nurse this week."

"I think I met her briefly the first night. A spirited Jamaican woman?"

Nurse Becky beamed. "Yes, that's her. She's unassuming but extremely good at her job. Patients love her."

Interrogation ranked at the top of Lizzie's skills. Patience was tough. She did not want to interrupt for fear it would drag on longer. She clutched her hands in front of her and merely nodded.

The nurse stood, stammering.

"Nurse Becky, let me help you."

She straightened her spine and her speech improved instantly. "Just Becky, please. Call me Becky. I thought I'd ask her to stay and tell you about it. But we had meetings first thing, then the policemen were here for Tyler. We didn't call them last night because we didn't have anything to report."

She held up a finger to suggest the nurse wait one minute while she took a few steps to peek around the corner and see that the two teens were still engrossed in their work. She returned her attention to Becky, who had held her thought in the air and continued the second she got Lizzie's nod to do so.

"But it wouldn't hurt to tell you. Right?"

"Right. Tell me."

"Nurse Nickeisha saw someone last night. But she's not sure what or whom. Since her story is this vague, I wasn't sure who I should report it to. She mentioned it to security. You know, to have them be more aware. There didn't seem to be more I could do when she told me this morning."

"What exactly did she see?"

"She saw someone coming down the corridor walking toward's Tyler's room. When he saw her, he left. Said she couldn't see much. He was tall, but not much more."

"Okay."

"That's it. But I thought you might be willing to talk with her. I asked her to come in at noon to meet with you in case you had concerns."

Lizzie exhaled, relieved. This she could handle. But she would worry, depending on what was going on. "Thanks Becky, I will see her. The cafeteria at noon?"

"Perfect. I'll let her know."

They walked to the corner of Tyler's room, where Lizzie checked on the kids, still talking about equations. She stopped Becky from leaving with a touch of her hand on the nurse's arm. "I noticed a small waiting area around the corner. If it's not in use when Jenny Lyn comes back for her next lesson, can they meet in there? I think it would make Tyler feel more comfortable."

"Sure. Anytime. We don't cater to house arrest. And his health is improving rapidly."

"Thanks."

Leaving Tyler at lunch time was no problem. He grumbled about his math homework, coming from a girl and all, he said. But he looked alert and active and challenged. He would be ready to come home soon.

While waiting for Nurse Nickeisha, she ate a small salad in the cafeteria, passing up grilled chicken and lightly sauteed vegetables. She and Delia were supposed to eat out later so she didn't mind saving on calories now. It was an unusual feeling, since in her past life she ate whenever she could, never knowing when she'd have time later. She smiled at the new normalcy. It was good to be home.

The night nurse bustled in, then dropped into the chair opposite, suppressing a large yawn, barely covered by her hand. "Sorry, didn't get much sleep last night but Nurse Becky convinced me to talk with you."

Lizzie offered her lunch but she settled for coffee. When Lizzie placed it in front of her, the nurse moved her silverware around, as if to help to organize her mind. She looked up, anxious to begin.

"I saw this man. It was after two in the morning. He startled me. A large one, he was. Six feet tall, and big. He was at the far end of the corridor, walking toward me."

She sipped her coffee, then licked her lips as if to fetch every drop.

"I turned the corner from the other end. I'm sure he didn't hear or see me at first. He had his head down but walked with confidence. Then he stumbled a little. Surprised me. Wondered what was wrong with him. He righted his step immediately, but he looked up and saw me. I didn't rush to help because he looked fine at that point."

"It does seem a little strange, at that time in the morning. What else?"

"What bothered me was the green scrub suit he wore. In this hospital we use them for surgery. The doctors may visit after surgery to check on a patient but usually do that during rounds, in the white jackets. And it was the middle of the night."

She looked wide-eyed at Lizzie, as if seeing him again in her mind. Her eyeglasses were a part of her face. One knew she wore them from morning to night. For now, they magnified her startled reaction, as if it was happening all over again.

She continued, "When he saw me, he stopped on the spot, and headed back toward the elevator just around the corner. I picked up my step to see him better before he left, but he was already gone. I called security and asked them to check around but they couldn't find anyone. The elevator stopped at the surgical floor, you know, third floor, but if he got off there, he could have walked to anywhere, down the stairs. And he'd done nothing wrong. I left it at that."

Lizzie frowned, her concern showing in the fine lines around her eyes. "Where exactly did you see him?"

Nurse Nickeisha looked up from her fast diminishing coffee. "Walking toward Tyler's room. No one in the next two rooms, or the one before Tyler's. So where was he going? That's why Nurse Becky thought you should know."

"Good call. I will look into it." Maybe stagger some visitors in Tyler's room. Keep him protected, assuming nothing would happen with others around. Weak. But it might help. Her mind swerved to the herb conference earlier in the year when her sister Delia helped round up volunteers to unofficially guard their friend Abby, in danger from an unknown killer. She could do it again.

"Nurse Nickeisha, you are truly a godsend. I had no idea that Tyler might be in danger. If what you saw turns out to be unrelated, it still reminded me that Tyler may have seen someone the night that drug dealer was found. Or possibly the killer thought he saw something, and has come to find out."

She deliberately left out that he probably came to silence Tyler. No sense in worrying the woman without the facts.

She rose. "I appreciate you cutting short your sleep to inform me. Can I get you another cup of coffee?"

The nurse pushed up out of her chair. "No, I'll be fine. A walk outside may do me more good."

Lizzie wrapped her arm around the woman's shoulders. "Let's walk this way. It always cheers me up to see new life, and provides me strength to continue." They walked the stairs to maternity. The head nurse recognized both of them and went back to her paperwork while they stood outside the nursery, enchanted.

Lizzie pointed to two underweight babies in the far corner. "They're waiting now for their foster mothers to pick them up. Been here a month and finally improved enough to leave. They were both addicted at birth from young addicted mothers."

Nickeisha studied them. "They're still underweight."

"Not as much. And the foster mothers know what to do." She sighed. "At least two come in a month. I hope my teen center will turn that around. Keep the teens from addition, and also their babies."

As they headed outside, Lizzie said, "Oh, I was thrilled to see Tyler was taken off his IV during the night. Is he able to go home now?"

The nurse halted. She grabbed Lizzie on both arms, raising startled eyes to her face.

"What are you talking about? We didn't remove the IV."

"He still has the port but the stand and IV are gone."

"No!"

They both raced to the elevator. Lizzie's mind flying. Tyler is fine. Tyler is fine. I saw him. What happened? She spoke her thoughts out loud so Nickeisha would understand her fear. "Could the man have come by earlier, removed the IV thinking it would cause repercussions, or death? Maybe came back to see the results but he saw you and stopped?"

As they waited for their floor, the nurse asked, "Is Tyler alone now?"

"I figured with the bustle around lunchtime that he would be okay."

The door opened and fortunately no one else waited to get on. Both women barreled out when it hit their floor, and sped to Tyler's room. And stopped. He sat in the chair with his food tray, laughing and giggling with one of the nurse's aides.

Lizzie barked, "Tyler, who removed your IV?"

He looked puzzled. Mumbled, "The doc did early this morning. "You know, the one you met last week."

Both women sighed, their breath whooshing out in obvious relief. Nurse Nickeisha pushed the call button. "Let's get that needle out of you then."

Tyler grinned at that. "Yeah, the doc said someone would be by."

The nurse grinned back. Then mouthed to Lizzie, "We'll keep him covered."

Lizzie saluted goodbye. Crisis averted. On to the next one. She didn't know what, but there was sure to be one.

CHAPTER 11

The bar reeked of what she hoped was spilled beer and liquor that had seeped into the floorboards. Hard to tell with all the crud down there. Delia surveyed her sister in the dirtied gardening pants and ratty watch cap. Her own gardening jacket from the trash topped the outfit, the dirt matching the one she wore herself. What were they doing here, looking as grungy as the rest of the patrons in this minus one-star bar that never heard of Michelin?

"His eyes look mean, angry," she said. The guy she referred to sat three bar stools down, staring down the bartender in what she read as anger.

"No," Lizzie said. "That's despair on its last thread. He probably didn't have enough money to buy any more heroin so he wasted it on a drink and now he blames the bartender."

"I thought you could get heroin for $5 a bag these days?"

"True. But you haven't had this beer." Lizzie pointed to the price sign behind the bar.

"Two dollars a beer?"

"And that's high for this swill." Lizzie looked around, though she moved mostly her eyes with a slight swivel of the head.

They hadn't made enough plans for this particular foray into the seedy side of life. Delia had been warned not to look conspicuous, or nosy, but what specifically could she to do, sitting on a bar stool, no less. She knew Lizzie had started her search for Tyler here, and hoped to find a lead to the killer. What they hadn't discussed was how this place would help.

She'd have to scrub her hair afterwards. Uncertain how to act and how to recognize a killer when she saw one, she swiveled her head to look around. Yet, it was her idea to accompany Lizzie. Her sister's skepticism on whether she could handle it cinched the deal. No way would she prove Lizzie right. She'd swallow this swill if it permanently damaged her esophagus.

Not a good time to tell her sister she'd never had a sip of beer, let alone this brand, she sipped again. The plan had been fuzzy at best.

Speaking out of the side of her mouth, she said, "Remind me of the game plan."

Lizzie squinched her eyebrows into a scowl. "To find the killer."

"I meant the detailed list. The one that made heading to a bar after midnight in filthy clothes worthwhile. I remember, to look for a guy holding a BMW keyring. Right?"

"You have the general idea."

"Should I dig in all their pockets?" She decided to be nice and switched topics. "You mentioned Ethan earlier?"

"I don't think we'll find him here. Maybe his dad, but I got the feeling they all fled town. I need to find more about the man. A picture would help."

"Emily said his name was Verge Innis. Maybe we could find out more in his neighborhood. Some areas in town the people are so close they know what each family had for dinner by later that evening."

"Good idea. I could pursue that tomorrow. For now, let's look for the face Tyler described. And listen."

Delia didn't normally do scruffy. She struggled to get in the mood. She hoped for a mirror over the wall behind the bar to view the room. No matter. It probably would have been too gungy to see in it anyway.

She'd been thrilled they served the beer in glasses right from the tap rather than bottles. Numerous hands must have touched those bottle tops. Until she saw the dirty glass. But then this place catered mostly to men. She scooched up to the bar and cradled the glass without touching it, hoping she appeared to want a better grip on her beer instead of needing to sit closer to Lizzie to speak freely.

Drinkers filled the bar despite the lack of amenities, such as a decent place to sit.

"These barstools are torn, lack in comfort, and require a jump shot to get your butt high enough to land on them."

"Sis, hush. Tough guys don't whine."

"These guys look more uncouth than tough. You know, lacking sophistication and knowledge of the finer touches in life—like razors, or good manners."

Lizzie shook her head and sidled sideways to study them.

A guy behind Delia kept waving his arm and bumping her back. His laughter held a cruel edge. She winced and reminded herself she was there to help her friend Emily. She roped Lizzie into it. The least she could do would be to assist any way possible.

She whispered. "But I can't picture this man, or your other suspects. Do you recognize the two guys you saw earlier? The ones you said were driving the BMW?"

"They're not here. I figured, it's the same night of the week; maybe they'd be back. Slim chance. It was worth the try. And quit harping about the BMW keys. I never saw them. I just saw the car as it tore out of the parking lot. Enough of them. It's time we became proactive here. Need to find who killed that drug dealer."

"What happened to the police? They can't do it?"

"If we find anything, we'll tell them. This is just an assist sort of thing."

"Good. I thought it might be a tackle-the-man-on-the-spot sort of thing. Of which I am not capable."

"Shush. Do you have to sound educated?"

"Excuse me. Should I call you a bad name and speak in exclamations, like that guy over there?"

"No but you could listen to him. See if he says anything about the warehouse, or drugs."

"Gotcha."

Lizzie shrugged one shoulder closer to her sister. She lowered her beer to the scratched counter, and spoke in her quiet, deep voice. "Fury described the dead guy. Wouldn't let me see him though. There's no way it was the dealer Tyler said stole his money in the warehouse. No scar."

Delia pretended to sip her beer and casually studied a few of the patrons. Maybe she could get used to this. Of course, she may have to suture her nose shut first.

"So, the guy with the scar could be the killer?"

Lizzie said, "Uh-huh, you catch on quick."

Delia inched her head closer to her sister. "Do you think we'll find him here?"

"Doubtful." Lizzie glanced down.

Was she observing shoes and not faces. Puzzled, Delia wiggled her eyebrows downward and asked, "So who are we looking for, now? And will he be on the floor?"

"No silly. I'm looking for another couple of guys. Professional geeks, I think. On drugs. Maybe they came right from work. Slick shoes."

Delia studied the floor. "If they were here before in business shoes with those smooth soles, they probably fell flat on their faces skidding around on the cruddy filth scattered here. Look in the hospital. Better chance."

"Hey buddy, you're not into your role here."

Buddy? Since they were masquerading as old men, what name should she call Lizzie? The lines on Lizzie's face were more prominent than ever, perhaps, Lizard?

Who would have thought that coming home would have caused her sister more grief than being in the Cold War and the ravaged countries where she suffered untold pain, mental and physical. She must help her find Tyler, and set up the teen center as a bonus. She deserved someone to help her for once.

They should have worked out code names. Could she dare say Tyler out loud? Unless she swiveled around backwards she couldn't see much more of the room. The one she'd dubbed Angry Man scowled back at her. His lips clenched and narrowed and she nudged her sister. "See, that's a sure sign of anger."

Lizzie lowered her chin, lifted the muscles in her forehead far enough to approximate a face lift, and glared at her sister.

"First, talk deeper. You're a dead giveaway for a woman. Second, he was depressed. Now he's angry because you keep staring at him. Remember, we're supposed to be low key here. Unnoticeable."

Delia muttered. "Yep. That settles it. I'll call you Lizard."

Lizzie's eyes widened. "Where did that come from?"

She muttered, "Can't hardly call you Lizzie, now can I?" Lizzie closed her eyes. Uncertain if that meant okay, or good grief, Delia sat and listened. And listened. Lots of grunts. Shuffling feet. Creaky stools. Very little talk.

She'd read up on as many kind of drugs as she could as soon as Emily mentioned Tyler might be taking the OxyContin. Every day there were more ways to ingest death, even inadvertently. Fentanyl, illegally manufactured fentanyl, oxycodone, morphine, heroin, heroin laced with other drugs.

Good old marijuana. She recalled a recent drug bust. Coughing to rough up her throat, she said, "Did you know they found 175 pounds of marijuana in someone's car last week?"

"And you're telling me this why?"

"The idea of death. Drug deaths. Sticks in my mind now. Back when weed was the drug of choice, you didn't hear of many deaths. Now, they're coming right out with it, naming one drug, Gray Death, a cocktail of opioids."

"Yeah. Life is more complicated these days. Tough on teens. More ways you can hide from the complexities of living. Let's help Tyler. We'll stay here a little longer."

Delia listened for any of the language that alluded to usage. As much as she read, she couldn't keep track. She studied the voices and the style of sentences. Actually, there weren't many sentences. Just abrupt phrases, difficult to follow. She whispered, "What about that guy that Tyler said stole his money in the warehouse. Didn't he say he had long dark hair plus that scar?"

"Yup."

Delia rose from her stool to wander around with her beer. Lizzie grabbed her arm and drew it downward, like the motion to tell a dog to sit. Normally, she wouldn't let her get away with the insult. But here? Maybe she was right. She sat on the stool sideways, hoping to find the guy with the scar at least. Lizzie lowered her eyes, appearing to be doing the same.

"You told me Tyler mentioned a Hector, someone who

befriended him and not surprisingly sold drugs on the corner near school. Any description? Should we look for him here?"

Their heads met in the middle again. In her own convenient low tone of voice, Lizzie said, "I got the impression he was younger than this group, though Tyler never said. Maybe an older student. Seniors have more freedom to move around."

"Remember way, way back, when I taught high school? The kids sure were different then. Though we had the angry, disillusioned students, too. Drugs were found in the lockers, usually marijuana in little bags. Not a fortune worth of heroin or opioids."

"But it's difficult to picture a student who made it through the full four years while on drugs."

Two hunched men waddled out the door. Delia hopped off her stool. Lizzie clutched her arm before she took a step.

"Don't wander off."

"Make sense, Lizard. You can't see much with your back to the room. That table just opened up and I'm grabbing it."

Her sister followed, slow and easy like a lizard, while Delia flew into the first chair she could reach at the table. Practically pulled it out from under a guy twice her size. A silent battle ensued between glaring eyes, until Lizzie came up, a lizard morphed into a dragon. They both sat.

The big guy left. The new view replicated the same mottled crew.

Lizzie spoke first. "I knew we wouldn't find Ben here, the big guy bully from school, or Chunky, the one who attacked Tyler, but you were right about Hector. I had hoped he might be here."

Moving her head in an arc to take in more, all that were visible were the dark, gaunt faces that spoke of alcoholic abuse and junk food, not drugs. Delia smirked, realizing even she could tell the difference.

The room harbored many blank eyes, as if the souls were gone and only the bodies remained. Others appeared haunted, as if something within caused anguish and pain. Maybe it was desperation. Lizzie could be right after all. Despair. Not anger.

"Look at that guy. He's got grooves under his eyes big enough to be a shelf for his glasses. The glasses are a part of his face, as if he wears them from morning to night. Pealing them off at bedtime probably feels like he's removing skin."

Lizard growled. "Stop being fanciful and look and listen."

"I was looking. That's what I saw. You missed my point. Take a whiff. Look at these guys. Their appearance suggests a bad life. Maybe things they did, or that got done to them. But they look drunk, not drugged."

"Maybe I would be more useful checking with Detective Fury on what happened to Hector. He could be in jail for all we know."

"You're right. Good job for you. I don't have the finesse."

One last scan of the crowd brought Delia to her feet to face her sister with respect and admiration, allowing her to admit defeat. "You know this isn't my scene. How about I help you listen to your phone conversation, so cleverly recorded, then hunt up some fourteen year olds at school who knew Tyler?"

"I was supposed to set the phone on record? I just left it on."

"Why else did you do all that?"

"So I could listen later?"

She tsk-tsked and shook her head. "Lizzie, Lizzie, it's a phone, not an answering machine. We have to get you modern phone lessons."

Lizzie mumbled soundlessly, "We used old satellite phones, less complicated. The last upgrade I saw had more buttons than I could count."

CHAPTER 12

Lizzie strolled down Cedar Street. Her attempt at casual a little jerky. She never did casual in her past work. But this time she wasn't looking for a killer, just a kid. A missing kid. Tyler said he lived on this street. She hoped to find Ethan before she brought Tyler home. Then she could surprise him with a visit from his old friend, Ethan. But first she needed to find him.

She planned to ask a child, or a mother out for fresh air with her baby, anyone on the street if they knew the family. It might be a bad time of day. No people. No dogs, not even barking. No joyous laughter from children playing. A few mowed lawns, but lots of weedy ones, too. No flowers, except for dirty dandelions drooping so low they portrayed the sadness of the neighborhood.

Ethan's family must have been through tough times, along with the rest of the block. Tyler and his mom and sister lived two blocks away. Ethan lived in the hardscrabble end of town for sure. Not much difference in living style, except for a few brightly painted homes, porches that stood solid and upright, sentinels to a hopeful world.

A few windows were free of curtains, but most were covered in patched together cardboard. The poor and down-and-out preferred privacy too. A home at the end of the block displayed bright lace curtains, and one of them twitched as she approached on the sidewalk. The hand that swiftly dropped out of sight was fine boned and gnarled from age or arthritis. Change of plans. This person probably knew everything that went on around here.

Time for a story. Just bend the truth a little, her forte. Her knuckles tapped on the door. A genteel approach. Not threatening. Who would feel concerns for safety with an 82-year-old woman in a country skirt and brogues at the door?

It opened with a brisk swing, halted half way as a safety shield, a weak attempt. She would need caution after all. A swift move into the story was best. "Hi, I'm here on behalf of a friend, a little boy who is laid up in the hospital right now."

The bent woman stood there, proudly leaning on her cane, and nodded.

Lizzie continued. "He has a message for a friend. A teenager, I think, fifteen, who lives on this street. I clumsily lost the house address. His name is Ethan."

The woman didn't twitch. But her eyes brightened. Her head lifted a little taller and she nodded.

Lizzie went for a straight forward approach. "Can you help me find him?"

The old woman opened the door wider, but didn't bid entry. Instead, she minced closer, to the stoop, far enough to raise her cane and swing it. Lizzie stepped back. The cane pointed the way Lizzie just came from.

The surprisingly strong voice said, "Ethan lived that way, several houses down, on this side. By the dirty ball in the weeds." Lizzie spotted it and left with renewed hope, dashed instantly as the woman said, "But he's gone. The whole family. Mom and dad and Ethan. Disappeared about a month ago."

Lizzie faced her, frowning, "Did they move?"

"Word is, the house contains the furniture from before. Not much money in that house. Same as the rest of us. I call it living on a shoestring. Some of them call it living on the dole."

Lizzie asked, "Did you hear any reason why they just up and left?"

The woman slammed her cane down in front of her, and lifted and dropped her shoulders in a hopeless gesture. "It happens around here sometimes."

"Drugs involved, do you think?"

The woman shook her head. "Can't say, though his dad, or at least the man who lived there, seemed shady to me. Hardly ever around. Some mornings. Often showed up in the afternoon. Gone at night. Coulda been drugs. Who knows."

Lizzie pushed in one more question. "Do you think Ethan was involved?"

This time the woman's face cleared of frown lines as she smiled. "Not that Ethan. He came by and helped me out. Won't take no pay. Good kid. Looks clean to me. Different than some of them down the other way."

Happy to hear that, Lizzie realized she was no closer to finding the kid. She thanked the woman, prepared to leave, though she had no idea where she would go next. But the woman raised her voice a bit and said, "I'm making a cup of tea. Want some?"

Lizzie stood still, thinking, I've been invited to tea. First time, ever. New world, new ways. Her breath hitched but the inhalation triggered a response. "Would love to. I started my search for Ethan two hours ago. Never dreamt finding a kid would be this endless. When the school said he'd been gone for a month, I became worried."

The older woman held the door open. "My name is Mildred."

Lizzie swallowed her grin. Who knew which of them was the oldest? She judged by means other than a linear age line. She entered and counted her blessings, thanking the Lord for her agility and active life. "My name is Lizzie Ort."

A twinge sheared through her. Strange to hand out her name. It had never been safe. But this felt comfortable. She paused inside the door to assess the small living room. Registered every do-dad that lined the mantel, the recliner and overstuffed side chair. Afghans everywhere. No clutter on the floor. It whispered comfortable and harmless.

Mildred gestured for her to follow into the kitchen. Cheerful orange and yellow paint adorned tiny cupboards. A four-by-four-foot table barely fit on one end.

Lizzie gasped, "What a delightful view. And the garden. You grow herbs. So do my sister, Delia, and I." She sat down when the woman pulled out a chair with her cane, but continued. "You must tell me what you grow."

Over an uplifting fine cup of green tea and homemade cookies they chatted about their herb gardens. Lizzie interrupted her own sentence with an, "These cookies are delicious. What's in them?" Lacking social finesse, she licked a crumb off her finger to emphasize her enjoyment.

A smile lightened Mildred's face, too benign for a grin. But not a smirk. Maybe just a pleased reaction to a compliment. She frowned inwardly, to hide her reaction. That was ingrained. But mostly at herself. Why did she view everything as a threat? Did she think this woman would poison her?

Fortunately, the woman had moved on, unaware of Lizzie's turmoil, and listed the few herbs in the cookies, her alteration of a butter and sugar cookie.

"Hmm. Lavender and dill, an intriguing combination. Light, but triggering a distinct change from the norm. Good idea. I'll have to tell Delia. She's the chef in our house."

"I'm happy you like them. I don't have many visitors. I used to make them for Ethan and a little girl from the neighborhood. She's only five but she tagged after Ethan whenever she could. I imagined an invisible rope attached to his ankle so she wouldn't lose him."

Lizzie swallowed the last of her cookie, eager to find out more about Tyler's friend. The news was sparse.

"He's what they used to call, a strapping lad. Lean muscle, tall for his age. I think from the little I heard that he helped out his friends when he could. It's sad, but in this neighborhood bad things can happen. He was a protector of sorts. I hope he is okay, wherever he is."

"His friend Tyler, who sent me looking for him, is younger and much smaller. Slight for his age. I suspect Ethan backed him up on occasion."

They sat in friendly silence for a few minutes. Mildred, who looked out at her herb garden, said, "It's a tiny garden. Two raised beds, but useful." She acted delighted to show off the flower combinations that also served as medicinal aids. She explained that she dried lemon balm and holy basil for help with her arthritis.

Lizzie vowed to bring back some of her and Delia's salve, made for soothing arthritis.

Lizzie didn't reveal the size of their acre-plus flower beds. The good Lord had blessed them with the property to grow many healing herbs. They took advantage of this gift that made it possible to grow herbs, such as chamomile that required much space for enough tiny flowers to dry for tea or salves. Calendula also took space, but provided enough flowers for a soothing tea. Delia used it often in bruise and wound salves, and the arthritis salve.

Lizzie said, "Our shrubs and plants are native to northeastern Pennsylvania except for the culinary and some medicinal herbs."

Mildred's eyes lit up. "Tell me more about your garden."

"Many of the plants are useful, for instance, bee balm and evening primrose, but we haven't yet found native replacements for others, like comfrey and anise hyssop. "

Mildred's head bobbed up and down in agreement. "Did you know that they say the twigs of bee balm were used for a purification sprinkling in ancient Jewish rites?"

"That's one I hadn't heard. Though I find the historical uses most intriguing."

Lizzie folded her napkin and shuffled her feet. "I could sit here forever but I've been gone a long time. My sister will probably be calling the National Guard any minute. I told her I just had a quick errand." She rose and moved toward Mildred, covering her hand on the table with both of her own. "It has been a great pleasure. I hope I can bring my sister to meet you soon."

Mildred smiled, widely this time, and Lizzie took it for pure joy.

"I would love to have you." She grabbed a scrap of paper from a pile by the napkins, and the ready pencil, sharpened by hand to a small nub. She scribbled a note and handed it to Lizzie. "Here is my phone number. Please do call and keep in touch."

Lizzie took one of the other scraps and wrote their home number. "Call for any reason, but please let us know if you hear anything of Ethan."

She poured the last of the tea in Mildred's cup. "I'll show myself out. Relax."

"Thank you. It was wonderful having company. When you head

back that way, watch out for squatters. I've been here forever, before some of their grandparents. I think I must be safe under the grandfather clause."

They shared a laugh over that. Lizzie added, "Or it's the triple locks."

Lizzie winked and left. She stood on the minuscule stoop and looked back to Ethan's home. She planned to pick the lock at Ethan's and see what clues she could find. She always carried lock picks, flashlight, and her gun, of course. And people wondered why she'd adopted these voluminous country skirts that brushed her shoe tops. Her dear sister had kindly custom built the pockets for her personal needs.

She drifted to the back of Ethan's house, feeling no one watching. Her old senses still functioned. The lock, a feeble attempt at safety, opened in a second and she stepped into a small porch off the kitchen. What was that sound? She'd known a few rats in her time. The human ones were the worst. Her rubber-soled shoes moved with stealth and quiet. She stopped.

She wasn't alone. One hand reached for her gun. Her eyes scanned counter tops for other weapons. Found signs of mice. Nothing lethal. Hmm? Why mice? There shouldn't have been food out if the family left a month ago. A flick of the eyes back to the counter revealed some bread crumbs. *Fresh* bread crumbs.

She tip-toed to the inside door. Couldn't see well into the gloomy room. She swiveled toward the porch as a young lad scampered from under the counter and raced out. She followed, swift and sure, as she slid her gun back into the pocket and grasped the bedraggled child from behind, one arm under his left one, and one over the right and across the chest. A stranglehold that wouldn't strangle. A rarely used hold. Today was a good resurrection.

"Stop, lad. You'll hurt yourself. I'm a friend. I've been called a Passive Mob creature. That's a good guy." He stilled, studied her face, went limp. In the past, this was an attempted ploy for escape. With this kid, who'd passed scrawny months ago, headed to emaciated, she sensed resignation.

She turned him around.

He dropped his chin further. "I didn't steal nothing. It gets cold at night. Warmer in here."

She smiled, urging him to continue.

"And I locked the door so no one could break in and take stuff."

That brought a grin. "Good lad. I'm Lizzie. Who are you?"

"Tony."

"Tony, could we talk? I need your help."

She reached for his hand and pulled gently out the back door. Keeping him near, she snicked the lock closed and headed to the street. "First, a stop. I just came from a lady down the block who makes the most scrumptious cookies. Let's go there to talk."

Hand in hand, they walked to Mildred's. She feared he would drop before they reached the door. His reserves depleted with every step, but prevented the humiliation of an old lady having to carry him the rest of the way.

She banged on the front door, and shouted, "Mildred, it's Lizzie. Please open up."

Mildred did. And looked way up, and then down. The smile didn't falter at the scraggly child that leaned against Lizzie's side. "What'r you waiting for? Come on in."

CHAPTER 13

Mildred asked his name and invited him to sit at the kitchen table. Her words and demeanor radiated kindness and respect.

"Tony, I'm glad you came along. I have this whole pot of chicken soup and no one to share it with. I get carried away sometimes. It's my favorite." She dished it out as she spoke.

Tony delved in. After half a dozen spoonfuls, he came up for air. "It's great. It's got noodles." He swallowed two more heaping spoonfuls. Then he studied the half empty bowl. "It tastes different than the stuff we ate."

Mildred beamed. "This soup is my own recipe. There's a secret ingredient." She bent her head low and whispered it in his ear. "There's pumpkin in that soup. Now don't tell a soul."

Tony's eyes twinkled. "We should eat it all before anyone figures it out."

"Could you eat some more then? Please." She doled out enough to touch the brim of the bowl. "Now you eat that while I talk to my friend Lizzie for a moment."

Lizzie had waited patiently in the doorway to the kitchen, just beyond Tony's sight, and delighted to see Mildred interacting with him.

Deep in the foyer, they stood out of hearing distance from Tony. "I found him at Ethan's house. No sign of family, though. His, or Ethan's. He appears to be homeless, and looked desperate for food and a warm place to stay."

"I happen to have a spare bedroom. He'll be comfortable until we figure what to do with him. We need to find out more, but we should probably call the police."

Lizzie backed away. That wasn't part of her plan. But neither was running into Tony in the first place.

"Can't we talk with him first? I need to discover anything he might know about Ethan and his family. Did you ever hear that his dad dealt in drugs? His name was Verge Innis."

"Sorry, I told you of his weird hours. I'm not that much into the gossip loop. Plus, you have to realize this area doesn't do normal hanging out over the fence thing. Everyone is secretive, or frightened, or just too sad to care because they've been out of work for a year and they're losing their home."

Lizzie said, "Times sure have changed while I was gone. The neighbor-helping-neighbor system must be totally gone."

"Around here it is. But then, I'm helping you—snatches of it left. Let's see if Tony will talk more about his situation. Did he say anything about his parents? Relatives of any kind?"

"I guess that's where we start. I'm renowned for my interrogation."

Mildred's scowl preceded her words. "He's a kid. How about I talk with him and ask some gentle questions? I was a foster parent when my husband was alive. Relieving young boys of information through kindness is my bailiwick."

Impressed, Lizzie motioned her back to the kitchen.

Tony finished the soup and rubbed his belly in appreciation. He looked startled when both women sat down at the table. Lizzie decided to give her new friend the lead for now.

Shifting the soup bowl away from the lad, Mildred asked in her mild voice, "Did you enjoy it?"

"Oh yeah. And I won't snitch on you. No one will hear your secret from me."

"Good for you. Now, we do need to know a few things. I want to help you out with food and such, but we must hear about your family and why you are alone today."

The air beneath the table vibrated from the shuffling of his feat.

His legs hang in the air and couldn't reach the floor. She knew nerves could make parts of your body move when you couldn't just up and flee. Or was it guilt for Tony? But she'd wait, with patience.

He spoke low, but at least he answered. "Dad died when I was a baby, I heard. Don't remember him. He had no job. That's what ma always said."

He looked at the soup bowl with eyes that revealed the depths of his empty stomach. Mildred knew how to reach a child, from her experience working with foster children. She read the discomfort, and signs of hunger. Rising, she wondered out loud, "Hmm. What could she have meant by that?"

"Probably blamed him for us having no food."

Mildred set a plate holding a half-dozen oatmeal cookies on the table. "Now, don't eat them all. Your stomach will probably get upset if you haven't eaten for a while."

He inched his hand to the plate and took just one. But ate big bites.

"How old are you?"

He raised his head high. "I'm nine. But I'm smart. I can live on my own."

Mildred said, "Tell us about your mom."

He answered, mouth full. "She died." He grabbed crumbs that had filtered out, and ate them, too.

Lizzie softened her normal voice. "I'm so sorry, Tony. When?"

"Don't know. February, maybe. No calendars at home. They had some at school. But I stayed home to help mom. She was sick for ever, weeks maybe."

Mildred patted Lizzie's arm with a touch that looked gentle but said, 'let me, remember?' She spoke to Tony. "Did she die at home?"

He tipped his head down to hide a tear, but when she pushed the cookies forward, he rubbed his face with his arm and reached for another. "Yeah. One night. When I woke up, she wouldn't answer me. I ran to the neighbors. The woman came over."

"Then what?"

"I saw her nod her head and then cross mom's arms. I knew she was gone. I ran and ran."

"No other relatives you could talk to? Live with?"

He'd eaten the cookies in between words. Lizzie took one and handed one to Mildred, leaving one. A tasty attempt at keeping the kid from getting sick.

Lizzie said, "The police will be looking for you."

His head jerked back. "Whafor? I done nothin' wrong." Then his eyes opened wide. "I didn't kill her. She was my mom!"

Mildred recognized that Lizzie had taken over, and kept quiet. She put the last cookie in front of Tony and cleared the table.

Lizzie explained. "Not that, my dear. You're missing, same as Ethan is missing. The police will look."

"Nah. They don't care about me. And they never came to look for Ethan. He left with his mom and dad. Legit like. Not missin'."

Some progress she thought, but she hoped for more. "Did you see them leave?"

"Sure did. I stayed in that dry gully near their house. Took some dead branches from around there. Covered up. Kept me a little warmer."

"How did you see them leave?"

"Couldn't miss it. His dad screamed so loud. He said somepin' like, you're comin' with us, so quit fussing."

"Any more you can tell us?"

"Ethan said something about missin' school. Can you believe that? Upset at missin' school."

Lizzie chuckled, but stayed on target. "You moved into Ethan's house after they left?"

He lowered his head again and nodded. "They left the door unlocked."

Both women looked at him without speaking.

"They did, honest."

And now she had just locked it. Was it breaking and entering if you're the one who locked the door? Hopefully, she wouldn't have to find out, but she did need to search that house. How likely was it that a drug dealer, or addict would leave anything behind to revel their guilt? Either way she couldn't let Tony return there.

He began shuffling his feet again. She had to continue. "What rooms did you go in?"

He scrunched up his face. "The kitchen. I looked everywhere there for food. Wasn't much. Some canned beans. Yuck. I ate every one. I found the bread in a dumpster down by the main road. Wasn't too bad. And Ethan's bedroom. I went in there. Rest of the house. Too spooky."

His feet tap danced in the air this time. "I didn't take nothin'. Just some shirts. But I did sleep on the bed. It had an old blanket on it. The holes didn't bother me. Lots better than dead branches."

"Tony, this is important. I'm trying to find Ethan. Did you see anything else in the house that might seem strange? Anything left behind?"

"Just a few old shirts. Small ones. Nothin else. I was careful what with the floorboards torn up in a couple places. Near the wall."

Lizzie beamed. Bingo. A clue. She'd go now. Tony had been reasonably clean when she found him. Surprising. She couldn't help but ask. It didn't compute.

"Lad, you appear neat and clean for living away from your home. You did well. How did you manage?"

"They had well water. And a pump out back. I used that. Washed the shirt. But I borrowed this from Ethan."

He pointed with pride at the oversized shirt. "I think he wouldn't mind. It looks too small for him. I saw him. He were a big kid."

Another trip out into the hall was required. Mildred bustled over to him and pulled out his chair. "You did good. But you have cookie crumbs on you. Now I want you to go upstairs. The bathroom is at the top, and you wash your face and hands real good. There's a bedroom just across from it. Take a look and let me know what you think."

He raced upstairs, looking earnest and willing to please, even if it meant washing up. Lizzie waited till he reached the top before she said, "Can you keep him overnight? I want to search the house. If we call the police now, they might want to look there."

Mildred pursed her lips.

Lizzie saw it as a sign of hesitation. "I promise we will deal with this soon. But I have to run, and Delia will go crazy waiting much longer. We'll work on a good plan for the child."

Mildred nodded and opened the door.

The tour through Ethan's house didn't take long. Empty was empty. But the floorboards revealed much. With everything she'd heard about Ethan, she doubted he did drugs. But under the torn boards she saw a fine powder. Not much. She didn't need more to recognize heroin. Just a touch.

So Verge Innis kept some for his own use, or sold it. No pills around. He probably had no connection to Tyler, and if he left a month ago, probably had nothing to do with the dead dealer. As she traveled home to appease Delia, and get food besides cookies, she fought feelings of defeat. Clinging to one more possible hope, she'd see if Delia found anything about Hector. At least they knew he dealt in pills.

At dinner that evening they discussed the volunteer brigade of teachers, nurses and Delia's friends who she'd assembled to occupy Tyler. Agatha had visited the hospital, bringing the custom herbal plan, and regaled Tyler with how wonderful he would feel. The time went fast, but not as fast as the food. Delia made an excellent stew, making it easy for Lizzie to clean her plate. As she cleared the table, she asked, "Anything on Hector?"

"Oh dear, I forgot. Yes. The guy is being held in jail. He ran when he heard the cops were after him, and they just found him. That nice Detective Fury told me they were holding him until the judge determined what juvenile facility to send him to since he was seventeen."

The next morning, Lizzie visited the jail. The day looked much brighter than yesterday. That Sergeant Torkless was on duty. This one she could manipulate.

"How nice to see you, sir. You have a fine young man in here, named Hector. Could I see him for a few minutes, please?"

"Of course not."

"I certainly won't do him any harm. Just a few innocent questions about a possible friend of his."

"Ma'am, it's not allowed."

"Sir, I have been discreet about a certain officer's lack of muscle tone. I sure wouldn't want to leak that information to Detective Fury. I see you've been working out, though."

His frown wove his eyebrows together right across his nose.

"I won't help him escape, or hand him a weapon. A teenager is missing. I only want to ask him if he knows anything that would help."

The sergeant's frown disappeared. He'd made a decision from his heart. And thus began her interrogation of Hector, gentle by anyone's standards.

"Hi, my name is Lizzie."

"Whoa lady. Who are you? I don't want no counselor."

"You should be ashamed. Old enough to graduate from high school, and you don't know you should say, 'I don't want any counselor.'"

"Well, duh. That's what I said."

Lizzie gave up and tried to stick on track. This guy didn't compare to any drug addicts she was familiar with. Clear headed, if stupid, and clean to boot.

"What makes you think I'm a counselor?"

"You're way too old to be a cop."

She sat at the rickety table. He didn't. No chains, no handcuffs. What were police coming to? Or maybe special treatment for kids? Or kids they wanted to serve as informants? She looked around for cameras.

"So how'd you get in here? You sure ain't my lawyer. Come to think of it, he's an old dude, too."

"I played the old feeble lady card. Besides, the cop out front owed me a favor for not ratting him out."

"Whatcha got on him?"

"I don't rat, and I'm not a cop. But, I'm hoping you can help me."

"What's in it for me?"

Lizzie said, "I hoped you could take your head out of your wallet and tell me what you know of Tyler Hopson."

"Tyler who?"

His eyebrows moved into his hairline. Which didn't take much, since his black hair was scraggly and long.

"He came to you for drugs on the corner by the school. He was bullied and said you were kind to him. Helped him. Gave him some pain killers." Lizzie mentally patted herself on the back for that one. Made it sound like he was a friend and not a drug dealer.

"Oh yeah. That kid. Thought for sure he'd be back a lot. But someone snitched me to the cops."

This had been a dead end but she had to check. As she rose, she thought of one more question. "Do you know where he might have gone if he couldn't find you?"

"Sure. The Wanton warehouse. That's where I go for my stash. Went. The no-name dealer; the scar-faced one, always has plenty. He's the middleman. Never saw his source. Woulda loved that."

"The cops know any of this?"

"Not yet. I'm bartering for a better deal. You keep it that way."

She nodded, and pointed her finger at his nose. "Barter quick. I give you one day."

CHAPTER 14

Metal clanged like cymbals. Glass shattered as it crashed. Lizzie leapt from her bed into a squat to survey her room. Silence. Maybe she hadn't acclimated as well as she thought. She'd slept barely four hours. In her past career, a pin dropped nearby would have had her on her feet. This was much more than a pin. This time it took an ear-splitting percussion of sound. Was she losing her edge? No time to think.

She raced low down the stairs on bare feet. She'd left her gun upstairs. She'd do without. She often had. Where was Delia? The danger? She launched herself toward the kitchen, knowing Delia often began her day baking.

"Don't move!" The words screeched out so piercingly high that she hardly recognized it as Delia's voice. Lizzie froze. She leaned forward to peer around the doorway into the kitchen. Delia looked startled, but not scared. Hand covering her mouth, she studied the mess on the floor. "I tried to be quiet and let you sleep."

Lizzie laughed. "You might need to work on that a little. Let me help."

No. Don't move. You're in bare feet. I'll have this cleaned up in no time. You want breakfast, then?"

In the time it took Lizzie to wash and throw on some clothes and shoes, Delia delivered a scrumptious platter of scrambled eggs and toast. That part of being home had been the easiest to adjust to. Breakfast every morning, lovingly made by her sister. Sometimes she would make motions of clearing the table. Today Lizzie rose with a shove from the table that moved herself back, and tumbled her chair to the floor.

Delia usually brushed her away, as she did now. "You know I've got my methods for cleaning the kitchen. Go visit Tyler and find a killer."

She righted the chair. "I've tons to do first. I could use your help."

Delia dropped the dirty pan in the sink with a splash, wiped her hands on her flowered apron and sat within seconds. "What can I do?"

"I need you to go to school and research Ben, the big bully Tyler mentioned. We gave the formal complaint form to Emily. If she didn't sign it and return it to the school, make sure she does and please deliver it to Mrs. Donegal, the math teacher."

Delia whipped off her apron and stood, ready to leave. "I'm on it."

"Hold it. There's more. While there, see if there's a way we can determine Ben's whereabouts the day before I found Tyler. Had he maybe skipped school that day? And ask if Mrs. Donegal knows, or suspects, whether he takes drugs. Next, find out what you can about Chunky, the one who attacked him at school. And figure a way we can learn if he could have been at the warehouse. Talk with other kids, maybe? Will you be allowed to do that?"

"Sure, if Elizabeth doesn't okay it, I can do a lunch room workaround. The lunch room guards love me because I helped out often. After I retired, I mean. I think they were in diapers when I taught there."

Lizzie offered a knowing smile. Age might be hanging on to their coat tails, but sometimes it had a stronger pull than others. Today, they would keep ahead. Just.

"Anything else I can do while there? Search the corners for drug dealers, or kids swapping pills?"

"Don't laugh. You see anything like that, call me immediately. Or Detective Fury. I should probably talk with him soon, too. Don't want him to think I'm disobeying his orders not to interfere. If you find any information, it might pave the way to a tit-for-tat."

Delia's superior connections in this area ranged far wider than her own, inspiring faith in her success. She had been a teacher in the school district, an administrator, a confidant, and a perpetual volunteer. Lizzie heard a continuous barrage of kind words about her sister's delightful personality and contributions of kindness, as if she didn't already know deeply of her good deeds. Leaving that aspect of the search in capable hands, Lizzie outlined her own plans as she prepared to leave.

"I'll drop by Tyler's room and make sure he's been working on his math and English. And accepting a girl as his tutor. And I need to stop and see Mildred and Tony and develop a game plan there."

She mentally finished the plans as Delia drove her to the hospital on her way to the school. First, she wanted to pick their brains about Ethan's dad again. His pursuit had inched to the top of the to-do list.

"Sis, do you think I should buy a car? I don't want you to chauffeur me around all the time."

"You know I don't mind driving you, but when we're both in a hurry, it might be useful. Let's think about it after we find this killer."

"Don't forget, according to Detective Fury, we're not looking for a killer. Just minding our own business."

"My business is helping you find a killer, but I won't tell him that. You're on your own if he asks what you're doing."

"It's nice having an older sister. *She's* always got my back."

"Hush. We're here. Get out. Do good."

Surprised, Lizzie found Agatha with Tyler, explaining that it seemed a good time to finalize the health program with him, what it would involve, and why. "I introduced him to the names of many of the items."

Tyler said, "She told me what each one does and why I need it. Who knew food could pack this much wallop. Oo-ee."

Agatha laughed and said, "We went through most of the foods and herbs. That should be enough for now. We covered the basics last time."

He said with awe, "Did you know that blueberries and grapes help my mitochondria? I read about those structures in *A Wind in the*

Door by Madeleine L'Engle."

Lizzie expressed delight and Agatha left some leaflets. She told Tyler, "Take a look at these while my friend and I confer privately."

Out in the hall, Agatha said, "Delia called yesterday to say Jenny Lyn was scheduled today for tutoring, but had a last minute quiz to take and couldn't get here. She didn't want Tyler alone, and we decided he could handle a preview now of what we hope he will do when he gets out. I'm waiting for the next volunteer now."

"Do you think he suspects we're not leaving him alone?"

Agatha glanced inside. Tyler leafed through the information. "He didn't mention it."

"I forgot to ask how they were covering nights without him knowing."

"The floor receptionists were forewarned; no entry at night unless preauthorized by the head nurse. The stairwells are locked and rechecked throughout the day. Personnel who use the elevator must have a photo passkey newly issued by security this week."

Lizzie, overwhelmed with support, stammered, "I need to find this killer! Many people help, yet that puts them at risk, including you."

Agatha shrugged. "That's okay, dear. I have my pepper spray ready night and day. Someone taps my shoulder this week to get directions, they're laid low with spray."

Lizzie laughed at the light tone. "Well, pull it out now. And be careful. Any idea who the volunteer is?"

"No."

Lizzie winced. "We were given a list. It said, 'Don't leave him with anyone except . . .,' but I forgot it."

The next volunteer, a chatty woman from Delia's church guild, arrived then, and Lizzie asked Agatha to drop her off at Mildred's. She briefly explained who Mildred was. "I wish she could remember more, or listened to gossip. Maybe she can steer me to someone else living nearby."

On the way there, Agatha said, "Delia told me you might need a car. You know Dave and Carmelita who run the herb farm now? They said they have a spare. You can drive it a while and decide if you want to buy it. Call them to work it out."

"Thanks so much, and for the ride today, too."

Once she arrived, Mildred came to the rescue after a pow-wow to discuss what they needed to cover today. She outlined how she could deal with Tony's future care, within the guidelines of the police, and Children and Youth.

"Tell the police you want to come visit with a young lad who has a story to tell them. Please don't mention my role in any of this."

Lizzie walked home to do online research about recent heroin busts. Maybe that would provide a new lead.

* * *

Dusk came early, brought on by the thunder clouds portending a wet drive home. Delia scuttled quickly from the car to fetch peaches and sugar from the local grocery store. If she hurried, she might beat the downpour. She loved Mr. Mancini's store, the scents, logical but unusual groupings of food, and his kind attention to each customer. He'd owned it most of her adult life. You walked through the door and entered a different realm, one redolent of garlic and tomatoes, as if they already filled the pot and were bubbling away. She often wondered if he didn't have a secret kitchen in the back, where the missus, as he called her, lovingly conjured up the scents of pasta sauce and fanned it up and down the aisles to catch the weary shopper unaware. It must be a subliminal trigger.

Delia sniffed the ripeness of fruit as she traversed the produce aisle. She needed peaches to bake a cake. She loved peaches, but they had no room to grow fruit trees. Usually, she bought from the local farmers and canned them herself, but she'd already run out this year. Now she wanted to make a special dessert for her sister. And searched for the perfect peaches.

She laughed quietly, thinking she probably ate too many peaches before they hit the pot last August. She'd have the cake in the oven and baking away first thing. Then she'd prepare Lizzie's favorite beef casserole with tons of their own oregano. She always grew it in the kitchen window to have it whenever Lizzie came home.

Delia was thrilled her sister was home to stay. Doing these favorite things might provide her the contentment to keep her happy here. She'd traveled the world and could live anywhere. Maybe the information gathered today at the school will help with Tyler. Then she would rally troops to support the teen center. She doubted if Tyler wanted to be a poster child—but that's how she thought of him—someone to spur on the community to provide more guidance for the teens.

She walked faster, head down, concentrating on a few other needed ingredients. She wanted to get out and home quickly. She checked out and charged forward, through the beginning rain drops, keys in one hand and the bags in the other. Another reason to love Mancini's grocery store. He always offered paper bags with sturdy handles to transport the goods. Dusk deepened the shadows in the parking lot.

A hand grabbed her around the waist, with the other forcing a knife to her throat from behind. She dropped the bags. Afraid to tug on his arm. She went limp. He cinched her tighter. The man's voice whispered a message. It was over in minutes. Mr. Mancini ran out. He helped Delia inside out of the rain and placed her on the nearest chair. She shook uncontrollably. He ran and found a blanket to cover her. She heard him call Lizzie on his way back out. She thanked him for that, and the blanket. He knelt in front of her and said, "I saw the groceries fall from your hands and a man. By the time I got here the car sped away, shooting gravel."

As he wrapped her in the blanket, he said. "My wife called the police."

She settled back for the wait, and took a deep breath. The first full one since she walked outside. Within minutes Lizzie roared up in Julia's son's hot rod. Delia didn't ask if he loaned it or she hot wired it. Best not to know.

Lizzie parked it half on the curb and sprinted in. Delia raised her eyebrows at Lizzie, nodding at the car.

Her sister looked chagrined. "I know, I need to get one of my own. What happened?"

The police arrived and asked the same thing.

She told them. "A man grabbed me from behind in the parking lot, held me tight." As if she just realized the danger of the attack, her voice halted, then steadied. "He shoved this large knife toward my throat. I thought I was dead."

They all studied her in silence, as if looking for the blood to begin its drip.

She continued. "But the knife stopped and he spoke, in a thin reed of a whisper."

The responding policeman asked, "What did he say?"

Her eyes swiveled to Lizzie. "He wanted me to give a message. He said, 'Tell your brother to stop investigating the drug scene. He's getting in our way. The dealers are laying low.' And he raced toward a car, threw himself into the passenger side, and left."

The policeman looked at the unspoken communication in their faces as they starred at each other. "Do you have a brother?"

They both shook their heads no.

He looked perplexed.

Lizzie announced Detective Fury's arrival as Delia spoke. Delia welcomed the warning and stopped.

The women were in the inside store entrance area, with Delia seated, apparently unharmed, on a chair shoved between the carts. She smiled as Lizzie moved closer, like a concerned guard.

The detective motioned for his man to give him the details. The policeman did. Fury stood in front of Delia. "Tell us the rest."
Delia finished her story. "He said to get on the ground. I pulled weak and helpless and said, "If you force this body down that far, it might never come up. You'd be condemned to hell for taking my life without leaving a scratch."

Lizzie gasped. "What a chance you took."

Fury nodded, but kept silent.

"He pulled me back to the bench in front of the store and sat me down, never once letting me see his face. In his gruff voice he said to close my eyes."

"I'm not stupid, I'd already catalogued his watch and clothes. As soon as he left I opened my peepers and saw him hurdle into a BMW careening by. Sorry, wrong angle to see the license number."

"Detective Fury said, "What do you think? The killer?"

Cautiously she raised her head, way, way up to study his eyes. "I don't think so. I'm still alive and unharmed." Then moaned, "Except for my soaked groceries."

The policeman kept writing in his notepad. "Can you describe him?"

"I saw his arms and the back of his hooded coat when he leapt into the car. He seemed rich, or had been at one time."

She dropped down a finger on each count. "He wore a Skagen watch, leather strap. Saw it in a gleam from the streetlight that had just blinked on. Minimalist dial. The jacket, hmm, a simple utility jacket, well-worn. It fit a tad loosely and didn't come off the rack. It had coyote fir trim on the hood."

The policeman interrupted. "You recognize coyote fir?"

She raised her chin. "In my day, I protested the killing of any animals for fashion. I knew them all."

The policeman backed away, chagrined. Fury hid his smile. He nodded for Delia to continue.

"The hands could have been beefy. I was scared."

The officer taking notes jotted it down and stood tall, as if finished. She noted Lizzie's restlessness, maybe wanting them to talk, but alone. She tried to end it, but Detective Fury threw in one more question.

"Size?"

"Large. Easily six feet tall. Had to hunch to hold that knife to my throat."

Even Detective Fury let his admiration leak out. "And I thought Lizzie was the cool one under fire. My compliments ma'am. Could my officer drive you home? I can follow in my car to pick him up."

Delia tailed behind the man as he shoved his notepad in his pocket and reached for her keys. He loaded her grocery bags into the trunk and escorted her to the passenger seat.

Fury shouted after Lizzie as she ran to follow. "I want to see you at the station tomorrow."

She saw the detective's eyebrows raise as she hopped into the hot rod and drove off.

CHAPTER 15

Lizzie followed Delia inside their home, and jostled the kind policeman who had driven her there. Distraught at what happened to Delia, Lizzie muscled her way past him. "Sorry, I must see to my sister."

He tipped his fingers to his forehead and moved away. Delia had swiveled around to catch the encounter and attempted to distract him from Lizzie's strength. "I must sit."

A minute later The policeman shouted from the doorway. "The detective is here. I left your keys on the table by the door. I hope you feel better soon and don't hesitate to call us if you remember anything more."

Delia raised her voice enough for him to hear. "Thank you officer. You take care."

Lizzie bustled her into the kitchen and offered a cup of tea. Delia returned her attention back to Lizzie. "I remember the last cup of tea you made me." She bounced up and filled the kettle. "I'm fine. Though it was scary."

"What didn't you tell them?"

Delia returned to her chair. Lizzie assessed her condition, an ingrained habit. Delia's steps were sturdy, but slow. She realized the 'scary' part probably held more reign than the 'fine' part and expressed her guilt. "I really am sorry. Sorry to involve you in this mess."

She waited thirty seconds, barely enough for her remorse to sink in, and repeated, "What didn't you tell them?"

"You know the BMW guys you described? I'm just guessing, but these men seemed different. More coarse."

Lizzie said a silent prayer to God for more than that, since she was out of leads. "And?"

Delia smirked. "And neither guy had a goatee, like you said."

Lizzie, ready to settle for that as her answer, noticed her sister still held the smug look. "And . . .

"And it was a sports car, all the way. Not a sedan."

Lizzie jerked to the back of her chair, sitting straight up. Neck elongated. "Okay . . .where does that leave us?"

When the kettle whistle blew, Delia prepared the tea. "This soothing herbal tea should calm both of us," while Lizzie analyzed the situation. They both excelled at stringing occurrences together to make sense. Delia didn't have her younger sister's strength, but their IQ's rivaled each others.

"I wonder how he, they, whoever, knew you were my sister?" Lizzie pondered.

Delia said, "Okay, we know he doesn't know who we are or where we live because he still called you my brother."

"True. But did he see me when we were at the bar the other night?"

"Doubtful, or you would have recognized him there."

Lizzie fussed with her tea, adding more honey. Delia introduced her to the use of honey long ago, but until this final visit home she'd never imbibed much. Right now, she didn't want to be soothed. She needed to think.

The natural color in Delia's face had returned. Lizzie thought out loud. "I wore that disguise twice. He must have seen me the first night I was at the bar. If he followed me to the warehouse, or was there before me, then he saw me put Tyler into the car. Your car. Maybe he followed that."

Delia rose and cut some bread. Lizzie knew she always cooked when she needed to think. The hope of one of her sister's delicious meals died quickly.

"Sorry," Delia said. "I had a great meal planned. Toast is what you get. There's fruit."

While Delia doodled with food, Lizzie remained still, praying for insight, or for Delia to have some. She couldn't specify with God, only wish for help.

As Delia pushed the toaster lever down, she turned. "You know what I think? I think they might have been the preppies you mentioned. I misconstrued the knife guy's hands as beefy, when they actually were long and lean like a pianist's hand. Or a professor."

"Tough to misconstrue when it's under your nose."

"I didn't want to sound too perceptive to the police. I also didn't want to mislead them completely. There was no sense of pending death, I but didn't know how to explain that to them. I feared they wouldn't understand. I gave them what I could. Shook a bit. I'm not sure if that made me look feeble or frightened. Seemed like I should hold information back until I could think better."

Her sister had led the police in one direction, leaving the better clues for themselves. To clarify, she asked, "What are you saying?"

"He had preppy shoes."

"We don't know what the killer wore. Nothing to compare."

"No. But we know the preppies were wearing shiny shoes. Now the killer could also have shiny shoes. But what are the odds. Come to think of it, my attacker's shoes were, you know, casual leather shoes, something you could wear to work. But not all that shiny. Maybe not preppy."

Lizzie stared at her. Amazed. And *she'd* been the secret agent. Who knew what she'd left behind all this time. She'd worked in U.S. counter intelligence for many years, and trained hard and long, eating dirt, racing till her heart stopped or learned to catch up, and studying nuances in perception while her eyes blurred. And here was her sister, who couldn't run a block, as capable of gathering intel as fast as she'd learned herself.

She'd missed growing to know her sister while gone, much more than she'd realized. Her many years of service meant seldom being home. Now she loved finally being there to stay, bum ankle or not. No time for mushiness right now. She said, "Too bad you couldn't follow him. We still don't know who it is."

"I thought of that, too. But figured it might be difficult seeing as he could have knifed me if I'd opened my eyes and moved off the chair."

"Oh Delia. I'm sorry. I didn't mean it that way. Just antsy for some progress. I am so glad you are okay."

Delia's comment had dragged Lizzie from her introspection, so she continued with a change of subject. "You know, Chunky's not chunky," Delia said as she cleaned up from their non-meal. "Not like peanut butter. He's extra solid. All muscle."

Lizzie jerked her head upright from sipping the last of the tea. "What! Where'd that come from?"

Delia hosed down the sink, then said. "Remember? That's what I was supposed to be doing today? Finding clues from the kids."

Lizzie shook herself into attention, wondering which one of them actually got assaulted tonight. She wondered if she felt more rattled because someone she loved was hurt, more than if it had been herself? *Dear Lord, I'm used to it being me in the crosshairs. This is a new experience. Please help me learn to cope. Or better yet, God. Keep Delia out of danger.* She voiced her concern. "I'm sorry dear. But it disturbs me that you were attacked and I wasn't there to help. Maybe this whole thing has gone too far."

Ignoring her, Delia sat down. "Uhh. Chunky? You want my report or what? Besides, I learned more from that shy young lad that Mrs. Donegal's assistant pointed out than from any of the others."

Lizzie was hooked.

Delia made her report. "First, the papers were filed against Ben. He's not in school right now, pending further decisions. Chunky is a huge trouble maker. His name is Charles Zeiler. According to school records, he was in attendance the day before you found Tyler. Since you located him after midnight, I assumed he'd been there since sometime the day before."

"Wise thinking. Though if he didn't arrive until evening, I suppose Chunky could have been around any time after school. Doesn't rule him out. I don't suppose he's in any after-school activities?" Lizzie winced at the inanity of the bully following the rules of any sport or club. Her sister surprised her.

"Close. He was in detention. His parents picked him up and took him directly home. He's skirting an expulsion and they don't want to take any chances." Delia finished her tea, pursed her lips and tilted her head sideways. She said, "You know, those assistants are a wealth of information."

Lizzie stored that in her brain for possible use with the teen center committee, then pulled out the cookie jar. "I can go for days without food if necessary, but when that happens I never have the call of a homemade cookie to make my stomach growl."

Unoffended, Delia continued, "That assistant also nodded discreetly at individuals in the lunch line that might be willing to discuss Charles. I shadowed two of them till I found them alone and learned that both feared saying anything. One trembled when I said the name."

Lizzie knew a few of those. "How did you deal with him?"

"I walked by his table and accidentally spilled soda on his shirt. The assistant helped him from the room and I circled around to meet up with them in a private room. He spoke as soon as we separated him from the others. The assistant described him as one of the shyest boys in school."

"Any light on the issue?"

"He said Chunky threw shade. I laughed until the assistant explained that meant he put people down. But he also said he had seen Tyler on the street corner with Hector, but he'd never seen Chunky there. He may have a different 'fam' altogether and not be part of the drug scene. He may just be high on power."

Lizzie already knew that term, fam, though it was difficult to picture Chunky with any kind of family. She swallowed another cookie, held the jar open to her sister, and when Delia said no, she covered it and put it back on the counter. Five was enough. Who needed drugs when sugar resided in her home. She leaned her back against the counter.

Delia asked, "So where does that leave us?"

"With a couple of thoughts. That Chunky is a bully and nothing else. And that the two other guys that he did see on the corner with Hector, repeatedly, might be able to tell us more."

"Jeesh Delia, you couldn't have started with that ripe tidbit?

What is this kid? A narc making reports?"

"Shoot me. I'm a linear person. And he's just a busybody. Observes but nothing more. Our dear assistant said she'd work with him to ID the guys if they're students, and she'll get back to us."

"Okay, we'll give her a day. Right now I'd better get some sleep. I get to be interrogated by our good buddy, Detective Daniel Fury, first thing in the morning. I don't understand why me. *You* were assaulted."

Delia smiled at her sister, swept away the crumbs, and disposed of them. Then drifted from the room. "But I'm a weak old lady traumatized by this. You're the strong secret agent who can take it when he reams you out," she said, this time not hiding that knowing smile.

The next morning, Lizzie learned that once again, Delia's words proved to be true. First she breezed past Torkless and pushed the door open to the detective's office. Show no fear. That was her motto today. She changed them at whim, but who was to know.

She'd wasted time and bravado. Detective Fury wasn't there. Torkless stood right behind her, grinning. "The detective said if you came in to take you to the conference room."

Puzzled, she feigned no emotion and left the ball in his court. At her silence, he barked. "It's down the hall on the right. He's been going through files most of the night. A friendly tip—though why I should bother to help you—don't cause any trouble today."

She swallowed her pride and gave him a slight lowering of her eyelids in acknowledgement. And hurried down the hall. He grimaced and slipped behind the front desk. What'd he think? She would hug him?

Fury sat amidst a dozen file folders, most of them opened with pages spread out. Disorganized, yet not. No folder touched the next one, no papers from each one overlapped any pages from the other folders. He ignored her.

Refusing to ask what he wanted, she pulled out a metal folding chair and plopped down as if it was a lounge chair. She didn't have all day but she knew how to act nonchalant. Of course, he was the molasses guy. He might be able to hold out longer than she could.

Change in game plan. "What do you want from me? I didn't attack Delia. Shouldn't you be looking for who did?"

He finished reading two more pages before he looked up. "Of course you didn't attack her, but maybe you know who did."

It wasn't a question. It didn't matter. Just because she'd made some guesses. It could be the preppy duo, or the killer. Didn't mean she knew them.

He leaned toward her, arms resting on forearms like he was confiding in an old friend. "Who's this brother he threatened her about?"

"We don't have a brother."

"So you don't know these people?"

"I don't, or why they threatened Delia." *My guessing is not the same thing.* The thought went through her mind but she knew it didn't flicker in her steady gaze. She said, "We talked again last night. I don't think I look like a man. Men don't wear their hair in a bun." She shook her head. "It's all a muddle. Was it the killer? We got no where."

Fury's friendly pose disappeared as he straightened and pointed his finger right at her heart. "What were you doing talking with Hector? You weren't supposed to go near the drug angle on this investigation."

"He didn't reveal anything except the logic of Tyler seeking drugs at Wanton Industries. Everyone knows that, including the cops who don't do anything about it."

She'd tried to turn the anger back at him but the words got stuck in his molasses treacle and they lost their force. Nothing seemed to rile the guy, except dear old me. She shrugged. "I didn't learn anything useful from Hector. And I convinced him to talk with you. Where's the congratulations—like, great job, Lizzie?"

His lack of response was expected. As much as she needed to know more about the dead guy, she knew today she'd get no answers.

She rose. "Is that what you wanted? To threaten me to be good?"

He shoved his chair back, placed his hands on his waist, elbows back, and steamed. "Stay out of the drug deal."

She'd dutifully waited outside the door for him to finish

admonishing her. She looked alert. He couldn't know that she was eavesdropping on the ragged couple walking ahead toward the exit. She overheard another officer warn them to stay away from Wanton Industries.

Like on rewind, Fury wrapped up. "Stay out of the drug angle."

She shrugged okay, as she eyed the couple leaving and followed them. Torkless, drawn to answer the phone, didn't notice her. Eavesdropping as the woman walked out the door Lizzie already learned she was an addict, and hated cops. This could be the break she needed.

CHAPTER 16

"I didn't got no 'shrooms in my pocket this time. They had no reason to arrest me at'all," the woman griped as Lizzie slipped out the door behind her.

"Quit your whining," the man said. "They didn't arrest you today. They told you they had questions."

"Yeah, but why me, Peter? "I'm clean now. Mostly. Broke too. Don't deal. Never did. Was just carrying those yellow and red ones for that Mussard guy."

Lizzie heard the woman refusing the ride home from the police.

"No way am I goin' to sit in one of those cop cars again," she told Peter. She'd raced out and had only gone three blocks before she started dragging her feet.

Peter traipsed along behind the woman till he caught up and patted her arm as he answered. "I know, Charmaine. You were mental and didn't understand what ya done. Let's get outa here."

Lizzie could have walked in the noisy woman's shadow they were both so loud, but followed as a needlessly silent tracker, a distance behind. The old lady's rants filled the surrounding air. The fellow with her appeared just as simple-witted, despite his younger years, as he moved forward, not noticing Lizzie. Those were guesses. She still hadn't seen their faces. And "lady" didn't fit the woman, but Lizzie attempted an open mind.

Charmaine sped up, and Lizzie barely heard the woman's lowered voice as she said to Peter. "We could stop at the shack and get a little help. Just one pill. I deserve one after that mess."

Lizzie saw Peter balk at that, digging in his feet and not moving, giving her time to drop down behind the nearest shrub as Charmaine turned to him.

"Come on Charmaine. We been through this afore. Let's get home and find some food."

Lizzie regretted not having her ragged old man costume with her, feeling exposed in her normal appearance. Besides, it had rained last night. She scrambled forward, attempting to keep her skirt off the wet ground, and her head out of view. Things were easier when tramping in Macedonia, where she hunted for the arnica plant to disguise her CIA operation. There were no sidewalks where she was in Macedonia. Everyone walked in the brush. The couple turned the corner and Lizzie's luck turned also. They headed down a rutted road, with trees. Shrubs, spruce, pine, straggling—cover, allowing her to creep closer, and upright now.

Peter snickered. "Sure couldn't believe how you snookered them cops. You knew who they was talking about didn't ya?"

"Shush. You want someone to hear ya?" She looked both directions but not behind her.

Charmaine must have thought it was all clear. She said, "I ain't never told no one about him, ceptin you. I'm not lookin' to die just yet."

Peter lowered his voice, "I never met him, but it had to a been that Damien guy. You know, the one with the scar who sold you them pills when your dealer didn't show up that time. You told me about him."

Charmaine faltered as she hit another rut in the road. "Why were they askin' me about that guy? They wouldn't say."

He gallantly grabbed her arm. "You shoulda took that cop ride. We'd ha been home by now. Eating."

The wind brought her another whine from Charmaine. "What'a ya goin' ta eat? We ain't got no food."

"I brought a couple cans of soup home yesterday when you wasn't feelin' so good."

Life for Lizzie turned rosier now that she saw new info piling in.

Were these two describing the killer? Someone they knew? What exactly did the police ask them? Or her? Peter didn't seem to know much. Maybe he wasn't an addict like Charmaine obviously was.

She let them get a little ahead, around the next curve, then prayed Delia would be free when she called her. She was. Lizzie thanked the good Lord for His help, and that Delia agreed to pick up a pile of groceries—all stuff on Agatha's list for addicts—and drive right over. Lizzie whispered, "I'll call you when I know where. And I promise. I take an oath, that I will arrange for my own car by tomorrow."

She raced to catch up to the bickering couple, following their voices like a trail of crumbs. They'd turned down a less traveled, but more open road, if you could call it that. She no longer had any idea where she was.

The couple hobbled into a small cottage off the road. Finding a scrub bush in the back of the cottage, she hunkered down to eavesdrop. A forsythia, struggling to bloom, was crowded out by a spreading yew that itched wherever it touched her. The forsythia was one of the few bushes leafing out this early in spring that didn't sprout needles. She hugged it close and listened.

Were they talking about the killer? The woman's voice was too soft. Where were listening devices when you needed them? But she did hear Peter say the man with the scar on his face, she was sure of it.

Charmaine cackled and her voice rose. "I sure did fool them cops, didn't I? Said I had no idea who used to give me drugs. Notice I said used to." She snickered. "They had no cause to keep me today."

Lizzie heard a couple bowls clink onto the table. Peter must have fixed soup. She heard them munching crackers. Her ears were attuned to their location now. And her stomach. Maybe when she delivered the food they'd let her share it. Mainly she wanted to bribe them into talking. Her phone buzzed and she rose and ran to the corner to talk. Shortly after, Delia pulled up. Julie's car coasted in behind her. Delia climbed out and motioned Lizzie in.

"Gotta run. Julie's giving me a ride home. When you come home, we can drive out to the herb farm to pick up that car. I don't care if it's a rust bucket. You need wheels."

Lizzie grabbed a bag of nuts out of the food sack, and shoveled a handful in her mouth, which was now too full to talk, so she nodded and took off. She pulled up to the cottage, hustled both grocery sacks into her arms, and kicked the door with her toes.

Peter opened it a crack and only eyes showing, said, "Who are you and what ya want? Before she could talk, the groceries started falling out of the bags. Peter caught a few before they hit the floor and swung the door wide. He didn't move. "Talk first."

"I followed you from the police station. Want to know about that man with the scar. I'm not a cop. Just trying to help a young teen and need to find the guy. Pronto. These are in exchange for information."

Charmaine called out, "Who is it Peter?"

"A woman who wants to bribe us with tons of food."

Charmaine shoved the finished soup bowl away and said, "Put it here. I want to see."

Lizzie laughed. A woman after my own heart. She opened the nuts and passed the bag around, sifting a few more into her mouth.

"Sorry, I haven't had lunch. What do you say? Can you tell me about him for this?"

The couple looked at each other and nodded simultaneously. "What do you want? He ain't no killer," the woman said.

"Okay, but he might have seen a killer, or a killing, or a stranger one day recently when he was at Wanton Industries. Now I can't find him to ask."

Peter didn't speak but turned to Charmaine.

She narrowed her eyes. When she whipped off the glasses to wipe them clean on a filthy corner or her shirt, Lizzie cringed, wanting to hold them under the faucet and rub them dry with a tissue. Instead she waited, and saw the woman eye's had a blank stare, as if unseeing until reunited with her glasses.

In the hopes of encouraging a response, Lizzie pulled out a chair and sat, facing Charmaine. She laid her hands flat on the table. "Please. There's a young boy who may be charged with that murder at the Wanton. He's innocent. Just got started using drugs out of despair and anger. I want to help."

Charmaine spoke. "That's sad. To be young and no where else to go. I know about those feelings. That's why I took drugs. Pushes everything bad out of sight. Poof. All gone. Locked behind a door somewhere."

Lizzie waited.

The broken woman continued, "When the drug wears off, the door opens. Sometimes slow. Other times it just hits you in the face. One big swat. You try to lock it back up. With more drugs. Peter helps me fight that now." She nodded to Peter and faced Lizzie. "I'll tell you what I know, if you promise you won't do that man no harm?"

Lizzie said, "I just want to ask him what he saw after Tyler stopped by. He told the kid he had a meetin' and to get out till it was over. The boy passed out and never saw anything after that till he was in the hospital."

Charmaine said, "He ain't at the ole Wanton no more. He moved out the day the man got kilt. Said too many cops would be hangin' around." She pursed her lips. "He meets up with clients now at the shack behind the 'Jumpin' Lizard.'"

Lizzie slapped her hand on her forehead. "Never saw the shack. Wasted my time inside the bar. Any idea when I can find him there?"

"Monday, Thursday, Friday, Saturday. Noon till dawn. Don't know where he is other times."

Lizzie smiled. Progress. She tipped her fingers to her forehead this time, in thanks. And left. Peter and Charmaine were too busy rooting through the groceries to say goodbye.

When she arrived home, Delia flew out the door and jumped in the sedan. "Let's go. Dave and Carmelita are waiting for us at the Kinney Herb Farm."

"I'm starved."

Delia handed her a bag crammed full with a sandwich with all the fixings.

Lizzie took half and drove one-handed, not talking until she'd finished. She sighed. "I'm not sure where I'm going with this Delia. Chasing a killer doesn't seem to fit in with my hope for helping people instead of killing them. And these people I'm calling suspects —they're often just sad people who didn't make the right decision somewhere in their lives and now can't change."

Delia leaned against the door and stared at her sister. "Your personal assessment's a little harsh, don't you think? You did mounds of good in your life. And now you're fighting for young kids to build strong lives and stay away from what you faced."

"I know you're right. Most of the time. I want this to be over with. Then I can return to the peaceful part of that."

Facing forward, ready to give directions, Delia said, "Sometimes peace and violence are close neighbors. We're coming on to the farm. Try slowing down. We'll get you a car and then decide what we can do next. You can tell me what you learned when we get home."

Lizzie swerved into the farm, not noticing the unpaved road leading to it until the last minute. Delia just clutched the strap and hung on.

"Huh. You're finally getting used to my driving and now I'll have my own wheels. It's not a real rust bucket is it?"

Delia grabbed the keys. "No but it's not a sports car either. I figured you needed a sedate vehicle with speed. They had just the thing."

They walked behind the farmhouse and sought the couple who now ran the farm. Acres of neat rows of herbs in early stages. Some with lots of green showed, but most, just sprouted green tips.

Dave found them admiring the comfrey and oregano. He looked more mature than he had two years ago, when Lizzie had seen him last. "I hear you're going to take this souped up car off my hands. Can't let the young guys use it around here. They've got no restraint."

Lizzie's smile crinkled her eyes it spread so wide. No sense in telling him about her speeding habits. Thankfully, Delia kept her mouth shut. Lizzie merely said, "Lead on." As soon as she saw it, she couldn't help it. She blurted, "It's a beauty."

Delia walked beside her as she inspected it. She whispered, "Great way to keep the price down, sister. Maybe you could demean the car. Say it's a horrid color?"

"Delia, it's the perfect color. It's a dark sage green. Won't stick out in the crowd when I'm doing surveillance, and it's still pleasing to the eye."

Delia shrugged. "Right. You study it. Keep your lip zipped. I'll go do the bartering."

Lizzie sat inside and studied the dials and buttons, the movement of the gears, and the fit of the seat. After kicking the wheels, she slipped up to Delia when she returned and whispered, "Is it mine?"

"It was a tough sell. He asked if you were trying to get a teen center started around here. When I confessed you were, you won."

"What?"

"He said, 'Great. We need a center. She can use the car for two months, and if she wants it we'll come up with a low price.' "

Lizzie reached for the keys in her sister's open palm, flipped them high in the air and caught them one-handed, as she opened the driver's door. She waved, smiled brightly to Dave, and tore out of there, raising gravel every-which-way, and tooted the horn.

CHAPTER 17

Time to pursue the man with the scar on his face. So his name was Damien. No wonder he never used it. Damien doesn't fit with drug dealing. Scoping out the shack when no one was around would help. Lizzie took it slow and easy, plotting her itinerary.

She slowed at the first cross road. A speeding ticket was out of the question. Any stop by police would prove embarrassing without a driver's license. She did know how to drive, sort of. Driving here didn't vary that much from driving in third world countries where she'd been assigned. Well, slightly different. This one had paved roads. And rules. And laws.

A quick lesson from Delia, and the fastest testing facility, were in order. She'd have to confess to her sister that she'd driven in Florida this winter without a license. She'd been in a hurry. Who had time to get a license in Florida? Didn't live there. Was heading home soon. But Delia would probably make a fuss. Maybe she'd bring her a present with the lesson request.

She made a left. Glad no one had seen her driving when she borrowed cars earlier in the hunt for the killer. Come to think of it, she was darn lucky they didn't ask for her driver's license for identification when she brought Tyler to the hospital. Handy having the old CIA card. She smiled at that, until she realized it might not work if a cop pulled her over for reckless driving. She slowed. Checked the speedometer. Inched up a notch. Heaven forbid a cop would see a little old lady driving under the speed limit. Probably pull her over on a senility check.

She planned while she drove but she itched to take a peek at the shack. Strange, but broad daylight might be the best time to snoop around. Normal occupants of the Jumpin' Lizard should still be out cold elsewhere—with luck. Delia awaited her at home. Probably with food. Her stomach might give her away if she took much longer. Better hurry.

The bar's appearance fared much worse in the daytime. Ramshackle. The weathered sign hung from one chain. One wonders how the other one became unattached. Then she saw the rust faded, softened letters, and knew the Jumpin' Lizzard harkened back to another century.

The stale beer smell permeated everything. She couldn't stand the putrid scent of liquor mixed with decaying trash. She didn't look closely at first, then realized she should watch where she placed each foot. Trash was the least of her worries. Drying vomit clashed with the stench. It penetrated the cracked tar and gravel along the building. This time the odor of beer won. Nothing worse than vomit she thought until she remembered the blood of slaughtered bodies on the bleak days in other countries. She stopped comparing.

The Jumpin' Lizard faced the street, surrounded by the parking lot on one side and woods on the other two. Almost serene. As long as one didn't breathe. Sometimes folks didn't have much to compare it to. She inhaled deeply. *Thank you God for all the bright spots you provided in my life. Guide me to help Tyler and his mom.*

Buried in the woods, the shack sat way off to the side. It lacked height, space, and accouterments, like siding and much of a roof. At first look. But underneath the weeds growing above and around the roof, Lizzie spotted a glint of metal shining in the sunlight. Could that be a new roof hidden under the weeds? Disguised? Why?

She edged around the outside of the shack, working toward the back near the woods. How far a walk through the woods would addicts have to trek if they came that way to hide their association with this guy?

A door hiding behind a tangled mess of ivy appeared as she approached the rear. Unusual to find the ivy here among more logical woodland plants. She knew it liked the shade. Still, set here for camouflage? She'd check the woods later. Appears to be easy access. She made a mental note to be careful when coming back tonight. The woods could be full of needy addicts waiting their turn.

A dirty hand clamped around her arm from behind.

Busted.

She attempted a move to face him. He jerked the other arm back. Tight.

"What da ya want here?"

No time to think. She came in with no knowledge of the enemy. Bad move. The kind that could get one killed.

Stall. "Looking for someone."

Now what? Worse, she was out of her old-crippled-man-in-gungy-clothes disguise. Maybe this man had an aging mother that he loved. On the other hand, he wouldn't beat her up, would he? He was alone. And she wasn't defenseless. No weapon needed. She decided not to break his arm.

He jerked harder. Crap. Who'd a thought anyone would be around and wide awake in broad daylight. Don't drug dealers need sleep? Dumb. She learned addicts sleep is constantly interrupted by the brain altering chemicals they'd introduced into their bodies. Many dealers were addicted to drugs and money. She should have figured it out earlier. Been more alert.

He tugged again. "Who?"

Yanking out of the one hand, she swiveled toward him. It was the man she'd been seeking. Even without the identifying scar along his jaw, the long dark hair and knife hilt sticking from his belt pretty much clinched it. Better not call him Scarface though. Play it simple —little old lady trying to track down a grandson maybe? Introduce myself? Ask his name? Shoot, what's my name?

She held out her free hand. "Hi, I'm Giselda. And you are?"

The wrinkles did it. When he saw her face he broke his hold. But he ignored her question.

"What da ya want?"

Quick assessment.

This wasn't the guy in the hospital. No one could think he was six feet tall.

Probably not the man that confronted Delia. He had no fancy watch.

Just because he was emaciated didn't mean he wasn't a killer. She could practically see his brain working behind those bleary eyes. They moved around, not sure what to make of her. Lizzie would try the grandson tactic. Concern. Fear.

"I'm trying to find my grandson. Someone told me he might look for drugs here. He's desperate. I don't want him hurt." She smiled, friendly, but not expanding into a grin. "I need to find his dealer. The one he saw at the Wanton Industries place."

His look was so sour it could have turned lemonade. He stretched his body to top height, which left her peering down at his face. "We don't sell drugs here. This is a bar."

As he shifted, a shaft of sunlight speared its way through the newly leafing trees and landed on the hilt of his knife. "I don't meet with anyone at Wanton. Or here. Never have. Don't meet with no addicts."

He continued. "I don't meet with nobody because I don't sell drugs. Now get out, lady. Before I kill you. Now *that* I'll do. Anywhere ya ask fer it."

In an unyielding tone, she said, "I don't care what you sell. I want to know if you saw anyone the day, or night the man was killed at the Wanton. You know, while you might have been walking by, meeting a friend in the area?"

"Get woke, lady. That's hot information. You don't look like no cop," he snickered, as he studied her aged body. "But I sure ain't givin' it away free."

"Okay, I'm not naïve. I'm trying to help a teenager from being railroaded by the cops. I'll pay. What do you want?"

He scratched his skull. "How about $500?"

"That should buy me the name of the killer and where I can find him."

"It buys you who I saw at the Wanton right after I walked past the dead man. Take it or leave it."

"I don't have it on me. I'll bring it tonight. Here. Tell me what time, and I'll hand it over."

The man said "midnight," his voice as rough as his face, and he drifted back to his hideaway.

Lizzie sauntered to the car. Then floored it. Time to regroup at home.

Delia didn't complain at her late arrival but beamed with good news. "The hospital called. Tyler can come home today."

"That is exciting. Did you tell Emily?"

"Right away. I confess. I bought her a cell phone yesterday. I told her it was for Tyler. That way he can talk with her anytime while he stays here."

"Brilliant, sis. Will they come to the hospital to pick him up?"

"If you can stay with Tyler for a short bit when we bring him here, I will fetch Emily and Heather and they can visit for the afternoon. We could have a party here."

Lizzie grinned. "Great idea. Do we have time to bake a cake or anything?"

"Right. What kind of cake will you make?" Delia responded with a smirk. They both knew Lizzie didn't cook.

Lizzie settled at the table, where her sister had placed a steaming lunch of roasted vegetables and melted cheese on her own version of herbed focaccia bread, liberally doused with a spicy sauce.

She savored a bite. "So no cake?"

Delia enjoyed her own meal before answering. "It's in the oven. Can't you smell it?"

Lizzie breathed in deeply, luxuriating in the aroma of lunch, the baking cake, and the pleasure of being here with her sister. She'd wait another day to discuss the license problem.

Later that night the contentment dissipated into a mental arm wrestling match. "I've said *no*, Delia, enough times. I have to leave."

"But I can drop Tyler off at his mom's and be with you in no time."

Lizzie smoothed the pancake makeup across the second cheek, extending the skin and causing a bruise to appear in a blue-brown blur. "Don't be ridiculous. On his first night here? We finally just got him settled."

Delia whined. "I'm afraid for you. I know something will go wrong."

Lizzie calmly placed her hands on Delia's shoulders. "Plans usually go wrong. It's what you do and how fast that matters. I'll take care of this."

A quick hug and she was out the door. She'd agonized over wearing the old man disguise. The dealer knew what she looked like now. But the bent, dirty man could say that the old lady sent him. She felt safer that way. And this jacket hid many secrets beneath its folds.

When she arrived there were no lights on this side of the bar, too deep and close to the woods. Probably well planned.

Three guys approached her from the dark side. Not one had a marred face, unless you counted the grooves from the squinty eyes and downturned mouths.

Was one of them the killer?

Was it the one who took main point while the other two flanked him? She didn't need much moonlight to see the shape of a defensive back in big league football. As he got closer she tried to see a sign in his face that revealed humanity. All she saw was skin stretched too tight over bone. She wasn't sure she could take him. He was tall, very tall, and heavy. She mumbled, *"Dear God, please notice my humbleness here and help get me out of this."*

Closer yet, she say the puffiness in the man's face, and more flab than muscle in the middle. The eye's revealed instantly that she could take him. They were flat. Dull from pain. What was he before the drugs, the pain? Why is he here, confronting her? How does he know she's involved?

And it didn't take long to figure out how. He growled. "That Scarface's a scum sucking leech."

Busted twice in one day. That was a first. She readied her stance. This didn't look good.

Head man combined a snarl and a shout. "What'd that rat tell you?"

She shook her arms loose. Wanted him to think she had no weapons, and she might need rapid movement any second. "That rat told me nothing. Said he would tonight."

When she scanned what she could see of his clothes in the darkness, he appeared downtrodden. He was rich, or had been at one time. A gleam of moonlight revealed a fancy watch, and an oversized tailored jacket. A quality guy, but would he strike?

The others stayed in the shadows, just beyond the pools of moonlight. But he had a scruffy, beard-stippled face—old enough to need to shave more than once a day. Should she confront them? Tyler might be in danger from them if they'd seen him at the warehouse.

They didn't seem the chatty type. And she'd promised the detective she wouldn't get involved with the drug part of the investigation. May be time to leave.

She never looked away from the front man. He spoke one word, firm and harsh. "Erne." Didn't withdraw his deadly stare from Lizzie. The short man on the left drew a knife.

He hurled it her way. But she'd already whirled around and launched her own into his side.

Not lethal. But his loud groans drew the other's attention for a second.

And Lizzie fled.

Collecting her car from the next street over, she considered heading directly to Detective Fury's house and get this settled. Ask who he was targeting for this, and what was being done. She'd tell him of what happened tonight, describe the one man, and use the ploy that they came at her. Tell him she didn't approach them.

She glanced at her filthy jacket, deliberately dragged through a mud puddle before she left home, and laughed at herself. Her anger dispersed in the wind from her window as she drove away. Right. I'm sure he'd come to the door and let this old man in.

No questions asked. At two in the morning.

She had questions of her own she couldn't share with Fury. Like how did they know to confront an old man? The scared guy would have said old woman? And what would they do next? And did all three do the killing? None of them? She needed answers. Maybe Fury would share. But not tonight.

Thank you, God, for pointing all that out to me. But tomorrow is another day. Okay, it's already tomorrow. Time to get hoppin.'

CHAPTER 18

Lizzie stomped around Fury's tiny office, unable to sit and blow off steam.

"It wasn't interfering in your drug investigation! I went to a bar. So arrest me."

Fury just sat there like a smug baboon, fingers laced and napping on the desk. This guy reeked complacency. Strange that his name was "Fury."

"Ma'am. Please sit down. I'm getting tired just watching you pace. Let's work this out."

Lizzie plopped into the chair so hard she thought it might break. Calm. Be calm. She whispered the mantra inside her head. But when her voice erupted, calm disappeared. She settled for strained and tried to explain. "I came to you in good faith. I was attacked outside a bar. Three lumbering guys. I barely escaped." She scooched deeper into the chair. "I need to know who you're targeting and why. Where are you in your so-called investigation?"

He drummed his fingers. Finally, a reaction. He said, "You don't need to know details of our investigation."

"Maybe one of these guys that attacked me was the killer. I *do* need to know."

She heard a faint growl. Okay, a discreet clearing of his throat, but maybe it meant he was reconsidering. She waited. And when he asked her to describe the men, she answered, with polite deference. Still angry? Yes. But she knew how to play.

"The lead guy was bulky, looked like a puffy lineman, six-foot-five and about 250 lbs."

The detective hit the record button.

She kept talking. "His face was scruffy, like he needed to shave, often. Or maybe he was down on his luck and didn't have a razor anymore."

Fury said, "What do you mean?"

"He was once rich, but poor. My opinion, he fell on hard times maybe? Or into drugs and then rough times." She sat. "He stood straight. Head high. Like he'd been somebody. Not necessarily a CEO but someone in commerce or office work, higher up than a line worker."

Fury nodded. "What about the other two?

"Shadows. Though I won't forget the face of the one. As he stepped forward to throw his knife, I saw him clearly. His jaw was so elongated that his cheekbones sunk down and in, trying to meet it. The other guy, nothing. Couldn't see."

He'd surged up at the word 'knife,'and looked her over. "How'd you get away?"

"My knife was more accurate than his. I left during the shuffle."

He remained silent for a full minute, but didn't drop his gaze. Finally, he said, "I didn't hear that."

He turned to his notes, giving her dribs and drabs of information. "We've staked out Wanton Industries ever since Hector confirmed that drug deals were conducted there."

She listened, but didn't confirm she already knew that from the friendly drug addict, Charmaine, who'd told him nothing.

He added, "We've interviewed any drug addicts we could, looked for any other local drug related deaths, overdoses or murders. We found one, a month prior to Jamison's death. This time it was an accidental overdose—of fentanyl. We tracked down his next of kin. They named Jamison as the dealer. The kid's uncle is suspect. He may have been into drugs but he's left his job as CEO at Lurtenck Industries under a cloud of suspicion. No one will talk and say why."

She nodded, intrigued now. New leads.

He continued. "We have a BOLO alert for him. Name and type

of car. Nothing else."

"His name?"

Fury hesitated.

Lizzie jumped up before he finished. "He could be the guy who attacked me."

"Which one."

"The head guy. The football player. Not the knife guy."

He shuffled through the files on his desk, jerked one open and pulled out a photo. "It's old. The family has been estranged for a while. Feared the man was on drugs since he was a teen."

He held it out. "Is this the guy?"

"You bet. You think we have our killer?"

He watched Lizzie's grin widen into a chasm. An enthusiasm gap he closed rapidly. "Settle down ma'am. What we have is simply information on the missing uncle of the young man who was killed."

Lizzie'd been having second thoughts about the scared man's involvement because he didn't show at their meeting. She was surprised he didn't gather up the five hundred dollars and then rat her out if he wasn't the killer. Or, there was still a slight chance that he left for some important reason, and these three men happened by. That idea led no where. Why would they attack a feeble old man? The scared man didn't know her disguise so couldn't have described her. Maybe the men had come for another purpose and she'd wandered in.

She wouldn't share her thinking with Fury though.

His friendly face had morphed into cop demeanor in an instant. "We might have more information about the uncle. As soon as you talk."

Lizzie quelled her internal victory dance and her chin dropped in defeat.

She parlayed. "His name?"

He offered it, slowly. "Troy Ryther III. Could you tell us why he attacked you? You know, since you were bar hopping and not interfering in the drug angle."

She knew it was time to combine their information and move forward. She told him of her meeting with Tyler's so-called dealer.

How he set her up, after telling her he knew who walked by him shortly after he saw the dead body.

He scribbled in his file, despite the running recorder. Old fashioned. Like her. "Now we know this uncle was at Wanton around the same time as the young man was killed."

"Sorry," she said. "We don't know that. He attacked me behind the Jumpin' Lizard."

Lizzie already figured he'd also been at Wanton, and thoughts on how to proceed and find the guy collided in her brain. She would wait until Detective Fury finished. Her hope for a clear path faded when he looked up, forehead furrowed deeply enough to plant seeds in it.

He spoke. "Thank you for your help" He accompanied it with a smile. "Now get out. And stay away . . . ."

She rose and finished the sentence as she walked out the door. " . . .from the drug angle." She scurried to her car. Bad time to mention she needed a license. Maybe next time, or next year, depending. Better yet, just take the test and get the darn thing. She jammed the key in the ignition. Hmm. It would be easier just to get a forged license. Not today, though. She had too many leads to pursue. Starting with visiting Tony and picking his brain. Hopefully, now that he'd settled down, warm and fed, he might remember more of his time on the street.

Maybe Verge Innes held a clue they'd all overlooked. Lizzie breezed through Mildred's door as her new friend opened it. She thought she hid her feelings well but Mildred must have noticed the hovering storm cloud and head motioned her toward the kitchen. Once there, Mildred suggested they have some tea. She said Tony was upstairs studying and she wanted to keep it that way.

Lizzie held her tongue, and smiled when Mildred set the cup in front of her. Lizzie shifted back in the comfortable cushions of the kitchen chair, let her worries settle down and her thoughts drift. She examined her friend's face and wondered if she dared call this woman Milly.

As she sat in her own chair, Mildred spoke with crispness that barely hid her joy as she presented an update on Tony's situation. "I'm happy to report that I am now sole custody of Tony as an emergency care giver through the county Children and Youth Agency."

Her grin spread. "We got them at a good time. Or a bad time, depending on who's looking. They are full up with dwindling numbers of willing foster parents on the one side and young babies coming in drug dependent. There's no room at the inn, and with my offer to adopt him as soon as possible, they couldn't resist me."

"I'm impressed. Amazed. Are you sure?"

"Okay. You can't take away my happiness. My husband and I were foster parents for so many years they led us slide right through."

"And you're serious about adopting Tony? Won't that be difficult at your age?"

"Sadly, even great grandparents are being enlisted to take custody of kin. Too many abandoned kids and not enough foster homes. I just have to prove I'm in great health and have a good backup system."

She pointed right at Lizzie's heart with her mug. "You and Delia are my backup system."

"We won't pass. We're too old. Whoa. I've never said that before."

"Actually, I know a young couple. They agreed to be my backup —on paper, anyway, but I figured you've got a few more good years in you for the tough stuff."

"That's it?"

Mildred's face turned serious. "They're doing psychological testing on him because of his home situation, looking for abuse or anything beyond neglect and poverty. The specialists tend to consider numerous aspects to pinpoint and treat problems early on. They call it toxic stress, and claim that extreme stress can cause brain changes that effect learning, health, and behavior."

Lizzie frowned. "You don't agree? It sounds reasonable."

"Oh, it's not that I don't agree, but I hope they won't delay too much. Tony seems well-adjusted for someone who lived on the streets for weeks."

"Has he talked about his mother, or father?"

Mildred shifted her hand to reach for a cookie, then backed off. "I leave them out for Tony, but they tempt me too often." Sitting back, she answered. "Yes, he seems open about their relationship. And misses his mom. He doesn't discuss the poverty. He's disposed to accept things and deal with them as he can."

"Must have prepared him some to manage when she was gone. Is he ready for the adoption?"

Mildred's face lit up. "Yes. We both want this to be permanent as soon as we can."

Finishing her tea, Lizzie rose to put the cup next to the sink. "Is he okay to talk with me now? I'd rather not wait. It's urgent."

"He's good. I'll call him down. But I think having a permanent place and 'mother,' so-to-speak, will provide him with the confidence he needs to become a great man, with wisdom and sympathy for those less fortunate than many of us."

Lizzie listened to Tony babble on about his days with Mildred, delighted that he appreciated her so much that his spaces between words shrunk to nothing. She notched up her hearing another degree and caught most of it.

When his words petered out, she asked, "Can you recall any details about your time staying near the Innes family? We must find Ethan and his father. Especially his father."

"Gee, I only saw him at night. Once though, he was leaving and I saw a bit because the light inside was on."

"Can you describe him?"

Tony scrunched up his face. "He was short. And had a crumbly mustache."

"What's a crumbly mustache?"

"Fuzzy. Like it wasn't clean, maybe. Not straight."

Lizzie took a deep breath. She'd interrogated the best of them. But this, a young innocent lad—nine years old—tough. She wanted to be kind, and had to work to keep the questions gentile. An effort that grated from lack of use in her field.

"Did you see his hair?"

He quirked his head sideways, and brightened. "He only had a little hair. But not bald either. Sorry. I couldn't see much in the dark."

She patted him on the shoulder. "You did great. See anyone else around? Maybe other friends of Ethan or his mom's?"

"I don't think Ethan liked it there. After school sometimes I could hear him shouting. Worried at first. Than I heard him holler mooshroom. I know mushrooms. We got real sick eating them once. But then he said cow critter. Later, I heard he was playing a video game."

Lizzie saw his frown. "Was that a problem?"

"No. He was an okay kid. He had a mom and dad. And a video game."

She waited.

He dropped his head. "And I was cold. A lot."

"It's okay, Tony. I get jealous too. My sister has tons of friends." She shrugged. "But she's the best person in the world." Lizzie wondered where that thought popped from. But it seemed to make the lad a little happier. Back to questioning him. "Did anyone visit Ethan? Or his mom?"

"There was a kid a few times. Smaller than Ethan. Didn't hear his name. Or, maybe it was Tom or something."

She nodded. "Tyler?"

"Yeah. That was it."

"I'll take you to meet him sometime. Anyone come see the dad?"

"One guy. During the day. Walked right in. He was tall. Looked rich. I followed him when he left."

"Why."

"I don't know. I thought about asking him for food. But he walked to the corner and a big car picked him up.

"Can you tell me about the car?"

"Well, it was big. And green."

"Big how? More than four regular doors on the sides?"

"No. Just very long and low. But it still looked big. And zoomed out'a there quick."

She realized he had little opportunity to study cars like some young kids. "Thank you so much Tony. You've been tremendously helpful." She waved goodbye to Mildred, and walked down the hall to the door.

Wistfully, Tony said, "Don't you want the license number?"

Lizzie whirled around. "You memorized the license number?"

He palmed his forehead and closed his eyes at her disbelief. Then he said, "Duh, yeah."

Mildred walked up and handed him a pad of paper and pencil. She looked at Lizzie but said, "Smart kid. Told you he was studying. Always thinking, this kid."

He wrote it down and tore off the page for Lizzie.

She bent and hugged him. Couldn't resist. And said to Mildred. "Give this kid six cookies. I'll buy you more."

Mildred's look would kill weeds. "These are homemade."

"Don't hold your breath on me making cookies."

Tony looked sheepishly at Mildred. "Store bought is okay."

Lizzie laughed. She said to Mildred. "I just came from a nasty meeting with Detective Fury. He can't expect me to run to him with every little bit of information I unearth. I'll just pursue this on my own."

CHAPTER 19

Lizzie fumbled for the cell phone she'd left on the passenger seat and veered to the side of the road. She stared at the phone a few seconds, trying to remember how to answer the darn thing. To date, she'd learned how to make a call when necessary. She could never remember whether to swipe at it or poke it.

She hit the icon resembling the headpiece of a phone. No surprise it was Delia. No one else knew her number. But the shrieking she heard was so unlike her sister that her heart rate doubled and threatened to choke her.

"Delia, please, repeat that slowly. I can't understand you. Are you okay?"

She heard her sister take a deep breath and release it. "Emily's house is on fire. Tyler's home." Her voice faded before she could say more.

Lizzie knew how to hone things down to the most crucial. "What? Are Emily and Heather alright? Was Tyler still with you?"

Delia's voice steadied. "They're both safe. They ran out when Emily saw the kitchen curtains catch fire. She called me right away."

"Where are you now?"

Delia's sigh came through the phone line loud and clear. "I'm standing out front."

Lizzie knew not to drive holding a phone but she didn't remember where the speaker part was so she grasped it and drove gingerly, making a U-turn off the grass and headed back toward

Emily's. She could hear Heather whimpering in the background as Delia talked.

"The whole place is burning. I'd just dropped Tyler at the herb farm to work with Dave."

Lizzie parked her car at a drunken angle, and reached the women as the fire truck pulled in. A paramedic rushed to Heather first when he saw her pumping her lungs, and raised an oxygen mask to the child.

Heather screamed when he hooked one arm gently behind her head as he approached her face with the mask. Emily held the child in a firm grip, bordering on frozen panic and didn't help. Lizzie noticed an ash-blackened Marcus and lifted him up higher with two fingers.

Loud enough to be heard over the child's crying, she said, "Marcus, you need some air. This will help you breathe." She motioned for the paramedic to swerve the oxygen over to Marcus's face. The paramedic did so and waited. Heather's screaming stopped.

After a minute, Lizzie said, "There Marcus. All better."

Lizzie nudged Marcus's head from behind to bring his mouth above the mask. She then tipped his paw to move the oxygen to Heather. The child grabbed it with both sooty hands, her pet monkey now tucked under her arm. The paramedic took over, with a nod to Lizzie.

Another paramedic tended to Emily, whose knees and clothing bordered on black. She pushed the mask away and spoke. "I don't need it."

He repeated, "Ma'am, are you hurt? Are you burned?"

"I'm fine. I'm filthy because she wouldn't leave without Marcus. I crawled through ashes on the floor, searching for him. It was hot but I'm not burned."

Immediately the paramedic looked around for someone named Marcus. Lizzie saw him and pointed to the monkey. She heard his sigh of relief as he turned back to Emily.

Charred bits of the home's wooden skeleton remained, with openings in the lath strips revealing the burning embers inside. Flames took some final licks at the blackened wood, caught a last bit of fabric from the window, long since shattered. The cloth had no chance as the fire flared up through the ceiling one final time. Little had escaped the fire, window glass littered everything, from the frames of furniture, to the twisted metal bed frames, and through the burnt floor to the ground.

The chimney collapsed to a crashing sound and everyone turned in unison to watch the finale. Lizzie lifted Heather from Emily's arms as the woman visibly shrunk, her shoulders curled downward.

Lizzie opened her eyes wide to the child. "Your mommy saved Marcus? She's a hero."

Heather's cries had ceased and the paramedic removed her mask. Before he left, Lizzie said, "We need to get mommy a hero badge."

The man withdrew a small firefighters badge kept for children, and put it in Heather's hands. She said, "Thank you." And pinned it on her mom.

"You a hero, mommy. You saved Marcus."

The fire hoses quelled the fire at the cottage leaving tons of rubble. Lizzie watched, analyzed, and mentally recorded her conclusions. The back corner walls had long since crumbled. The lath dated the house prior to the 1950s when drywall rapidly replaced the earlier method because of the construction speed needed following the war.

This fire was the opening volley of another war—one on Tyler and his family. Lizzie motioned to Delia and passed the child into her arms. She needed to talk with the lieutenant to learn how the fire started. When she walked away, she knew one thing for sure, though the fire lieutenant would make no firm conclusions. Between what he said and one glance at the conspicuously large pile of burnt ash near what had been the back corner, Lizzie knew—arson.

The question was—why?

Settling Heather and her mom ate up what was left of the afternoon. The few neighbors that gathered expressed sympathy, but none had extra room. Most already housed large families in tiny cottages. Delia insisted on bringing the frightened woman and child home with them for the night.

Emily stood still, eyes glazed. Delia shrugged one shoulder in question to her sister.

Lizzie responded, "Let her be. She's in shock and needs to work through everything in her brain. She may do this often as she remembers. They didn't have much. But it was hers, and now she doesn't have one set of clean clothes."

She felt no need to tell them her fears of arson. She'd hoped to tackle Detective Fury today. Arson lit up a whole new angle to pursue.

However, Delia requisitioned her to pick up Tyler. She said, "I'm scrounging some clothes for Emily while I wash hers. Tell Tyler about the fire. Please be gentle and compassionate."

"I'm offended you don't think I have compassion."

Delia just stared at her.

"Okay, so I had to be cold and hard in my job. That doesn't mean I don't have empathy."

"I know, dear sister. But it's a bit rusty. Tyler might be fourteen, but still a child hiding beneath that bravado."

Lizzie nodded and took off. On the first day Tyler was out of the hospital Lizzie took him home to gather some of his clothes and other possessions. He had little, but was delighted to have his own things again. He would be okay for now.

Lizzie figured Delia would have used her endless resources to obtain necessities for Emily and Heather by the time she returned home. Their shock had been palpable. She drove carefully, at first composing what she would say to Tyler. No sense in blurting it out. But her mind drifted to what she wanted to say to Detective Fury. He probably heard about the fire. She knew there would be a connection between the drugs, the killer, and the fire. Would he sense it, too? Maybe they could work on it together. For now, the best she could do was leave phone messages until he deemed to call her back.

After the uniting of the family and a great dinner by Delia, activity in the house had settled down. Lizzie hadn't. While Emily helped Heather with her bath, Lizzie fit in one more quick self-defense lesson with Tyler. When he'd seen her doing her exercises one morning last week, he'd asked if he could learn.

Ever since, she allowed him to accompany her, and set aside a time where she could train him in protecting himself. She provided knowledge explaining each move, but also general martial arts beliefs.

"Mental strength is crucial to a teenager. It's essential for one growing into a physical strength, like you are." She added the mature guidance to the moves that would help him develop fully. She hoped he would be able to continue training with a martial arts master.

Later, she peeked in on Tyler in his bed, with Heather snuggled up next to him, Marcus, still marred by unremovable remains of black ash, firmed her resolve. On the surface, the two children exuded peace, and she shuddered at what could have happened.

Still unable to reach Detective Fury, she moved to the dimly lit kitchen and wrote a list. Maybe it was time to go it alone again. Delia's notepad on the counter beckoned to her as she realized the enumeration of ideas no longer required stealth. In her new role here at home she could write down her thoughts without fear of them reaching enemy hands, like in the past. Unless one counted Detective Fury. If she didn't hear from him soon, she may cross him from her friend list and move him to the foe one.

Their's was a strange relationship with no written rules. He functioned as a fully responsible policeman with methods of finding the enemy and serving justice. They both fostered and protected the goodness in people. She needed to accept that and work within his boundaries whenever possible. But to keep Tyler and his family safe, her skills provided a means to do more than house them. What should she do?

Delia tiptoed in, ensconced in her fluffy blue bathrobe. "I heard you mumbling to yourself. Care for a cup of soothing chamomile tea? I'm making some for me. Hopefully, it will calm me after such a busy day."

Staring at the blank sheet a little longer, Lizzie raised her eyes to her sister's, unable to hide the despair in her own. "I think I need more than tea."

Delia halted. "I've never seen you in such agony since Jeremy kicked your butt in second grade at the ring toss. Let me write the notes for you."

Lizzie held back a snappy reply. "I can write fine. Just can't think. I have to be missing a clue."

Delia put on the kettle and set up two mugs with strainers filled with the loose chamomile flowers. She sat. "Okay. Talk it out. How has the fire changed things? You've been tense since you arrived at the scene."

"That's easy. It was Tyler's house. Not some random fire. The type of blaze indicated arson."

Delia reached for the pen and calmly wrote ARSON in big, bold letters. Then waited.

Lizzie said, "So who? And why?"

When she didn't answer her own questions, Delia said, "Someone fears what Tyler knows. They set the fire to keep him quiet."

Lizzie didn't hesitate. "Or kill him to ensure he kept quiet."

Delia nodded, her hand barely shaking as she waited for her sister to begin her mental elimination process.

Lizzie concentrated and tried to follow a path to the fire. According to Tyler, his first contact had been Hector. Though the teen confided in Lizzie that he never saw Tyler again after the street corner transactions, she put him back on the list of concerns.

She merely told Delia, "Write 'check on Hector and where is he now'."

After another moment of review she said, "Add those two guys trying to buy drugs from the man at the table at the Jumpin' Lizard. I know those men headed for Wanton Industries but I never saw them again. Maybe they killed the drug addict.

"Put him on the list, too—the gungy man whose body trembled intermittently while denying the men their drugs. He's real doubtful, but I don't want to miss anything this time around."

Delia waited. She drummed her pencil on the table. Lizzie finally noticed.

"Sorry. I've been filtering everything through the old brain."

"Any more suspects come to mind?"

Lizzie sighed. "Too many. Remember the preppy ones I described while we were at the Jumpin' Lizard? The geeky ones?"

"You mean the ones that had you looking down at everyone's shoes?"

"Right. We never found them. And they were users. They could have killed the guy in a fit of anger."

Delia stifled a yawn as she poured more tea. "Long night. But if they were users, would they waste good drugs by stuffing them in the guy's mouth?"

Lizzie perked up. "You're right. We probably aren't looking at addicts at all. I'll move them down further on the list. And I need to hunt up that scar-faced dealer again. He's less than trustworthy. He'd have respect for the cost of those drugs, but maybe his users were drying up because his own use made him unreliable and he went crazy."

Before Delia could speak, Lizzie continued. "I'm going bonkers myself, right?"

Delia raised her brows, opened her eyes wide, but said nothing.

Lizzie could see her biting her tongue, the way her mouth was pursed. Wise woman, and it brought out a laugh that released some tension.

Delia added the dealer to the list and looked her sister in the face. "What about that man the nurse saw in the hospital. Did you learn any more about him?"

"No further news. No confirmation that he was the one with the knife to your throat at the shopping market. It seemed likely that he was the one from the hospital, since he could have followed you from there." She sniffed in a miff. "Add to ask Fury if they have any idea who it was." Lizzie hung her head. "I'm glad he didn't hurt you. I did so much better at my job than I did protecting my own sister."

Then Delia rose gracefully from her chair, pushed it in with a gentle tap, and said, "Bedtime, sis. You're exhausted. Let's go."

Lizzie blinked, nodded, and followed Delia's lead.

Delia turned out the lights before her sister could change her mind.

As they walked to the foot of the stairs, Lizzie said, "Tyler wasn't in the house. Thank the Lord. This accomplished nothing." She breathed deep.

Delia patted her on the shoulder as they moved upward.

Lizzie whispered, *Thank you God, for protecting everyone. We'll get back to helping you out in the morning.*

CHAPTER 20

Delia hit the kitchen as soon as the sun flickered in anticipation of morning.   She would prepare a feast for her house guests. Nutritious food fed the body and kept the brain functioning on high alert. Her other firm belief—great tasting food uplifted the soul providing what the body needed to help the brain decide ethically.

When she saw the note by the coffeepot, warm brew still wafting its scent through the room, she smacked her hand on the counter. That loner sister of hers took off already, without seeking help from her declared partner on this crime. She should have gotten her partner status in writing. The woman used to work alone. Maybe she'd need to embroider a reminder on her bed pillow.

She jerked down a bowl and flung some flour in it. Her usual neat style flamboyant now in her anger. Delia huffed some more as she worked. That woman never slept. She wouldn't see the pillow. Maybe I'll tattoo it on her forehead. Then smacked her own forehead, forgetting the flour on her hand. "That wouldn't work either. She never looks in a mirror."

Seeing the flour on her hand, she realized what she'd done and breathed slowly to calm herself. Two deep breaths and a wash-up of hands and white-powdered face, got her back on track. Planning. Feed the crowd. Tackle Lizzie. She chuckled at that. Fat chance. Her sister could withstand boulders. If she attempted a tackle, she'd probably be the one to crack into tiny pieces.

As she picked up the note to move it out of the way, it flipped over. Her sister had revised the list. She glanced and pondered changes as she completed biscuits and heated her largest iron skillet for bacon. Eggs followed soon in a bowl for a scrambled concoction that included fresh tomatoes, onions and peppers, followed by parsley, basil, thyme and marjoram.

The guests stirred. Delia straightened her shoulders, and firmed her resolve to keep these folks safe. But she also needed to help Lizzie find the killer and renew her path in life through a teen center. The center was a new item on the day's itinerary, in capital letters. She wondered how that had gotten onto a suspect list.

It appears I need a hefty breakfast myself. She added two more eggs into the mix as Tyler hopped down the stairs. She stalled for a second, smiling. She already recognized the cadence of his step.

A sleepy Heather spoke at the top of the stairs. Low, almost fearful. "Wait up, Tyler."

His clatter stopped in an instant. She was proud of him. Knowing he loved his sister, the experience of hearing it in his quiet response, made her *proud*. They whispered as they tiptoed the rest of the way. As they entered the kitchen, his sheepish grin caused her to hesitate.

"What's up?"

"We don't want to wake mom."

"Great thinking. Why don't we eat and plan our day."

Tyler studied the table and chairs while she poured more than half the scrambled eggs into the waiting pan. He brought two of the plumpest cushions from the living room, and squared them up on one of the chairs.

"Here, Heather. Jump up and I'll get you in place." Once she looked secure, he nudged the chair under the table, then settled next to her. "Now don't wiggle or you'll fall off."

Delia poured three apple juices and put one glass between Heather's hands. "I think you are a big enough girl to drink out of an adult glass without breaking it, right?"

Heather's forehead rose, eyes wide as she closed her mouth tight in concentration. She gave a quick nod, as if afraid to take her eyes off the task. Delia knew that glass was safe, but she also didn't want to test the child too much.

"Why don't you and Tyler drink up now while waiting for the rest of the food? I don't think God will mind if you start a bit before we say grace." She hadn't been around children much but had already learned plenty from Tyler. Maybe Heather was too young to understand praying thanks to God for a meal.

She asked. "Heather, do you know how to say grace?"

The child looked up, a ring of apple juice on her lips. She said, "Grace."

Delia and Tyler laughed, then turned toward the living room as soft footsteps sounded on the stairs. Emily came in, her eyes somewhat crusted from sleep, looking more frail than Delia had ever seen her. Worse than when she reported Tyler missing. A good breakfast was in order. Delia headed back to the stove.

Tyler said, "Sorry, mom. We were trying to be quiet."

Emily's face lit up. "Oh, baby. You didn't wake me up. You're both great kids. You came downstairs without a sound. I hope you didn't pester Miss Delia." They'd agreed on that name when Delia refused to be called Mrs. O'Neary by the children.

Delia clutched a full skillet of eggs and served them onto plates. She answered first. "Don't be silly. These children are charming and well-behaved. I hope eggs will suit you. The bacon's on the counter right behind you, and that bowl of cantaloupe."

Emily reached for the bacon and fruit and centered them on the table. "This looks scrumptious, right kids?" Noticing the lack of a fifth setting, she asked, "Isn't Lizzie here?"

"No, she left early. Eat up. We have a big day ahead of us."

Delia sat, offered a brief but heartfelt prayer, and wondered how she would keep these people occupied while she took off to solve some of her own questions. At the top of her agenda was finding out more about the guy who drew a knife on her and threatened her so-called brother, Lizzie, in disguise. It had to be someone from the bar, or the sordid occupants of the defunct Warton Industries. No one else knew of Lizzie's guise as a feeble old man. She mulled her options, grasping the bacon plate and offering it with a smile to each at the table.

Once the others were occupied, she would call Lizzie, and hope for a response. Her sister wasn't known for holding her phone at the ready like today's teenagers. Or should she leave her be, in case she was moving amongst the realms of the defeated. The ones innocent of the killing might still object to her unearthing their secret lives.

Maybe she'd call that nice Detective Fury instead. Or that sweet Sergeant Torkless. She asked Emily to pass the bottle of mixed herbs on the table and sprinkled them on her eggs, holding back a grin that would seem unfitting for eggs.

"Can't have too much parsley," she said, while planning her attack.

Torkless it was. And a lightbulb went off in her head on how to protect those here. Maybe the parsley cleared the mind. Did she need to coax her temporary family or just announce her plan? She studied the glum faces as they ate. Though Heather was bubbly. And ate every bite.

Firm it was. "I've got a great idea folks. Tyler, would you care to bring your mom and sister to the Kinney Herb Farm? Show them where you work and what you do? I can call Dave now and see if that fits his schedule."

Tyler jumped up to clear the table, surprising his mom and delighting her also. Emily's pride in the boy shown through her earlier gloom. Tyler cleaned off the plates and dishes and kept talking the whole time. "You'll love it there mom. It smells wonderful. And they say that in the summer it looks like it, too. I guess it's the bright colors. Most of it is green right now." He lifted Heather off the chair, bent down in front of her, eye to eye. "But if you look real close at the young plants, you see lots of different greens. You can't touch anything, though, okay?"

Delia left the room to make her call, explaining to Dave about the people she'd be bringing by for some R and R, and that she wanted time to tend to matters away from their attention. She decided to be forthright. "And Dave, they need to be secure from the outside world while there. The fenced in areas of the farm will be fine for that."

Dave and Delia were old friends and he began his career in herbs with her help. He often said he owed much to her, but she didn't usually take advantage. Today, she needed time to investigate. To check up on Lizzie. To pick up those clothes the thrift shop had ready for her. She didn't have to explain to Dave. He just said, yes, without question.

She rushed about and changed into her take-charge outdoor shoes, mumbling over and over how she could do this. No wonder Lizzie rambles on to God. This type of investigation and sneaking about was stressful. You need any help you can get. Starting with the top was a good plan. Once God was on your side, the enemies would fall into disarray.

Dave gathered Tyler's family in through the gate, hustling them off to the work sheds and other employees for introductions and a tour. Delia drove away to visit Torkless, mumbling her list of needs into the air as if it was a tape recorder. Once said out loud, she would remember.

First, con Torkless into spilling the beans. Do they use that term any more—spilling the beans? Next, try to connect with Lizzie. She would not go to Wanton Industries alone, though. Third, get the donated clothes for Emily and Heather. And don't forget the car seat. Heather absolutely must have one. The thrift store probably carried them.

Just as important—convince Lizzie that the Hopsons must stay with them at least until the killer was found. *Oh, and last, but also important, God, is to find a nice house or apartment for the family. You know that implies an income for Emily and day care for Heather.* Screeching brakes of the car in front of her tore her from her thoughts and mental wanderings. She slammed on her own brakes and stopped inches short of the red Corvette's rear bumper. A tall, elderly man removed himself from the driver's seat. His lean frame and gentlemanly manner soothed her fears. This didn't look like a killer, though how would she know?

Delia fluttered her fingers in front of her face to release that fear. Add to that the stress of a near miss on the road.

The man stepped up his pace. "Ma'am, are you okay?" He opened her door.

She could have had ten broken toes but wouldn't have admitted it to this stranger. Stalwart, she answered, "I'm fine, though you startled me a bit."

"A bit! If that happened to me I'd be looking for the nearest bottle."

Now she was flustered, but managed to say, "Why, whatever do you mean?"

He pointed to the slight gap between the cars. "I mean I've never seen anyone with such driving skills. I was sure I'd have at least a crumpled bumper."

She smiled. The good Lord must be watching despite her lack of concentration. "Just luck, I guess." She wanted to see this tiny gap and swiveled sideways to exit the car.

"I want to take you to lunch as a thank you and an apology."

"Sir, thank me for what? I almost hit your car. And, it's ten o'clock, a long way from lunch."

He grinned and reached for her arm to help her. She stepped out gingerly, looked around, and realized there was no one else on this old country road.

"Please, ma'am. We could start with a drink, maybe a coffee, and move slowly toward a meal."

She walked to the front of his car, still slightly wary, and saw nothing wrong. "Sir, why did you stop?"

"Didn't you see that deer run across the road without looking?"

Though she finally believed there was no ulterior motive, she took brisk, though dainty, steps back to her car. "Thank you kindly. But I'm on a mission and can't delay."

She took an agile hop back into the driver's seat and patted her trusty blue sedan. No need to tell him that Lizzie had hired someone to beef up the engine a bit. And fine-tuned the braking system. She leaned her head out the window and said, "But I will take your name in case we need to discuss car repairs."

His face contorted into a frown, probably wondering what repairs, since the cars hadn't touched. But then it opened and brightened. He handed her his card. "I'd be glad to hear from you again, ma'am."

She dragged her purse up from the floor where it had been

tossed by momentum, and shoved the card into her purse. As soon as he walked back to his car she wrote down his license number on the notepad kept handy on the dash, then rolled up the window and sped off. Her mind reeled with so much to do, while his cheerful facade seemed to crumble as if he recognized his lack of success in wooing her. Or worse. Delia headed immediately to the police station.

With a peek through the window, she delighted to find Sergeant Torkless staffing the front desk at the station. She rumpled her clothes a bit and tilted her daisy hat at an unstylish angle for effect.

"Dear Sergeant Torkless, it pleases me to see a kind and familiar face. I would have felt embarrassed talking with a stranger."

He stood in an instant, a frown line of concern forming on his forehead. "Please come over here and take a seat. How can I help you Mrs. O'Neary? Whatever happened?"

She waved her hand in front of her face fanlike. "Why, I close to hit a man on the road."

"Is he okay?"

"Of course, he was in his car."

"Then what's the matter?"

"He wanted me to get out of the car and look. I was afraid you know. After the man with the knife."

He patted her arm. "I understand. You are safe here. How can I help now?"

"You could check out his license plate number. See if it belongs to who he says he is."

The sergeant brought her a glass of water. "I'll do that. You wait right here. A minute later he came back with a sheet of paper. "His name matches the Aaron Alexander Ballard on the card you gave me, if that is any comfort. I did a quick check on the internet. He's a long standing contributor to the community in many ways."

She breathed a sign of relief. Now for the rest. "Please tell me you've made some progress on my transgressor at the supermarket. I haven't been able to bring myself back there since it happened."

"Actually, ma'am, a witness thought he recognized the car. Our men tracked it down but it belonged to an elderly couple, who had reported it stolen."

She rose. Well, at least she could take the new man off the list. One more attempt before she left.

"That Hector guy. Do you still have him locked up?"

"Oh yes. He's been moved, but definitely under our control."

She sighed. "I almost wish something would happen to move this investigation forward, then I remember the fire and know that's not what I want after all. I do have nightmares about that scar-faced dealer though. The one Hector knew about."

The sergeant walked her to the door. "Now don't you worry ma'am. We've been following him based on Hector's information. He was arrested a day ago on drug charges."

She smiled back. Bingo. She'd eliminated three items on the list. Lizzie would be proud of her.

CHAPTER 21

Lizzie's excitement evaporated the moment Delia answered the phone. Before she could say more than 'Hello,' Delia growled, "Where have you been? What happened to, 'We're partners?'"

"I just left an impromptu meeting with the nurses. It began as a simple check for more information on the stranger lurking around Tyler's hospital room last week. It turned into a delightful blessing for us."

Despite her sister's angry voice, Lizzie wanted to share the news with her. "Delia, you won't believe it!" We already have a team set up to help the teen center. The hospital nurses jumped right in and offered ideas and help. I can't wait to tell you about it."

Her sister sounded baffled, as if caught off guard. "What? Lizzie, what are you talking about? I thought we were tracking down the killer. Remember the dead guy? We wanted to clear Tyler and prevent any more incidents. Uhh, like fires."

Lizzie deciphered her sister's disjointed sentences, though the cause was still unclear. "Where are you dear? I'm at home and no one is here. What happened to the homeless waifs?"

Delia fumed, "I'm sitting here in an abandoned gas station parking lot talking to my sister who disappeared this morning without a word to me. I'm on the way to pick up everyone from the Kinney Herb Farm where I parked them while I went out to track down the killer."

Oh my. *Dear Lord take care of this woman. Who would have thought she'd go off to find a killer on her own?*

"Delia, please head right home. I'll go pick up the family while you start lunch. Is that okay?"

"It's better than me gathering them up while you make lunch."

Relieved to hear the return of humor to Delia's voice, Lizzie went to find everyone and see if Emily knew what Delia was up to. Or Dave. She did feel slight remorse at not telling anyone where she was going this morning. Habits were tough to break. This one, of taking off on her own, was ingrained over many decades. Yet, it should be easy to adjust to someone caring where she went and wanting to help in any way. She'd try harder.

She drove to the buttercup-yellow house. The new fence wrapped around part of the property. A spurt of laughter from the far side drew her toward it, enjoying the earthy scent of recently turned soil. Green shoots in straight rows, contrasted with her sister's hodgepodge herb garden with surprises tucked in nooks, a delightful mix of colors, spring through fall. But then, this was business. Straight rows were more economical.

Her wave caught their attention. Tyler raced toward the fence but stopped to put Heather on his shoulders after she followed and stumbled. Dave pointed to the gate, a few yards down, and said he'd meet her there.

Puzzled at the gated fencing, she tilted her head sideways and asked why the security. Trying to keep out the deer?"

"Delia mentioned possible danger so we stayed in the fenced areas. We're experimenting in the largest areas with motion-activated lights instead."

She walked through the gate. "How's that working out for you?"

He waved her toward the gathering in the corner. As they walked, he said, "The deer seem to enjoy eating by candlelight. I'm working on adding the sound of gunshot to the mix."

She covered her mouth to hide a laugh.

After setting Heather down, Tyler came barreling up. "We've had a great time showing mom and Heather how the herb farm works, and talking about who we supply what. You know, the tons of meadowsweet we grow for people with arthritis."

When he saw that his sister had stopped to look at some newly emerging herbs, he lowered his voice and said, "Mom's real interested. You know how she's been since the fire—kind of dull. But now there's more. . ." His voice stumbled reaching for words. "More life in her face."

Lizzie patted his shoulder as she asked the rest of the group. "Does anyone know what Delia's been doing? Where she went this morning?"

Dave said, "She just said she had a lot of errands to run."

Lizzie nodded. No help there. "Time for lunch. Delia's cooking away as we stand here." Emily, Tyler, and Heather separated themselves from the others, and walked closer to Lizzie, who nodded to the rest of the crew and mouthed a silent thank you to Dave.

When they got to the house, overflowing boxes of clothes in the living room greeted them. Child and mom crept close in awe. Heather wanted to delve in, but her mother stopped her, afraid to touch the soft fabrics with the quiet designs and brilliant colors.

Delia waved her spatula from the kitchen toward the boxes and told Emily. "We gathered some clothes for you and Heather. See what you think. I'm not sure all of them will fit. Take them to the bedroom to try on later. We're eating in ten minutes."

Tyler lugged boxes to the bedroom. Tears tracked down Emily's face. To mend fences, Lizzie hugged Delia from behind. A move she'd hadn't made in many years, it reminded her of a time in childhood when she would squeeze her sister from behind and thank her for a kind gesture or small gift.

Delia laughed, her memory easily going back the seventy years. "What do you want this time?"

"I want to apologize for not telling you where I was going. I'll do better. I promise. May I ask what you were up to?" Lizzie sat at the table while Delia stirred a mixture of zucchini, onions, and tomatoes in a skillet on the stove. The herbs in the glass on the table became an aroma blending with the vegetables.

Gathering her thoughts to report first while Delia concentrated on cooking, she said, "I went to see Nurse Nickeisha. You remember, she's the one who found the strange man lurking on the fourth floor at the hospital? She called at five and asked me if I could come over before her shift ended at seven. I headed over there before anyone woke up."

Delia faced her. "Tell me. What did she want?" She swiveled to open the oven door and check on her honey mustard chicken.

The sweet scent of the rest of the herbs wafted into the room. She continued, "The security men tackled a guy hanging out on the second floor late last night. He was just a weird man who had no where else to go, and in his sick mind he thought he'd be safe and warm in the empty rooms. He'd move about constantly, hiding. The police arrested him."

Delia turned off the stove, pulled out the chicken, and organized it on a platter. She asked, "Did Nurse Nickeisha see him?"

"Yes, and it was the man she saw near Tyler's room. One suspect off the list."

Delia smiled at Lizzie and offered the platter. "While you were gone, I visited that young Sergeant Torkless. Take two more suspects off the list."

Lizzie stood and reached for the platter, stuttering, "Who? What? How did you get him to talk?"

Delia's eyes twinkled. She stepped into the hallway and called from the bottom of the stairs. "Lunch is ready. Wash up please."

Scooping the vegetable mix into her favorite yellow-flowered pottery bowl, she set it on the table, then enumerated on her fingers: "One, the guy who held the knife at my throat, must have 'borrowed' the car because it was stolen. So he's still out there. Two, Hector is engulfed somewhere deep in police facilities. Can barely speak some days. He's stoked on drugs, doesn't make much sense, and couldn't have set the fire."

The family settled at the table and Heather said. "I say grace." She didn't seem to mind the stifled giggles. She bowed her head and said, "Grace, thank-you-for-food." When she raised her head her eyes sought approval. She didn't have to wait long as everyone chimed in with praise. They all controlled their laughter in different ways. Tyler merely stuffed his mouth with food as the others filled their plates.

Lizzie finished her tale. "While at the hospital I spoke with Nurse Joy. She pulled me to the nurse's lounge where we met up with

Nurse Becky and some others. They had talked about the teen center and offered a few suggestions."

Tyler's head rose and he stopped eating. "A teen center? Totally lit." Joy on his face gave the only clue to the old-timers as to what he meant.

Lizzie continued, "They want to offer their time in helping out. With special programs on health and nutrition and drug abuse. Some will concentrate on assisting addictive parents of pre-teens and teens to clean up, while monitoring members to keep them healthy. With the rise of opioid addicted mom's giving birth to addicted babies, others said they'd zero in on working with pregnant women to stay clean. Plus, they said they could serve as supervisors."

She stabbed a piece of chicken and held it aloft, like a flag. "And the best for last, they know of an abandoned building now owned by the town, that they think would be ideal."

With a sigh, Delia acknowledged that her sister did have a fruitful morning. She praised her sister, then urged another serving of vegetables on Tyler and Heather. Tyler balked on taking more, his eye on the cookie platter behind Delia on the counter. She said in her firm, quiet voice, "I could find that list you got from the nutritionist, and the one from your herbal addiction counselor, if you need it."

Tyler filled his plate with more vegetables. Heather followed his example and added a smaller pile to her own. He smiled at the makeshift family gathered around the table, then filled his mouth with food.

Delia removed empty platters and replaced them with a small plate of five lavender cookies.

The herb added a wonderful aroma to the cookies. Lizzie knew it also helped reduce stress and anxiety. They all could use that today. Maybe she could entice her sister to let them have a few more later.

"Where will the teen center be?" Tyler asked.

The possible building is set back a little, one block off of Main Street."

He perked up while simultaneously trying to snitch Heather's cookie. She poked his arm until he dropped her cookie. She caught it and left it in her hand while she finished the rest of her food with a wobbly fork in the other hand. But she was smiling. Little sister—1, Big brother—0.

Lizzie lowered her lids to cloak her amusement, and said, "We should schedule a meeting soon with the town counsel. First we need an official teen center board."

The others began to clear their plates from the table, while Delia drew her sister into the next room. "Lizzie, what on earth has caused this fervor since yesterday?"

"I heard on the news last night about a drug company founder indicted in a opioid conspiracy, back-to-back with a local story about a nineteen-year-old boy overdosing in his mother's bathroom."

Delia placed her hands on her hips and said, "Okay. What can I do to help?"

"I want it to stop."

"That might take a bit. I'll rephrase. What can I do, first?"

Lizzie laughed. *That* was her sister.

"Could you get Agatha on board, to give a simple report on how herbal addiction treatment works, and then entice her to be on the board? I plan to tackle ole Torkless myself, this time with the license plate number that Tony gave me."

She added, "I haven't pursued Fury's lead because he didn't give me enough information, and I figure maybe they can follow this one without help. If they're right, we'll all be relieved the killer is in prison."

Delia pursed her lips. "Brilliant thinking. And, finally, you are working with others."

Throwing up her hands, Lizzie said, "I was never on the opposite side of the police, you know." She appreciated her sisters ensuing chuckle. There hadn't been enough laughter from her usually ebullient sibling lately.

Lizzie added, "If they are wrong, then we need to know where these other leads go. If nothing else, I will have gathered valuable information on the drug addiction scene in this area."

"Ahh, the trust in cops lacks total conviction."

"You know me, sis. The only one I'll totally trust without thought is you."

Delia picked up a pile of newly washed clothes for their guests but gave a one-armed hug for Lizzie as she left the room. At least Lizzie thought they *were* guests, though it appeared Delia had offered them a permanent home.

Lizzie drove out, listening to the monotonous thump of the tires on the road. She'd read that in most places the tires hummed, but this was Pennsylvania. The one break in the thumps was the thwack, thwack as the car jounced over potholes. Maybe Torkless would help her. Or Fury. Or God.

Speaking of you, God, I'm worried I can't fight this battle while staying within the law, and still keep my new relationship with You. The teen center's a given. It's finding the killer that bothers my concept.

CHAPTER 22

"That's poison! Don't touch it!" Delia heard the shout shortly after she brought Emily and family to the Bittersweet Herb Shop. Agatha's disembodied voice mumbled something else as she laboriously crawled from beneath the counter.

Agatha told her it was okay to bring Emily and her family to the shop. Second thoughts rushed in. Delia grabbed Heather and Tyler's hands and they all stepped back in unison. Emily plowed into them from behind, sliding the last few feet as she hurried to her children from the other end of the store when she heard the shout.

A disheveled and breathless Agatha rose from the cubby behind the counter. "Sorry about that," she said, as she shoveled bracelets with her gloved fingers into a bag, clearly labeled, SAFE DISPOSAL.

She studied the children. Since she'd already met Tyler, she smiled at him, said hello, and waited, her eyes on the girl. Delia stepped back. Gallantly, Tyler bowed, and said "Ms. Agatha Hartman, meet my sister, Heather? He looked behind him. "This is my mom, Emily Hopson."

Emily inched forward, eyebrows arching downward at the jewelry still hanging on the lip of the bag. She reached to shake the owner's hand, and jerked back. Agatha wore gloves. Delia watched Emily's eyebrows lower further, but hoped Agatha could handle this.

Emily said, "Hello," but added, "Why would you have that on the counter if it was poisonous?"

Agatha winced. "They shouldn't have been there. I was cleaning the cupboard and found them tucked way in the back. When I reached up to put them in the bag to destroy them, the bag toppled over and I set them on the counter till I could get up. Not as easy to do these days."

She explained, "The bracelets were bought by the former owner, probably thirty years ago from the looks of the tags. She probably didn't know at the time that they are made of what is commonly called Rosary Peas."

Everyone looked puzzled and stared at her. Delia said, "Maybe you could tell us more to explain the odd name for the poisonous seeds."

Agatha did. "The beads are extremely deadly when scratched to reveal the inner core of abrin, a ribosome-inhibiting protein."

Heather's face looked blank.

Agatha pushed the poisonous bracelets deep into the bag, removed her gloves, and added them to the bag before tying it tight. She came around the counter and squatted down to Heather's level. "You see, if you eat one little seed and chew it, you will become ill and die."

Heather blinked. "Why you keep them?"

She stood, and spoke to her as if she were an adult. "I was reading through some old record books from 1970 and saw that the owner had bought more than she sold. I scoured this whole store till I found a secret storage container in the back of this cubby."

"Wow, a secret place? That's nice," Heather said.

After they all laughed, and agreed, Agatha said. "I plan to clean the cubby out, then maybe I will ask Heather, here, what we should use it for. But I think you came for another reason—to learn about the life-giving herbs and foods for Tyler, right?"

Delia said, "I thought you could help Tyler explain to his mom about the program. He seems to be making the right choices in food, and taking the supplements you provided, but he could use your help in clarifying the importance of each."

The shop owner escorted them to a nook surrounded by books, all on health issues. It was just large enough for an old wooden table and four chairs. She fetched a copy of Tyler's customized health plan and made them comfortable at the table, providing Heather with a coloring book on vegetables and a four-pack of crayons.

"Young lad. You go through the plan with your mom, Emily is it? I'll be up front with Delia, and if either of you have questions, you can send your messenger here to find me." When she pointed to Heather, the child giggled and nodded, ready to make her first run.

The instant they were alone, Delia cajoled the woman into a spot on the teen center board before she could even swallow one sip of coffee. It helped that Agatha was eager to provide insight into the teen drug problem, and would offer programs to the teens, and their parents, once the center opened. Agatha, as the owner of the Bittersweet Herb Shop, and a long-time community advocate of health care, would supply permanence to the board and center.

Heather raced up and tugged on Agatha's sleeve. "Tyler needs help with valer-something."

"My messenger is here. Are you finished twisting my arm?"

Heather gripped her arm and pulled it out straight. "Better now?"

The child filled Delia with joy. That did it. They must stay with us until we can find adequate housing for the family nearby. As they trailed behind Heather to the back table, Delia realized both she and her sister needed this elixir of youth.

Agatha filled in Emily on the herbs for detoxification, including valerian to treat the insomnia that accompanies withdrawal. She added, "Special foods and herbal supplements would also relieve any withdrawal symptoms of addiction."

Tyler finished by explaining the need for passionflower for anxiety, a side effect of withdrawal. He'd already learned that from her in the hospital and Delia helped him make some tea when they arrived at her house.

Agatha emphasized that the herbs used in the recovery process worked most effectively when combined with nutrition, relaxation, and exercise.

Delia said to Emily, "That's one of the many reasons why Tyler works a couple of hours several days a week at the farm. He earns an allowance, and gets his fresh air and exercise, too." She said to Tyler,

"Which reminds me. Today's your day off work because, ta da, it's tutor day. He groaned, "Not with Jenny Lyn again. When can I go back to school?"

Delia herded them out the door. She shared a look with him before saying, "When can you do polynomial expressions?"

This time his groan went bone deep.

When they got back to the house, Jenny Lyn met them, and she and Tyler settled at the kitchen table with herbal pumpkin cake slices nearby. Delia asked Emily and Heather to finish sorting through the clothes to set aside those that didn't fit.

After her conversation with Emily last night about neighbors and acquaintances that might know Ethan and the Innis family, Delia sat out on her favorite garden bench and scrolled through her handwritten phone directory. Noting the date she'd entered on the day she bought it forty years ago, she thought tenderly about all the friends she'd gained over the years.

On a mission to help Lizzie find Ethan, she settled down to business. She found a name Tyler's mom had mentioned and started calling. Lizzie had concentrated on finding men associated with Vern Innis. If she found Ethan, maybe they could clarify much of what was happening.

On the third call, she found what she needed. But it took coaxing. The woman was adamant Delia not reveal the source, and especially, not put the family in jeopardy.

She explained the situation with Tyler, then added, "I swear, Ethel, we just want to make sure Tyler's friend is safe. Tyler's having a rough time and could use an old friend right now."

"Well, why didn't you say so? They are hiding from Ethan's father though. They were threatened by a man who did business with Verge. Verge knew to get them out of the house, but as soon as he squirreled them away, they took off and hid from him. They could no longer trust him."

After hanging up, Delia sat back, relaxed for a minute, and viewed the beginnings of her spring garden. Should she visit them immediately? Maybe it would be best to call Lizzie and decide together, like partners. Her sister's cell phone rang and rang. No answer. Where could she be? She tried one more time. And it rang and rang. Silly to expect she set up a voice mail. Technology had never been her strong suit, but sheesh, it's a cell phone for heaven's sakes.

Little Heather came running outside. "There you are. I looked and looked for you."

The little girl gave her a big hug. Delia waited. Then she prompted with a gentle question, "Heather, did you want me?"

"Oh yeah, Misornery."

The poor thing kept trying to say, Mrs. O'Neary. She reminded her. "Dear, why don't you call me Miss Delia. Remember, your mom said that would be okay. Now what did you want?"

"Oh, mommy said to tell you there was a phone ringing in Missort's room."

She gave up trying to think of an easier way for Heather to say that. In a calm voice, she said, "Thank you, Heather. You are a good messenger."

The little girl laughed as she trailed back inside. "I tell mommy me good."

There wasn't much she could say about her sister. You'd think she'd remember to take the phone with her. Now what? She did tell me she would visit that dear John Torkless to find out about the license plate number on the car by the Innes house.

She breathed deep, then called the police station. "Why hello John. How are you this fine afternoon?"

"My God, it's Mrs. O'Leary. Don't you two ever quit? Find someone else to pester? This time it backfired on your dear sister. I was out when she came in and Detective Fury took over. They're trading words in his office. I can tell. He's shouting. Her name comes out loud, then muffled, but boy you sure can tell he's upset."

Delia barely uttered "hmph" before he started in again. "What did you two do this time? Rob a bank?"

She managed half a sentence this time. "Now dear John, please calm down, before . . ."

"Oh yeah, that's too straightforward for you."

"John, John, take a deep breath. You'll hurt yourself. I'll bring you some passionflower and lemon balm tea to calm your nerves and help lower your blood pressure."

He settled enough to say "hmph" himself. She continued. "Now sir, these two feeble old women, who are used to being alone, have a family living with us right now because their home burnt to the ground out of a sick man's attempt to silence a young boy. Please, please forgive our anxieties."

She could almost see his look of humiliation as he stuttered an apology. She was good at this. Combining her usual soft nature with skills she learned from Lizzie would make her into a formidable spy and partner. John fumbled for more words, and she planned her next move.

She'd found her sister. That's why she called. She'd originally wanted to talk with her, but asking if she could come to the phone might set John off again. Switching to a more subtle tone, she said, "Do you think she's all right? I know she wanted information on a lead she got, a license plate number that might help us find our poor Tyler's closest friend. He's missing and a neighbor boy remembered the license plate number of the car at Ethan's home just before he disappeared. It's a slim lead, but maybe it will take us to a new address."

The sergeant cleared his throat, torn between being kind to an old lady and being a stern sergeant. His decision went in her favor. "I see the number here. I don't know if Detective Fury checked it or not." He cleared his throat. "They could have become entangled in another conversation first."

She pleaded. "Could you check it now? It might help us find the boy. Since his parents also disappeared we can't consider him a missing child. Tyler just wants to make sure his friend is okay. He has enough worries now. He's fourteen but his mom is ill and he has this adorable little sister. He wants to find work."

Okay, she already knew Ethan's new address from her friend. And this was the car Tony saw. But it was important, too. And might help Lizzie, who'd be in a real funk when she left Fury. She heard Torkless tapping the computer keys and offered a silent prayer to God, *Oh yes!*

Torkless spoke while he worked. "You know Tyler needs to be in school?"

"Yes, and my sister arranged a tutor for him right away. They are working on something called polynomials now, whatever they are. He will be back in school soon."

Torkless started to growl in frustration, then quickly lowered his voice, probably afraid the detective would hear him. "Okay, here's an address for you, 18 Morton Road. It could be an old one so don't count on this Ethan being there. Memorize it. You never talked with me. Right?"

She wrote it down, smiling with every letter. Another thank you to God and the sergeant, who'd become dear John long enough to help an old lady. She went inside, wrapped cookies to bring to him later. She wrapped more for Jenny's family, thanked her for her time, and walked her to the door. Time to devise a game plan, and wait for Lizzie.

Delia heard her arrive—couldn't miss her screech of tires, and didn't give her time to think. She accosted her the minute she walked in, telling her about the license plate and the name Torkless had given her.

Lizzie smacked her own head. "I can't believe I left without that information. That's why I went. That darn Fury barged in when he saw me standing behind Torkless's computer. I mean, the kid was gone and no one around. I thought I could figure it out myself. Why bother anyone?"

Delia giggled. She couldn't help it. "My heavens, woman, you can't use a cell phone properly. What made you think you could use a computer?"

Lizzie switched topics. "What about the suspicious guy's license plate?"

Delia grabbed her arm, pulled her toward the door, and spoke to Emily who'd just come downstairs and entered the kitchen door. "Emily, you're in charge of dinner. Hunt through the cupboards and find what you need to make one of your favorite meals. Hopefully, there'll be all five of us, so plan accordingly. Of course, if you over guess, I'm sure Tyler can help out with the leftovers."

Emily nodded, wide-eyed and looking flabbergasted.

Pointing at the phone on the wall, Delia said, "I'll call on that if anything delays us. Oh, and write a note to remind us to get you another cell phone."

She couldn't help but tease her sister. "You, Emily, would probably remember to keep it on you when you go somewhere."

Delia tugged Lizzie forward and spoke with zest. "Let's go. I'm driving."

"That's okay, my car's right here."

"No way. Besides, I've already prepped my car."

Delia tucked her into the passenger side, and the car moved before Lizzie could protest again. She did manage, "What? How?"

"I put mud over my license plate. That way, if they see us scoping out the house, they won't be able to find out who we are."

Lizzie smirked. "Honey, it's broad daylight. They'll *see* who we are."

Delia swerved around a corner. She reached behind her with one hand and grasped two huge bonnets, plopping one on Lizzie's head.

Lizzie turned stunned eyes on Delia. "Who *are* you?"

CHAPTER 23

"Shoot! Neither one looks like our tall, rich guy, and that sure isn't a long green car they're tearing away in," Lizzie said.

Parked down the street, both women sunk low in their car as two men waltzed out of the Morton Street location Sergeant Torkless provided. As soon as the men got in their car, Delia sped off, turning the nearest corner, right before the men's house. Lizzie lurched upright and shouted, "What are you doing? They'll get away."

Delia hunched over the wheel, an old lady driver, barely able to see. "Trust me. I can do this."

Afraid to ask what *this* was, Lizzie had no choice. Grabbing the handle above the door, she started to pray. A good thing, prayer. It kept one from wanting to strangle her sister. And she wasn't about to pinch her sister's neck to put her out of commission, not while she was driving. On the way over, Delia had explained how she'd gotten the address from the sergeant. Brilliant thinking. Too bad she hadn't thought of it, herself. Might have saved her from a ripping apart by Detective Fury.

Delia had started to tell her about Ethan's new location and how she'd discovered it while they were on the stake-out of the man seen at his former home. Then these strangers appeared and Delia hadn't talked since she slammed on the gas. And sure enough, she could do *this*, after all. They swerved around another corner, and came up right behind the crumpled sedan that had pulled away from the address they'd been watching. No way could the guys feel they were followed when the women appeared far away from the start.

"How on earth did you know which way to turn?"

"The time, and the fat guy with the buttons ready to pop on his shirt. Dead giveaway. They were headed to the nearest fast food place."

Delia was a natural spy. Who would have known. As they waited outside, Delia called Emily and suggested the family start to eat without them. They'd arrive later. She started her tale of finding current information on Ethan. But then the fat guy returned with a huge bag of food. He licked his lips and lumbered into the car.

When they entered the suspect's house, the sisters slunk back into their original stake-out location. Their silence worked well for a while, but Delia, not used to such things, nudged Lizzie.

"Why did Fury sound as if your demise was imminent?"

Without turning her head, Lizzie raised her voice in surprise, "How do you know that? You didn't go to the station, did you?"

"While speaking with the sergeant I couldn't help but hear a ruckus in the background. He kindly explained that you and the big man were butting heads. Who won?"

Lizzie sighed, and rubbed her noggin like it hurt. "I think he did."

The silence no longer comfortable, she started her tale. "Torkless wasn't at the counter. No one was. I thought I'd look up the license number myself on his computer, to find the address and maybe look this guy over."

Delia snorted. "Right. You and a computer. Tell me, how'd that work out for you?"

"I couldn't get into anything."

"I'll bet you couldn't get pass the guy's password."

"Didn't know I'd need a password."

"So what happened?"

"That nasty Detective Daniel Fury came in. Found me. Practically spilled his hot shot coffee from Starbucks. Guess the department coffee wasn't good enough for him."

Delia patted her arm. "Focus, dear. Is that when his yelling commenced?"

"That began after he pulled me into his office and slammed the door. He . . .wait, did you see that movement at the side of the house?"

Thank heavens for old cars, she thought, as she silently hand-cranked the window down to see better. She pointed, "Over there, behind that shrub."

"Can't see a thing. It's dusk now—hard to see your shadow, or anything lurking in the trees." Delia's sentence ended with a loud stomach growl.

Lizzie straightened her spine, mentally and physically, and said, "I'm going out to look. You stay with the car. If anyone leaves, follow them. But just to find out where they go. Don't leave the car. I'll find my own way home."

Sputtering indicated her sister wanted to argue. She responded with reassurance. "This is what I do. I'll be fine." She slipped from the car so silently Delia barely heard her. She'd decommissioned the door light connection the day she got home and borrowed the car. They were nasty, useless appendages that gave oneself away. She couldn't abide them.

And then it was all for nought. A rangy, bedraggled dog of indeterminate breeding slunk from beneath the shrub and crept away. So much for showing off clandestine spying skills. Lizzie slipped back into the car. And finished her story.

"As I was saying, Fury caught me, keys in hand, so-to-speak, and railed about my interference. Unlike you, I hadn't been quick enough to say I was trying to find Ethan for Tyler. I had to stand there and take his anger, since I couldn't jeopardize our useful relationship with Sergeant Torkless by claiming it was his fault for leaving the area unattended." She grimaced, "And, of course, that Fury had to remind me to stay out of the investigation. Somehow I didn't feel it was a good time to ask where they were on that."

Settling back in the seat, she looked around. Her sister remained mercilessly quiet. The street either catered to empty residences, or the people inside were all dead. No lights. No noise. No cars.

Delia's stomach grumblings were the loudest sound in the neighborhood. She asked her, "You want to go home?"

The engine revved up instantly. She wondered if Delia had already been turning the ignition.

Her words as she drove soothed Lizzie's soul. "It was a smooth move, leaving the paper with the license number by the computer. That's how John could find the address for me. We make a good team. Right?" Then she jerked upright with an, "Ohh."

Lizzie didn't know where the danger came from so turned to her sister.

Delia said, "Sorry. Didn't mean to startle you. I realized that in all this racing around I forgot to tell you where Ethan and his mom are hiding with an old friend. I didn't want to say anything in front of Tyler. I was waiting to ask you what you thought we should do."

Again, Lizzie marveled. Who is this woman? I'm gone for a few hours and she solves half our problems. Well, maybe less than half.

Delia kept talking, trying to clarify. "I spoke with Agatha today and we all had a productive time at the Bittersweet Herb Shop. Figured I could fill you in on that at home, since they were there. But the Ethan thing—how do we handle it?" Her stomach rumbled louder in emphasis.

Lizzie laughed. "We eat first, talk later. I'm astonished at all you've accomplished and we will have to go to Ethan and his mom soon, to warn them what's been happening. If they're not safe where they are, we'll still be able to arrange a reunion between the two boys, but we also need to find everyone a safe haven till all this is resolved."

Delia nodded as she pulled the blue sedan next to Lizzie's dull green car and hopped out. Their cars suited them, both somewhat faded and dark, fitting for the night—or the ravages of old age. Lizzie's stomach never reacted to lack of food, because over the years it never knew when it would get any and learned to take what it could get without complaint. But Delia operated on a fine balance of proteins and healthy carbs. In other words, regular food.

The sisters ate after Emily and Tyler served. Realizing the difficulty in cooking in someone else's kitchen, Lizzie praised the chef about different aspects of the meal. Delia said, "I love the balance between carbs and protein in this sweet and sour tuna casserole."

Lizzie, on the other hand, mumbled between mouthfuls of tuna, "Great addition of pineapple. Love it."

Tyler beamed through the whole meal. He smiled like the owner of a restaurant, as if he'd hired the chef himself. And the kid in him added, "I helped her find all the food." Mom and son cleaned up afterwards.

When Tyler yawned, Emily urged him to bed, following afterwards. She shushed him as they walked past her bedroom door, explaining, "I put Heather down in my bed. This way you'll get a good night's rest. You have to work early tomorrow."

As silence settled, Lizzie made sure to compliment Delia. "Your reaction time amazed me, and your keen thinking put us where we needed to be with those two guys. I bet they're in for the night but we should double check."

"Thanks sis. I appreciate that, coming from a pro."

"We must discuss some fine points, though, if you plan to continue in this line of work."

Delia put on a pot of water for tea and sat across from her sister. "What?"

"As fantastic as your observations were, you could learn to discern more from the details. It may seem unkind, but for now, we'll call the one, Fat Guy. You noticed his size and large face, and determined where he might be heading. That's a great start."

"But . . .?"

"But rather than being fat, his face was huge and florid, most likely from an overabundance of liquor. He carried a large gut, but his whole body was firm. His jacket hung loose, causing him to appear more rotund, but instead, it covered his gun. His hands were big, but hard. It guaranteed he served as an enforcer for the guy in the house."

The teapot whistled. When Delia returned with two steeping mugs, preoccupied with her thoughts, Lizzie could tell she was cataloguing everything covered, maybe saving it to draw on for the right occasion. Then her sister gulped and finally spoke. "You're right. I need tons of work. Much training. But I can do it. What next?"

"When the others are asleep, we split up. Lock up the house tight, set the alarm, and we go. You get back to that house on Morton Street and just watch. See if the man Tony described leaves the house.

That's it. No daredevil attempts at capture. Got it?"

Delia sipped the last of her tea, saluted her sister, and changed into warmer clothes. "I don't want to keep the car running. Might give me away."

"You'll do fine, sis. I need to find what's happening over by Ethan's old home. If anything. And then maybe head over to Wanton Industries, aka the Drug Dwellings, and look for some of our old friends."

Delia's eyebrows reached her bangs when she heard the term 'friends' but merely said, "Yes, boss."

Lizzie parked a block away from Ethan's, rigging her car to beep if anyone touched it. Better to be safe if she needed the old gal in a hurry. She sat on a log two homes down and listened to night noises, logging each as she identified it. The purring chirrup of a contented barn owl complemented the insect sounds of a peaceful night.

Then she saw two figures lurking around Ethan's old house. The heavy one said, "No one's been here for ages. I"m tellin' the boss to forget it. The kid's not comin' back and the mom, she's long gone, too. No sense in scoping out this place any more." This one was brawny, like the fast food addict with the bulbous nose, but harsh and rough, more muscular in street clothes that blended into the night.

His partner replied, "Yeah, we got bigger fish to fry. With Innes all smashed up, we have to find someone else to deal with that drug shipment next week."

They stumbled in the dark back to their car. He plopped into the passenger seat, and from the door light Lizzie thought he looked like the skinny man they'd seen with Bulbous.

He said, "We wouldna' had to do nothin' if you hadn't beat him up so bad."

"Boss said to teach him a lesson. He shouldna' been lookin' for his kid instead of tending that stash. Lost mucho bucks on that."

"I know, I know. But we can't use the guy's family as leverage if we can't find 'em. Glad you're the one who gets to tell the boss."

Instinct told Lizzie to nab them and make them confess everything about the shipment. But she wanted this one done the legal way. She walked further away, pulled out her cell phone, and called Detective Fury. It helped that Tyler had showed her the quick dial area and loaded in the detective's phone number, and then Delia's. Ones he thought she would use the most. Smart kid.

She whispered, "Just heard two guys talking about a big drug shipment coming in next week. They were scoping out Verge Innis's old home looking for leverage to get him to come up with the cash he lost regarding the drugs. They're leaving now."

His shouting bled out of the phone and she mustered a stern and lethal, "What? You want them to hear you? Shut up and listen. I think they're heading back to the big guy at 18 Morton Road. Not sure how far up the peg he goes. But I'll follow them and you get someone to intersect."

She hung up, then speed dialed Delia, hoping she would answer. Could answer.

She did, in whispered tones that said she was freezing her tush off, nothing had happened, but she'd seen a tall blond guy walk past one of the windows.

"Okay. Get out of there fast. I'm following Bulbous Man and his sidekick back there, and the police should be fast behind."

Delia hung up. Didn't wait to say, "Yes, boss."

CHAPTER 24

The agony of defeat depressed Lizzie as she crept from the police station sometime around three in the morning. She heard that early hour claimed the title, "darkest hour of the night," because it hung, drenched in darkness, with no hint of dawn. No light—no hope. She imagined addicts often felt that way, when alone, and nearing with— drawal. Or those bent on suicide.

Tonight she understood the despair. She'd spent hours with po— lice explaining why she lingered around Ethan's old home at night. She used Delia's line about needing to find closure for Tyler as to why his friend, Ethan, deserted him without a word.

Answering how she knew the identity of the two men was diffi— cult. She explained how they'd followed a car seen at Ethan's and it took them to the Morton Street address. She left Torkless out of it again. Boy, was he going to owe her.

Lizzie also told them she'd seen the skinny guy before, who she thought of as Torpedo, since he had not one bulge of fat on him and he stood straight and tall. She described him to the police. She said, "That's him—not willowy lean, just stick lean, and hard."

They moved on to worse questions. What did she know about a drug shipment, what kind of drugs, where? She knew what she over— heard, and she'd repeated it again and again. Trying to do this the le— gal way seemed a bad idea. They interrogated the men while she was told to sit and wait, and they still didn't know when and where the transfer would go down. And they had nothing on the guy in the Morton house, except when they raided the place, it was locked up tighter than a jail and held enough guns to qualify as an armory.

Detective Fury came out and asked her about the guns they'd found.

"I know nothing about the guns. Never went inside."

She jumped up and shifted her glare to him. "I'm an innocent by—stander. I knew nothing about drugs or guns when I checked out the place tonight. I was looking for Tyler's friend. Tyler's been down in the dumps since the fire."

Fury motioned her to sit back down. That did it. She thought, *God I've been trying to do this the right way but I'm losing here. Help me out.* Her mind hadn't caught up with the spiritual aspects. She lost it and shouted, "Fury, this is harassment. Arrest me or I'm out of here."

He glowered at her. Didn't say a word. She walked.

Strange that Bulbous wasn't there, just Torpedo and a guy she'd never seen. Time to head home and talk with Delia. Maybe she knew more than the police. The odds were good, the way things were going. New turn of events, and attitudes, and people, to cope with constantly—the strain of normal life wore her down.

Fog draped around tree trunks like a shroud as she drove. She would have acquired the necessary information and moved forward by now if she'd dealt with the men herself. Instead, she dragged herself home. Maybe if she sat in the living room, surrounded by mementos of her past life where she had control, she'd be able to absorb it. It was a refuge of nostalgia and antimacassars, from the scimitar on the wall, to the jade bear guarding the mantel. She understood better, now, those who did anything for the next pill or fix. Without it, they've lost control. With it, the illusion of control returns.

With all this extraneous activity going on, it had been difficult to concentrate on the teen center, but the more she learned, the more she knew that guiding them when young could save them. Otherwise, they may still be walking around when older, but not living productive, happy lives. The men captured by the police did not appear to be addicted. Their focus and movements radiated strength and control.

Of course, she abhorred loss of control. She barely drank coffee for fear of being addicted to it like some people, and seldom took medicine for the same reason. She didn't do woozy well like what can come from pain pills. They dosed her once while in the hospital with her broken ankle. She laughed at the following incident with the nurs— es. She'd lost control. Once was all they got—she took no more drugs. And she survived. With the special exercises, her strong body, and will power, the ankle neared perfect, though she received a permanent weather predictor in the bargain.

She went inside to sit and plan. First, coordinate information with Delia, if she was up. Not normal at this time of night, but then maybe she would be lucky and find her unable to sleep.

She tip-toed in the back door and shut it slow and quiet. An in— grained reconnaissance move. Always worked. No one ever knew she was around. She stepped in silence toward the sink. From the moon— light coming in the window, she caught Delia's glare.

Lizzie's hand automatically finished the sweep to find the switch and brought light to the room, lessoning the affect of her frown lines. "What's wrong? Are you okay? When the police didn't mention you, I figured you got away safely."

Delia motioned to the kettle. "Water's hot. Make a drink. There's rum in the cupboard behind the canned beans if you want a splash in the tea."

That brought a smile to her face at the end of a long day. The start of a new day if one looked at the clock. "What, you have a secret stash?"

"Figured it's safe behind beans. Nobody takes those, friend or foe."

A loud rumbling sound escaped from Lizzie's mouth. It evolved into uncontrollable laughter. Her sister looked up toward the ceiling, to re— mind Lizzie there were others in the house, hopefully still sleeping. Lizzie stifled the sound with both hands until the laughter stopped.

She strained her tea and plopped into a chair, despair morphing into exhaustion. "Thanks. I think I needed that. Puts life back into balance. Still, there's much to do."

"Tell me what happened."

And she did, finishing with, "I am so furious with that man."

"You must mean Detective Fury. Appropriate, don't you think?"

Lizzie glanced up from studying her tea cup. "I'd laugh but I'm worn out. He knows I'm not involved in drug smuggling, trading, or using. Why treat me with the inquisition?"

Delia leaned forward, "My guess would be so it's on record he showed you no favoritism. So, moving forward, what's next?"

"Your part of the story. Did you see anything?"

"Bulbous Man came tearing out of the driveway just as I turned the ignition and started past the house. Scared the bejesus out of me, I can tell ya. But he headed back to the fast food place and didn't follow me. The cops must have come right afterwards. I saw a few cars racing through the corner stop sign just after I made my turn and headed home. I didn't hang around to watch. That's probably about when you showed up."

Lizzie nodded. "Good job. You followed instructions exactly. Now I know why they didn't have Bulbous Man in custody. But that means he could contact the others to cancel the shipment. Things may still be brewing in that situation."

Delia added. "Too bad we don't have a photo of Verge Innes. He could be any of the three guys in custody."

Lizzie refilled both cups with fresh tea and a dollop of rum. "Which brings us to Ethan and his mom. We need to go see them in the morning, find out what's going on from their perspective, and maybe relocate them if necessary. And I never got to the bar or the Wanton Drug Dwellings"

Delia said, "I doubt the police would love your new title."

"Tough. I'll put the visit on hold, though."

They discussed what to do, and a way to keep Emily and Heather busy while Tyler was at the herb farm. She'd call Dave in the morning and ask if he could pick Tyler up and put Emily to work in the herb drying room. Heather would be safe there, too.

Lizzie said, "It's a plan. If we're not back, Dave can return them here in time for Tyler's next lesson with Jenny Lyn."

Delia rinsed the tea utensils and pot, clicking off the light as she headed out of the kitchen after Lizzie. "And to complicate matters, oodles of people have called interested in the teen center meeting. I'd asked if they could schedule a meeting. One of the nurses called tonight. We're on for seven tomorrow evening. I mean tonight." Then she grumbled. "Now we get four hours of sleep and we'll be raring to go."

Lizzie ignored the sarcasm. Old people didn't need scads of sleep. Too much to do before they died. She was thrilled at the response to a teen center. A hope for protecting kids rather than destroying them. She knew that half the new drug users were under eighteen. If she could help the local kids stay away from drugs it would cut into the need for supplies and hopefully put a dent in local operations.

Two hours later, she left Delia a note and proceeded to the Wanton. She poured a bag of mixed dried herbs, a formula straight from Agatha, into a gallon jug and covered it with boiling water. Part of the approved withdrawal program, the mixture as a good will offering might pave the way to much needed information from a desperate drug addict.

Lizzie parked in front of the Wanton Building. No more discreet parking blocks away. She didn't expect to find another unconscious teenager, but carrying Tyler that far was a one time only situation. This time her trusty car would be handy for a quick getaway, no matter the cause. She lugged the herbal concoction with her. If the residents laying against the ripped up walls noticed her, they may think she was a fellow drunk.

An old man slept on a cot of planks and a ratty comforter, in the front room, just off the hallway to the back. He scrunched his face like he was in pain, and rolled over. She walked past in silence. Two sections further, three men sat lumped together cackling to each other incoherently. Lizzie eavesdropped, unnoticed, just inside the opening. She heard little information of worth. Two of them only had a few teeth, greatly hampering enunciation. All three acted erratically, most likely from drugs. It was too dark for her to see track marks on their bare arms, but their goofy, then distraught behavior, reflected the height of euphoria on the down side. Good for pumping them for intel? Or not.

Who else is here? Amazing that none of these people showed themselves the night Tyler lie close to death in the corner. Maybe they were all here when the man was killed and Tyler collapsed. She halted. What did they see that caused them all to skedaddle out that night? She glanced at her gallon jug, her only weapon, her only item of value. But most often she worked with less.

After a cursory search, Lizzie returned to the entrance of the warehouse. She shook her head in sadness. Nobody capable of talking in here, but the first old man snorted awake. She stopped in front of him.

"I bet you'rn one a them old ladies trying to get me to quit doing drugs. Well, you're too late. I don't got no drugs no more. Sure weren't my choice, though. Nor'n cause of those do-gooders neither. That young kid who got me my stuff done up and left. Probably cause, well, ain't goin' there. . . ."

Liz knew it. The man saw something, or heard something. Ease into it. *God, help me find the words to help this old man, and in doing so, is it okay if I get help for Tyler? Please.*

She hunkered on the ground next to the man, like sitting in dirt was her favorite pastime. "You're in a fix then. Those withdrawal pains are killers, they say."

"What do ya care?"

"I'm one those ladies you were talking about. The ones who want you to quit cause it's bad for you. Of course, I ain't old like them. and I'm here for another reason."

He laughed at that. Maybe believing the same thing. "I heard you're not old unless you think you are."

She said, "I have a plan. Not for you old guys, mind ya. But for the teens around here. My plan is to keep them from doing drugs at all. Going to set up this town with a sweet teen center."

He fixed his bleary eyes on her face. "And how will that keep them from doin' drugs. Snarfing those pills down to feel better, safer, smarter. Whatever. I been there. How's a building going to stop them from needing that thrill. Takin' the pain away."

"The building won't do it, old man. The people in it will. Doing stuff together, special stuff, to make them feel better, or safer, or teaching them to be smarter. That will do it."

She lifted her head in assurance. Her conviction stopped his questioning look. Pulling her jug forward, she motioned to his bag stuffed full of what he considered basic needs. From his bad breath and body stench she figured it didn't include a toothbrush or soap.

"You got a cup in there? What I got here will soothe those gut-wrenching cramps."

He tilted his head, uncertain. "How you get that e-lix-ir?"

"A friend of mine grows all kinds of herbs and flowers. Certain ones help with withdrawal pains, others help you sleep." She saw him take note of that and how he was jerking around.

He pulled out a dented tin. God knows what had been in it. She hoped the herbs would do some good. She knew he would need more than one jug, but that problem could be dealt with later.

He slugged some down and reached out the tin for more. She re-filled it. While he sipped, more slowly this time, she said, "Why ain't that guy—the one with the scar—why ain't he around any more to give you what you need?"

The man sat up straighter, as if settling in for a tale. He didn't disappoint. "He tore out a here soon as that young man got kilt. Hap-pened the other day. Maybe two weeks ago now, though it's hard for me to tell. Don't got me a watch no more."

She just nodded to keep him going.

"He and everybody else trotted out real fast that night. Even I dragged me gear out a here, once'n ole Peter stopped long enough to tell me what the scream was from."

He offered up the tin again and she topped it off. "I couldn't sleep that night. Before I left I heard the shouting. Saw that man lope outa here so fast he tripped on my bag. The moonlight gave me a good look at his face. Boy, was he scared."

She shifted casually, relaxed as if listening to a good yarn.

"Seen him before?"

He hacked some. Poured more from the jug himself this time, fingers shaking. "Never. That guy weren't from around these parts."

"How so?"

"His sharp clothes. Bigwig type. You know. Fancy watch. Good shoes, though looking a little scuffed, they did."

"Never been here before?"

"Naw, had the look but he weren't no druggie, or alkie. Not from around Wanton anyway. Yet I saw specks of white powder on his hand. Was ready to lick it, I was. But he'n took off before I could blink."

"Ya think he killed the guy?"

He slunk back down on his bed. Closed his eyes. "Yup."

CHAPTER 25

"Where have you been?" Delia cried as Lizzie slumped through the door, grabbed a chair and swirled it around. She leaned her head on the top while still looking at her sister.

She answered, "I don't know how old people manage to live with nothing, in dirty, cold places. Ugh—the Wanton Drug Dumpster. I'm weary, and I was barely there a couple of hours." She closed her eyes and sighed. Just for a second.

Delia sniffed. "Could be the lack of sleep you started out with. Why did you rush out before dawn? And alone? I'm assuming you mean the old Wanton building."

"Thought before dawn would be a good time to find people. And I knew we needed to deal with Ethan and his mom early this morning. Am I late?" She grinned appearing unconcerned. Waiting for a good time for the punch line.

Delia noticed immediately. "That look. You're not exhausted. You're excited." She plopped down in the nearest chair.

"What did you find?"

Lizzie couldn't help smiling. She *was* elated. Her smile spread wide. "I found someone who saw the killer. An elderly man. Sick. And withdrawing from heroin, I think."

Delia patted her hand in a quick congratulations. She expressed sympathy for the old man. "Can you trust him?"

"Seemed extremely lucid to me. Made me wonder what he did

before he spiraled down into the trench of addiction. Couldn't bring myself to ask."

Delia poured Lizzie more coffee.

Lizzie gulped. It wouldn't hurt to warm her insides a little. She may be climbing the walls by bedtime, but was grateful at the moment. She continued with her tale. "He'll identify the killer if we find him. We now have a description. And some information. But he was holed up in the Wanton building."

"Tell me. Do you have a name?"

"Not *that* lucky. He said the suspect was clean cut, tall and lean. And he saw his face clear in the moonlight."

"Great. Great. Let's call Detective Fury."

Lizzie grabbed Delia's wrist. "Hold it. He's on my persona non grata list. I do plan on telling him, but I want to protect this old man first. Too bad he didn't see it happen, but if they have a suspect, this old man can place him at the scene at the right time."

Delia settled back in the chair. "Ahh."

Lizzie continued, "I'm afraid he won't last there long. I'm surprised the killer didn't come back to shut him up. The guy said the killer ran out scared. Maybe he didn't notice our man in the corner."

"Do you think that is an indication of the man's nature, that he felt fear after taking someone's life?"

Lizzie held the rest of the mug for lingering warmth on her fingers while formulating an answer. She'd heard how arthritis can cause aches in a variety of spots. Maybe the finger joints would go first. She held them up and studied them, twisting each one in the light. And maybe arthritis would never catch up with her if she kept active. Ever since she retired she expected ennui to set in, lazing in the sun. She practiced her series of forms, kicks, and moves every day just in case. Tyler enjoyed the time with her since she'd taught him some basic self-defense.

She reached for Delia's hand, and focused on the possibility of the killer feeling remorse. "Sorry, honey. You didn't see the body. No reverence there. Anger maybe, or revenge, according to Detective Fury. Remorse at taking a life—not likely. The fear could have come from realizing he might get caught. That's why I want the old man out of there. Before the killer rethinks everything in a clearer light."

"So we find him a place to stay. What did you say his name was?"

"He didn't exactly introduce himself. That's not the way of these places. But I noticed a card with his name on it when he withdrew a mug from his battered old bag. The card said 'Lennie.'"

"Okay, we get Lennie out. Somewhere warm. Dry. And with medical attention. I know just the place. Maude takes in the old and feeble. And she's a former nurse. I'll call right away."

Delia jumped up and grabbed the phone.

Shaking her head in amazement, Lizzie realized her sister knew just about everybody in town, and her friends slept less than she did. The clock clicked to seven-thirty. *Who am I to talk? I've been up for hours.* She walked past her sister to pour one more cup of coffee.

Before she dialed, Delia looked her up and down and held her nose. Getting the clue, Lizzie said, "I'm heading for the shower. Then we can leave as soon as the others eat breakfast. She took the cup with her."

Ten minutes later she returned to the kitchen, dirty clothes in hand and headed to the laundry room. "They're all waking up." She said over her shoulder. "What's our plan?"

"*Our* plan?"

"I figured you'd have one for both of us. The day is overloaded with extremely time-constrained and necessary things to accomplish. And we can't take 'our family' with us," she added as she nodded toward the stairs. "I feel terrible dumping them every time we go somewhere."

"I think they're safe here, from this killer, using the added safety of them being around a bunch of people. but . . . ."

Lizzie set the table. "So it's back to the herb farm? How is Dave taking it?"

Delia finished mixing pancake batter and tested the pan for heat. She looked at her sister. "That's the wonderful part. The man wants to hire Emily in the gathering room in the morning and the office in the afternoon. I developed a salve for her back and mix jugs of tea for her to drink throughout the day. Emily thinks she can handle the work now. Carmelita is thrilled with the extra office help, and is willing to train her. It will finally allow Carmelita to return to work outdoors."

Happy that Tyler's family found new direction in life following his drug and health issues, and then the fire, she asked, "What about Heather?"

With the pancakes poured into the pan, she took a second to face Lizzie. "The best part—he will let Heather stay with Emily until the child starts school. The bus comes right by the house because two of the workers have first graders."

Lizzie said, "We also have to find housing for them. I'm sorry I've done nothing on that yet."

Delia turned back to the stove. "I'm working on it." She slipped a plate of pancakes in the warming oven. "As soon as we drop them off at the farm we'll go pick up Lennie and get him settled at Maude's. Then we can find Ethan."

That seemed over-simplified to Lizzie but she figured they could adjust the plan as needed.

And adjust they did.

When they arrived, Lennie didn't want to leave. He stretched out on his pallet and shook his head. "No ma'am, not going."

Delia handed him another bottle of herbal mixture. "My sister said you appreciated this yesterday. Thought you might need more."

He harrumphed. "Who said I liked it? I was thirsty, that's all. Been dried up like a prune."

Delia laughed. "That's just old age setting in. You need to move around. Get those juices flowing again."

"Lady, I can move when I want to. Just don't want to right now."

Lizzie stood over him, arms akimbo. "I understand, Lennie, you're comfortable here on your bed. You enjoy knowing what's going on in this hellhole, you have your things, and you feel safe. Why on earth would you want to leave?"

"What do you know? This ole rock pile you call a bed, ain't comfortable. And nothin's been going on in this hellhole since that dealer got shot. The other guy who had them pills and heroin? He shook the dust off himself the same day and never come back. So no one else does. What's the use?"

"So it's safe here, then? No one coming round to bother you?"

He shifted to a half sitting position. "Lady, you don't know nothin. It ain't safe here. Cops don't come by no more."

Waiting to see what Lizzie was playing at, Delia positioned the gallon of herb tea next to Lennie in case he wanted a swig. She stepped back into a nook that might have been a closet long ago.

Lizzie kept roping Lennie in. "That should make you feel safe. Keeps the bad guys away."

Lennie pulled out his dented tin and dribbled some tea in it. Both women made no move to help. He swallowed, then said. "Dumb cops. Newbies. They make such a racket ya here 'em comin' all the way from the street."

"So what?"

"So what, lady? All the bad guys scuttle out before the cops git here. That's what."

"Are they here all the time?"

"Sure, they hang in the back. Rough me up sometimes."

Lizzie smirked. "So it's not comfortable, you don't have much in the way of things, nothing's going on to keep you occupied, and it's not safe."

The old man pursed his lips. "Ya think you're smart, huh? I saw what you was doin'. Was just stringing you along."

She walked toward the nook to talk with Delia. Considering the direction she headed, she hoped he would think they'd left and reconsider real fast. Motioning her deeper into the corner, Lizzie whispered, "Stubborn old man."

Before Delia commented, Lizzie saw movement, just a shadow maybe, through the broken slats on the opposite side of the nook. She thought that direction led to a door but noted, instead, a long hallway. Through ragged tips on the ripped boards she saw a silhouette of a man move. If she stepped beyond the partial wall the person might see her, so she held as still as a deer sensing danger.

Delia, raised her voice to get her sister's attention. "Lizzie, what's going on. You didn't hear a word I said. You're the one that started whispering."

The shadow jerked, and drifted farther away, down the hall.

Before Lizzie could follow, a ruckus ensued by the old man. *What next, God? I'm trying to do the right thing here. A little assist, a smoothing of the way, might help, please.*

She'd heard two distinct thugs stroll into the old man's space. One walked with a swish of his feet, the other stomped his way about. Peering around the corner she could barely see them in the dim light. They weren't the thugs who'd confronted her before, but from their squinty eyes and growling, she figured they were angry, looking for an easy victim, or just itching for any activity. She halted, deer-like, again.

The old man didn't wait to be attacked. He sat up straight. His left hand reached behind the pallet he rested on. The thugs watched the old man's face, and one of them reached for his bag. Before he had it fully in his arms, the old man struck. But the stick could only hit one of the two. The second guy lunged at the old man while the first, in pain, dropped the bag.

Lizzie advanced. Just in time, before Delia plowed into her backside. The men barely noticed her—until the first one pulled out a knife. Her kick knocked it into the corner.

Delia picked it up and didn't waiver. The now knife-less guy zeroed in on Lizzie and charged her with a fist. Within seconds, the burly man crumpled to the floor, holding his jaw and whimpering. Delia aimed the knife like a gun on the thug lingering over the bag. Lennie unfolded his long form to stand and shoulder the two-by-four, ready for any pitch that came near his makeshift bat.

Lizzie reached into the side pocket of her skirt and pulled out her cell phone. She pressed one button and notified police of the altercation, with a request to come for the ruffians—with an ambulance. She said to her wide-eyed sister, "What? You told me to carry my cell phone with me all the time. I just learned to keep it on silent in dangerous places." She pointed to the men. "This qualifies."

Unfazed by the troublemakers, Delia nonetheless seemed stupefied by what Lizzie said. "You know how to put the phone on silent?"

"When I help Tyler with sociology, he helps me with technology."

She knelt next to the man on the floor and eased his hands away from his jaw. Staring him in the eyes, she soothed. "Now, now. Stop the whimpering. It causes more pain. Breathe very slowly through your nose."

He tried to speak.

"No. No. That will hurt." She ripped off a section of her skirt and made a sling for his jaw.

Sirens wailed, coming closer. Delia said, "They came lickety-split."

Lizzie shrugged as she walked to the entrance. "Helps when you have the police on speed dial."

After giving her name and number to the police, she suggested to Delia and Lennie that it was time to go.

Lennie grabbed his bag and stick and followed meekly. Once ensconced at Maude's, with strict instructions to follow her house rules, they scheduled an appointment with Agatha for herbal advice.

Lizzie said, "She'll have another gallon of withdrawal brew for you.

The sisters hopped in the car for their next leg of the day's chores. It was time to pick up Tyler for his late afternoon session with Jenny Lyn, then an appointment with the administrators and teachers at the school to clarify guidelines for Tyler's reentry into the school's regular classes. And they still needed to visit Mildred and Tony before they could deliver Ethan and his mom.

Lizzie asked Delia as her sister drove away. "You've been looking somewhat frazzled all day. What's wrong?"

"I felt like I'd forgotten something important. Couldn't remember it for anything. Besides, we've been slightly busy."

"Okay. No big deal. Happens to all of us."

Delia grimaced as she made the next turn. "I'm glad you can say that. I just realized what it was."

Lizzie turned an expectant gaze to Delia.

Lizzie saw her body maneuver a slight shift to the left, away from Lizzie. Looking straight ahead, she said, "I was supposed to tell you that the nurses set up a meeting with some of the movers and shakers of the community to discuss the teen center."

"That's good news. Right?"

Delia shifted her look to Lizzie and winced. "It's tonight."

CHAPTER 26

Lizzie whispered to her sister as she stood near the podium ready to jumpstart the teen center meeting. "What are they doing here? What is *he* doing here?." She didn't have to point to the audience. Despite the diverse crowd that included nurses, teachers, and students and parents, The familiar scowl on her face as she stared at the cops and Detective Fury showed who she meant.

Delia said, "Stop that fire in your belly, sis. This is an organization meeting to establish a teen center. It's to entice useful volunteers, not clients. And those guys will be great volunteers. They can help the kids from their experience dealing with what can happen to them. Talk with the kids before they enter the age of the drug scene."

Lizzie hid her face from the crowd. She mouthed to Delia, "We can *use* these guys to our benefit for once?" Her smile formed before she finished her sentence. *Now that's more like it God. Working together can go both ways, right?* She didn't get an answer from God, but then if she had she'd have probably collapsed. Not the way to start a meeting.

Carmelita and Dave sat front and center, offering silent support. Lizzie squared up at the podium, resting her hands on the surface, and cleared her throat. "Thank you all for coming here tonight, for your enthusiasm to such a needy cause, and for Nurse Suzie Joy, who organized and gathered you all for this meeting.

"You already know that teens experiment. That's how they learn. What we want to do here is set up an environment where they can observe and investigate the nuances of life amid those who will guide them to a healthier future than they would have with drug addiction."

She began the meeting with words of encouragement, hoping to maintain the enthusiasm the audience brought with them. "Experimentation is a fact of life. Because teens try drugs or alcohol doesn't mean they are addicted, or will become so. It's more crucial to understand why some teens are tempted to explore this element. And most important, why others feel the need, more often, the urgency, to continue with alcohol or drugs."

Lizzie motioned to Nurse Joy to come forward. "We have some experts here who have dealt first hand with addicted teens and can tell us more about the need here in our community. Nurse Suzie Joy. . . " She frowned at the name card. "Oh, your *last* name is Joy."

She inclined her head to Nurse Becky in puzzlement, "Your last name is Becky?"

"No, My last name is Hebblethwaite."

Nickeisha laughed. "Don't give *me* that look. My last name is Clarke."

She looked at all the nurses, then back at Nurse Joy standing patiently next to her. Why are you Nurse 'Last name'?"

"Because I got sick of being called Suzie Q. I paid for a new name badge. Nurse Joy works fine for me."

When the crowd stopped laughing, she finished her introduction. "Ms. Joy is an emergency room nurse and can enlighten us to the ravages of addiction. She relates to the teens because she actually knows all about Minecraft games. She deals with teens addicted to drugs more than most nurses because of her job in ER at night."

Lizzie stepped back and the nurse grabbed the audience's attention with her first words. "At the hospital we see unconscious teens brought in with only a glimmer of life in them. Their bodies are wasted, and their minds are floating elsewhere. For many it started with a few painkillers stolen from the home medicine cabinet. Or from doctors attempting to reduce their pain after an injury. But the need for many leads to addiction.

"Drugs were originally created to help, not harm people. Some things in life have more ramifications than anyone can know—until later. By then the addiction runs rampant across the world and cannot be contained. Did you know that morphine was developed to replace the addictive form of opium, and at the time was considered the miracle drug?"

"Nurse Joy added, "For instance, out west, in the time of Kit Carson and Wild Bill Hickock, both strong users of opium, the medical community offered opium to overcome addiction to liquor. Aiding health is a learning experience to this day."

Lizzie studied the crowd as the nurse spoke, pleased to see such a wide variety of community attendance. Next to Sergeant John Torkless and Detective Daniel Fury sat a contingent of high school employees, Miss Bruell, the principal's assistant, and Mr. Arsenault, the English teacher, with Mrs. Donegal. Jenny Lyn's family sat enraptured in a large group of teenagers and parents.

When the nurse finished, Lizzie followed up with a few of her own thoughts, including her belief that the increase in drug use comes from many causes, but the growing addiction to video games where all is fantasy, helps kids distance themselves more and more from reality.

Groans from the younger side of the audience eventually faded. Meanwhile, one of the officers came to Lizzie identifying himself as the detective responsible for the drug unit, and had some information to offer. Lizzie stepped back and motioned him to the podium.

He began with the common reason kids abuse drugs, naming curiosity, peer pressure, stress, emotional struggles, and with a nod to Lizzie, added, the desire to escape reality. He continued, "We attribute the recent surge in drug use to numerous causes, added together to form an epidemic. One is the low cost of drugs today. In the 1970s, a pure bag of heroin cost $30. The average user was a 28-to 30-year old urban resident. Today, the same amount of heroin costs just $5-10, no longer pure, and the average addict is a white, middle-class teenager."

He motioned, hands downward, to still the rustling crowd, and continued, "What makes it worse, is the dilution of street drugs with everything from baking soda to cheaper, more deadlier drugs."

Later, Delia suggested the abandoned building now owned by

the town could make an ideal teen center, and brought forth the zoning officer to discuss a few structural concerns. When she mentioned the possibility of an existing building, and the ability to create a center sooner, rather than in the distant future, joyful murmurs filled the room. Lizzie saw it, and knew that their plans would be welcome locally—at least by the young crowd.

Delia concluded, "Many of you here have proposed special programs, on health and nutrition and their relationship to drug abuse, on herbal and nutritional help for those in withdrawal, and activities to entice teens to be active, physically and mentally, in their free time. What's better, many of you have offered your time in helping out, in supervising and leading this community to a better future for our young. Thank you."

The nurses attended to lines of volunteers eager to sign up to help the center become established. Lizzie said that from these names, and the information the people provided about themselves, they could set up a board to develop and run the teen center. Nurse Joy reached Lizzie as they walked away. "I'd like you to meet my daughter, Eleanor." She looked around at the close crowd, and whispered, "The one who's investigating that career we talked about."

Lizzie nodded hello. "You give me a call anytime with questions."

Delia and Lizzie snuck out toward the back, but the detective accosted them before they could leave the building. "I saw that grimace when you noticed me in the crowd, Miss Ort. Don't deny it."

"I would never lie to the police," Lizzie replied, repressing her smile.

"Nice to hear that. I only need a minute. First, have you uncovered anything new since we last spoke?"

Lizzie quelled her smirk before it showed. How interesting that he politely asked what she'd done recently. Makes me wonder what's wrong. She motioned to the crowd of people back in the meeting room, and said, "This has kept me busy."

He smiled. "Wonderful job, too." Nodding to the two officers in the line to volunteer, he said, "We plan to be involved. Let us know what we can do."

"Thank you detective. We will do that. Anything else?"

"In a small narcotics sweep at Wanton we accosted two addicts trying to hook up with a dealer. Said they'd been sent there by an old man last week at the Jumpin' Lizard. They were pretty sure it was the night our victim was found, but said they never saw anyone. The place was deserted."

She looked him in the eye and didn't react, waiting.

"Wondered if you came across them in your time at the bar, or Wanton."

"Why detective, you act as if I hang out at the bar. And God forbid, at the Wanton hell hole."

"Just thought I'd ask. They drive a fancy BMW. Look like young business execs in the making. The rest of my news might not cause too much joy. Remember that relative of a young adult who died of overdose? The guy we thought might be our main suspect in the Jamison's death?"

"Yeah, I know. The uncle who might be out for revenge."

He swatted back that tawny pelt of hair in what looked like a stalling gesture. "Um. We lost track of him. I wanted to give you a photo of the man, to share with Tyler and his family in case they see the guy."

"You mean, in case he comes after Tyler or his family?"

"Well, that too."

Lizzie snatched the photo from his hand, said a swift prayer of thanks to God for keeping patient with the detective, and walked out. Delia followed, brows raised as she passed the detective.

Lizzie crossed her fingers as she punched in the numbers of Mildred's phone. She spoke to Delia as it rang. "I hope she's still up. We must see her and ask about taking in Ethan."

She spun away from the open door to block out some of the noise. "Mildred, I'm so sorry to bother you this late, but, can my sister and I come over for a bit?"

On the way, Delia laughed. "Didn't you mention seeing those men the night you found Tyler?"

"Sure did. And I've been hoping to find them. I guess Detective Fury has some uses after all."

They quickly discussed how best to convince Mildred to shelter Ethan and his mom if necessary. Maybe they were already safe, but both wanted a contingency plan. They also plotted what they could do regarding future housing for Ethan's and Tyler's family. Lizzie shook her head. Too much going on and no time to deal with any of it properly. As her head moved back to center, a swift movement caught her eye coming from the dark woods. She braked just before a deer bounded across the road inches in front of her car. She'd remembered how bad the potholes were, but had forgotten about the deer. They were darling, Bambi replicas, until they strolled in front of a car, or ate all the flowers. No wonder Delia had their back yard enclosed by a seven-foot fence.

As Delia bounced back in her seat from the momentum, she cried out. "Great reaction time, sis. We couldn't have sustained another dent in this rust bucket."

Lizzie smiled. "Probably saved your neck, you ingrate. And this so-called rust bucket just stopped in a second. Count your blessings."

"Hey. If my hair wasn't already gray it would be now."

"That's okay, dear, it's a nice hazy pewter. Better than gray."

They parked in front of Mildred's. The front light was on. Sweet woman. At least we can't be mugged in the dark walking in. Glancing at her sister stumbling out of the car, she decided not to voice that out loud, in case Delia wasn't aware of the nature of the neighborhood. Delia had been a brick through this whole adventure. Most of these activities were outside her normal routine.

Mildred opened the door and silently motioned them to enter. The bright-eyed woman hugged Delia. "So glad to finally meet you. You got top billing from your sister regarding herbal information. I can't wait to sit and have a long talk with you."

She looked at Lizzie. "I imagine that's not why you're here tonight, though. What can I help you with."

Lizzie winced. "You've already helped enough for a lifetime. But you are correct. We need your help, again. We found Ethan and his mom. Or at least we know where they are."

Mildred waved to the kitchen chairs and the whistling tea kettle. The sisters sat and Lizzie continued while Mildred fixed the tea.

"Good news. Right?"

"It gets complicated. I happened to be around Ethan's old home a couple of nights ago and heard men talking about how they needed a lead to find Ethan and his mom. They hoped to kidnap them to pressure one of the others, Ethan's dad, to replace some missing money. Thanks to Delia, we have the family's location, hopefully before the men who are involved with a drug dealer, learn it."

Lizzie sipped her tea and took a deep breath. "To make the story short, Verge had been beaten, and not around when the cops subsequently confronted the men at their base camp. They arrested a bunch of them and the dealer. We fear he now could be out looking for his wife and son. His anger issues might turn toward them. Staying with a relative won't keep them safe from Verge now that most of his gang has been arrested."

Mildred nodded, as if she already knew the answer to the unasked question. But she waited. Delia took over. She explained how they felt the neighborhood might now be safe for Ethan and his mom, since the men were gone, but didn't want to risk moving them back into their old home with Verge still out there. She asked Mildred if there was any way she could shelter the two people until the sisters could find a permanent home for them once the they found the killer.

Mildred agreed, rose, and looking at Lizzie's drooping eyelids, said, "I'll be ready any time. You two get some sleep first. See you tomorrow."

Lizzie pulled out her keys and Delia swiped them, getting behind the wheel of the rust-bucket. "We're going home to sleep. Sleep by vehicular death is too deep for me. We have an agenda for tomorrow."

CHAPTER 27

Waving her hand in front of Delia and herself, Lizzie said, "Hi, we're emissaries from Tyler with a message for Ethan and his mom."

Based on the elderly woman's scowl, Lizzie readied her foot to block open the door, but before anything debilitating happened, a bubbly Ethan came from behind and pulled the door open all the way. Eyes bright and face grinning, he said, "It's okay, Miss Sylvia, let me talk with them."

Sylvia stepped aside, but stayed nearby. Ethan motioned them in. Tall and lean, reminding her of the sucker growth shooting up off a tree, he asked, "Who are you? How is Tyler? I've missed him."

Lizzie ignored his questions and asked, "Did you know he took drugs?"

Ethan leaned back from the waist, the skin on his face stretched tight. "No, not Tyler. I know he'd gotten thinner, but I thought that was from not having much food."

His eyebrows pulled down together, reflecting the tautness of his body. "I tried to give him food whenever I could." He looked sheepishly at his mom who had entered the room. "Sorry, mom. He was starving himself to leave more food for his sister and mother."

"It's okay, son." His mother moved forward and introduced herself. "I'm Mary Innis. And you are?" She looked inquisitive more than demanding.

Delia answered, "We are friends of Emily. I'm Delia, this is Lizzie. Tyler disappeared for weeks and Emily came to us hoping we could help. Lizzie found him, unconscious in a drug infested warren of rooms in the decrepit Wanton Industries building."

Ethan interrupted. "Oh no! Will he be all right?"

Mary invited them to sit at the table, introducing her friend, Sylvia, who'd offered them temporary housing.

Lizzie recited the recent events briefly, wanting to let Mary know why she thought they were in danger and needed to get out of there immediately. Then she told them of Verge's connection with the drug lords arrested just yesterday.

Mary said, "I feared that. He never would talk about his work, but then men started coming to our home. They weren't kind men. When Verge hauled us out of there one evening, I knew it was time to escape."

Ethan walked to her side, patting her shoulder in support. His mother continued, "At the first chance we were alone we took off with what we could carry and walked here to Sylvia's. Verge never met her. Didn't know exactly where she lived. She's an old friend, from my past life."

Sylvia stayed in the background, but nodded an agreement.

Lizzie explained that men were searching for Mary and Ethan. "They wanted leverage to force your husband to come up with some missing money. Now that some of the men were arrested, your husband may be desperate to find you. And the goons will be hot on his tail."

Delia interrupted her before she could stress the seriousness of the situation. "A car just drew up out front. Time's up."

Lizzie rose, motioned for silence with a finger on her lips. Glancing out the window from the side of the curtain, she saw Verge being dragged from the car by two men.

Sylvia peered from behind her. "The neighbor's must have ratted on you." Grumbling, she said, "Those no good juveniles," and pulled on Lizzie's arm and ran as fast as she could with her limp. "Back door."

Ethan grabbed their two duffels and followed. They all raced down the stairs behind the pantry in the kitchen. Sylvia said, "Out the door and through the woods. Mary, I'll tell them you'd been here but were gone days ago." Lizzie watched her pull her body up the steps in a rapid, rhythmic shuffle, then heard the banging on the front door. She shut the cellar door quickly and herded the women and young boy. No one looked back till they were hidden deep in the woods.

An hour later, after lingering in the woods and stealthily following Lizzie's lead, they made it to her car. Following her standard policy, it was parked two blocks over. She believed in a surprise approach, thus catching the prey off-guard, sometimes with beneficial results. This time it allowed their safe escape.

With Mary and Ethan ensconced at Mildred's, Lizzie and Delia advised them to stay away from their old home, no matter what the temptation. Lizzie explained, "You both need to keep inside Mildred's house and the immediate outdoor area, staying out of sight as much as possible until they catch the killer. If you desperately need items from your home, I will fetch them for you. Promise me you won't go there."

They both nodded, and Mary further reassured them. "It wasn't my home, just a place where we lived. I"m sure the landlord will fill it soon with new tenants and it will be as if we were never there. We took the few things that meant anything."

Delia added, "We promise to set up a meeting between you and Tyler soon. He's been extremely anxious to see you."

"Great. I miss him. Would ya tell him I'm sorry I couldn't say good-bye. Dad pulled us out without warning one evening."

Tony bounded down the stairs, surprising the newcomers. "I moved my stuff into the other bedroom that Ethan and I can share, ma'am. And I put clean sheets on my old bed for his mom."

Mary appeared flustered, and finally spoke. "That's so kind. You didn't have to bother." She faced Mildred. "You didn't say we would be putting any one out."

Tony piped in. "I'm just a guest here, too. Miss Lizzie found me camped out at your old place." He looked sheepishly down at his T-shirt, then at Ethan. "I borrowed some of your old shirts when mine got torn. You can have them back if you want, though now that I see you clearly, they would have a rough time stretching over those biceps."

Ethan laughed. "No problem. I outgrew those a while ago. Why were you camping out there? When did you see me?"

Tony's appearance shifted from open and sharing to a shuttered countenance. He stammered, "I was sleeping in that ditch near your house for a while. I saw you a few times. I watched you leave. The house was empty. I went inside. It was warmer there."

Mary said, "You should have come to the door. We would have let you stay."

His stutter increased. "Your old man didn't seem the type help anyone out. His friends barked and growled all the time. The ditch was safe."

Mary stepped back. Now she appeared mortified, as if she'd forgotten about Verge. Then she smiled and thanked Mildred for taking them in. "Just tell me what I can do to help here."

"It's time for Tony's extra class work. He's back in school but needs special tutoring to keep up for now." Mildred walked to Tony and palmed his shoulders. "This young man has agreed to be adopted by me. I have more paperwork to fill out. Maybe you two could supervise Tony while I catch up," she said with a hopeful look.

Ethan stepped behind him, one hand on Tyler's shoulder as they walked up the stairs. "Sure thing, Tony. What are you working on?"

"Math." The one word and the pouting mouth said it all.

Ethan laughed. "You'll live. If I can make it through ninth grade math, anyone can."

The others moved on to their tasks of the day and Delia and Lizzie prepared to leave. Getting into the car, they both sat back and sighed at the same time. Delia giggled. "I just hope that means we're tired and not depressed."

Lizzie started the car, but swung her face toward her sister before pulling out. "Sis, we don't have time to be depressed."

* * *

Late that night Lizzie stood in the dark by a young woman's bedside. Unconscious, battered and bruised, the woman had curled into a fetal position under the covers. Lizzie didn't recognize her, but felt the pain. The nurses, used to Lizzie being at the hospital from her weeks with Tyler, had let her travel unhampered to Carry O'Donnell's room.

The cop at the door needed a little convincing. He hesitated when she said Detective Fury sent her to take a look, see if she knew the woman. When she offered to phone him and he saw his name on her speed dial, he relented. He grumbled, but said, "Only for a few minutes, and leave the door open."

The twitching fingers and saddened expression on Carry's face convinced Lizzie of no need to stay long. She had hoped the woman had come to and could tell her about the man who beat her. But not tonight.

Lizzie had her suspicions, and Detective Fury had called her to give the latest information. "They found the girl on the ground, not near Wanton Industries, so we don't know it's related to our drug case. We thought we'd wait to ask her before we left her alone in the hospital. A man had called in a quivering voice and gave her name and location. Research had revealed that in the past she'd been known as Troy Ryther's girlfriend."

The detective had said Miss O'Donnell was under guard at the hospital with strict orders for the guard to call him the second she gained consciousness. Okay, that wasn't the same as suggesting Lizzie should go and visit. *Sorry, God. But I was polite. To both the detective and this cop. Didn't hit the man or anything.* She nodded as she left, shaking her head as if to say, "didn't know her." Which she didn't.

Once outside, the hand fell on her shoulder with such lightness that she didn't twirl and kick. She rotated around slowly, to observe first. The young man stepped back in deference.

"Didn't mean to startle you. I wanted to ask if you saw Carry. Will she be okay?"

Lizzie hesitated, accessing the situation as she studied the man and looked around. He appeared to be alone, though the fog had crawled in on her way to the hospital and hid most of the area from view.

Lizzie took in the man's tall but slight frame, with no muscles to speak of. Intelligence dominated his facial expression, bruised a little with fear, maybe. It lacked the hollow stare of an addict.

"Who are you?"

He shrugged his shoulders. "A friend of Carry's. Used to be a friend of the guy who did that to her. No more."

She wanted to jump up and pump her fist to the sky. Finally, a real lead. But it was late and she was tired. Instead she said, "You may be warm enough in that thin T-shirt but this frail old lady needs to get out of the damp air. It's been a long day. Do you mind sitting in my car?"

He laughed uproariously. Strange reaction. And he led her to the car. He must have watched her arrive. What was she getting into? On the other hand, there could be no gun in those tight jeans and snug shirt. She'd chance it.

They sat facing each other in her car. She tilted her head down to the side in question of the laugh. He smiled, then said. "I stood behind the bar when Ryther confronted you. Frail you're not."

She studied his build. Certainly not the linebacker. And not the one with the knife in his arm. "You were the shadow. Why didn't you attack?"

"He was my friend for years. This whole mess warped his mind, yet I found it difficult to abandon him. But I wasn't going to attack an old woman for him, despite the male cloak of appearance, by the way. Like I said. No more. His beating Carry? Not forgivable."

She relaxed. Offered a sheepish smile. "No one else noticed. Was that enough to bring you to ask me about Carry? How did they know I'd be near the shack that night?"

"Damien was stupid enough to let that info escape when we came to visit. He took off after that. Troy said he wanted to stop you from hunting him down. I wasn't going to come but I saw him bully Damien into handing over two bags of heroin. He gets crazy when on drugs."

"Most people do. Will you be okay?"

"Yeah, I'll hang around to see what I can do for Carry. Then I'm out of here. I've stayed off the drugs. Now it's time to blow this scene altogether. Watch out for Troy, though."

"Still?"

"He kept asking me to check out Wanton for anyone searching for him. He worried about that old man near the front. And the kid laying in a stupor who you picked up that night. Kept yammering on about them. How they were going to talk to the cops."

"Tell me what happened."

"I'd seen the kid. He was out cold. Later, I went back one more time to get away from Troy for a bit. Saw you with the old man. Figured I'd better listen in. Then I saw you break that guy's jaw. And fix it to lessen the pain. I could trust a person like that."

"Did your friend kill that dealer at Wanton?"

"Yeah. The real dealer. Not that wanna-be, the guy with the scarred face."

"You saw it happen?"

"You ain't no cop. You can't hold me for nothin', right?"

"Right. I just want to know what happened. And to protect that kid I picked up. I think your friend is trying to kill him. Did he set the kid's house on fire?"

"Troy went berserk when he found that dealer. Man, I couldn't believe what he did to him. Then Troy palmed some of the stuff before he left the warehouse. Later, he said it was automatic to grab the drugs. Troy said he tried to throw the pills away but they drew him in." Though inside the car, he shivered while continuing, "The killing must have tipped him off the edge. I couldn't sway him to stop any more."

Lizzie turned the ignition to heat up the car. The warmth from the sun left long ago, but the night didn't offer enough chill to cause this guy to shake like that. She hoped this man wasn't on drugs. Her years of experience told her no, but she was learning that all the brushes she had with addicts in foreign countries didn't foretell what to expect from the yuppy crowd. She nodded for him to continue.

The Shadow man nodded. "She's a bright girl, that Carry. I mean. uhh, cheerful. And loyal. She stuck with Troy even while he used. And kept with him through withdrawal. Then, he heard about his nephew. He really loved the kid. Left work and hunted till he found the dealer at the Wanton. Shouted at him. Blamed him for everything.

Later, I saw Carry with a cut on her cheek. She tried to hide it with her hair." He shuddered. "I saw that hair tonight. All bloodied. I called the cops but I couldn't stick around. Didn't want dear Troy Ryther III to pound on me, too." He added, "It wasn't bad hair. Long, brown. Maybe a plain brown, but when the lights caught strands of it, it glowed in spots. Troy called it muddy. Always put her down. But I saw the wound on her face. In her eyes. Hair can't hide that kind of pain."

Lizzie interrupted. "Someone had washed her hair. It laid on the pillow, clean and wavy. You're right. She has nice hair. But tell me more about what happened. I could barely see her arms. The covers hid the rest of her."

"Troy stayed home after that night. He didn't want me around." His voice rose in a plaintive cry. "We grew up together, but he forced me out."

She saw the hurt in his drawn face, lowered eyes—as if defeated.

He twisted his head sideways, but whispered. "Carry stayed with Troy. He must have gotten angry. Looked like he trampled her."

A car drove by, startling them. He jerked.

Lizzie said, "We need to find a way to trap Troy. Get him off the streets before he hurts anyone else."

He opened the door. "Go for it. But I'm outta here."

CHAPTER 28

"I just found out who the killer is."

Delia managed to comprehend Lizzie's mumbled words as her sister stumbled through the doorway and collapsed on the sofa.

Delia stepped closer and placed a pillow under Lizzie's head as her eyes closed. She leaned closer to hear what she murmured while shifting her head to get more comfortable.

"Functioning with no sleep doesn't work any more. Affecting my brain."

Delia knelt next to her. "You want me to do something about this killer?"

"Nope. Gotta find him first. Later. We gotta keep you all safe." She rolled over and snuggled into the back of the sofa. Delia barely heard, "Need to sleep for a few . . . ."

Lizzie sunk deeper into the sofa and was gone. Didn't respond to a touch on her arm. Delia covered her with the homemade afghan and moved to the kitchen to think about what to do next.

Not much she could do about the killer until Lizzie gave her more information. She compiled a list while the water boiled for tea. Lizzie had been attempting to keep Tyler, Heather and Emily protected from an unknown man who apparently feared Tyler might have seen what happened in the warehouse. The guy must be deranged, she thought, if he believed the kid could harm him.

Studying the situation, she realized he probably didn't know where they were staying since the fire. A huge relief there, but it was no time to relax their guard. She opened her address book and contact list. Time to pull in some help. If this worked out, it would protect Mildred and Tony, and Ethan and his mom, too.

When Lizzie awoke, they would have to discuss how she found the name of the killer, and where he could be. She also didn't know if her sister had ever shared Lennie's information about seeing the killer with the police. They would need to check on the man they coerced to leave his spot in the abandoned warehouse.

Okay, number one. Talk with Lizzie. Has she told anyone about Lennie. Make sure Lennie is still safe.

Two, find protection for Tyler and family and get him back in school.

Three, convince her sister it's time to involve the police. Get Detective Fury and Lizzie to cooperate. Whoah, that might be the kicker right there.

She'd regroup. What could she do without Lizzie? Hmm. I can protect the people Lizzie cared about most. And provide the two of us private time to plot. She grabbed the phone.

Agatha picked up immediately.

"This is Delia. If I recall, you hold programs for the public all morning most weekdays. Is this one of those days?" Once she heard the answer, she phrased her question as succinctly as possible. "Great. Could you use some free help, setting up, managing and cleaning up afterwards?"

Agatha's enthusiasm triggered her guilt complex. "To be honest, I have an ulterior motive. What we need is a public place full of people. I want to hide my friends in the crowd. You know Emily and Tyler. And I'm sure you'll love Mildred. As a bonus you'll get a few people who are staying with her, too."

"Delia, you're a godsend," Agatha replied. "Two of my employees called in sick this morning. I've been scrambling. How fast can you get here?"

"Thank you. We're on the way."

Delia called Mildred, tiptoed upstairs, aroused her house guests, explained why they needed total silence with Lizzie exhausted in the living room, and raced down to make a grab-and-go breakfast muffin and juice for everyone. They were out the door and picking up Mildred and her crew within fifteen minutes.

Once they arrived at the Bittersweet Herb Shop, the kids veered toward the sitting area where the programs were held. Tyler and Ethan leaned on the wall, catching up on each other's lives. Delia pulled the women aside to enlighten them, and Agatha, as to the problem and concern. "Lizzie needs some time when she knows you're protected, and she can recover from her exhaustion. We need to further our search for this guy. The man has become brutal. Loses control. Lizzie's instincts are to protect."

The women straightened their spines as if on puppet's string.

"What can we do?" Mary asked.

"You can protect yourselves here for her. There is no way he could know you're here. But if the man comes, the dozens of participants will provide distraction and protection by numbers.

Agatha pulled Delia aside once the others began setting up for the first program. She handed her a bag and said, "Here's a tea to give Lizzie when she wakes up. It's a pick me up. An energizer. She'll feel more able to continue."

Delia opened the bag and sniffed. And smiled. "It's got rosemary in it. What a pungent scent. And is that Jing Jie in there, with it's peppery, earthy aroma? Thanks so much."

"You're good. Most people don't know Jing Jie. If you get bored, feel free to come and work here, anytime."

After taking a step, she turned back. "And Delia, don't forget to include the police. Lizzie no longer has to do things alone."

"I know. Once she wakes up and explains what's been going on, we will call the police to alert them. I think she found the killer's name but not where he is."

Later that morning, when Lizzie stirred, Delia temporarily switched roles with her sister, and held firm. "We're calling Fury. We need help."

Lizzie sat up and shook out her tangled hair. The bun had disappeared while hairpins decorated the pillow Delia had slipped under her head. She looked upright but when she spoke, her brain must have still been in fuzzy dreamland. Delia stood, arms akimbo and waited for her response.

"What?"

Delia pulled her up by one elbow and marched her to a kitchen chair. "I'm making you a cup of special tea to open your eyes, and a full eggs-and-bacon, breakfast. When you wake up, I mean alert awake, we will talk about Lennie, and the killer, and us. About what we *all* will do to solve this." Her firm resolve withered as she looked at her sister, and she finished. "Okay?"

Lizzie, grabbed the tea and poured it down her throat as soon as Delia brought it over. Strong. It seemed to revive her. When finished, she rose, poured herself another cup, and said, "Okay. I'm going to clean up. Call me if I don't beat the food back here."

Delia smiled in satisfaction that her sister bowed to her wishes. She fried bacon and slid in two eggs. The bread sat in the toaster ready to brown. She steeped tea for ten minutes to maximize the benefits, and served it with honey. Delia had never seen Lizzie that tired before and felt relieved that she exhibited signs of life. She bustled about and turned with the platter of food. Ready to shout for her sister, they sidestepped a crash as Lizzie rushed in the kitchen door and plopped down at the table, timing it with the landing of the plate in front of her.

Delia sat, palms on her cheeks, and stared at Lizzie while she ate. She waited a minute but couldn't hold her curiosity back any longer. "So who's the killer?"

"It's the one the cops suspect, that Troy Ryther III. But he's missing." Not taking the time to say more, Lizzie kept eating, swung her left hand in the air, and swirled it around to prompt Delia to talk.

She started with the list she'd made. Lizzie interrupted when she mentioned Lennie.

"No, I haven't had time to talk with the kind detective, recently."

Delia didn't miss the purse of Lizzie's lips as she said 'kind,' but let it pass. She moved on to her worry about Lennie. "If he saw the killer, then the killer saw him. He might be in as much danger as Tyler."

Lizzie swallowed and said, "True, but he's secluded at your friend's house. No one followed us there."

"Then I'll just call and warn Lennie the guy is still out there. You finish eating." The conversation didn't last long before she burst out laughing, covered the phone and giggled, "He's complaining because my friend put him to work cleaning the place. Wants to know when we can break him out of there."

"Remind him about the killer and tell him to pull up his britches and quit whining."

After relaying the message she hung up and proudly said, "I temporarily took care of Tyler and his family, but you may want to find a more permanent solution." She explained about the herb shop programs and added, "Ethan, his mom, and Mildred are there, too."

The widening of her sister's eyes and the slight smile was all the thanks she needed. "Now, we're back to dealing with what happened last night. Who did you see? Who did you talk with? Did you fight or injure anyone?"

Lizzie dropped her fork and plopped hands on her waist. "What a thing to say!"

"Is that a 'no'?"

"It certainly is. I didn't hit anyone. Although the killer did. I visited the poor woman at the hospital that's all. She's under guard but I needed to see her. Hoped she would talk, but she remained unconscious."

Delia cleared the table and poured more tea. "That's it?"

"An ex-friend of the killer, who had called an ambulance for the beaten woman, stopped me outside the hospital."

A raised forehead and questioning look from Delia urged her to continue. "He's the one who told me that this Carry O'Donell was the killer's girlfriend. The killer, Troy Ryther III, got angry and pounded on her. Ryther must be back on drugs. This guy decided to break loose from the old friendship."

"And you believed him?"

"He seemed extremely anxious about her condition. I think he's had feelings for her for a long time."

Delia pulled her pad forward. "We add visiting Carry to the list and hope she can tell us who her new best friend is. Let's hope she's conscious."

Lizzie rose and looked at the clock. "Don't we have an appointment today with the school principal about returning Tyler and Ethan back to school?"

Delia hurried after, brushing down her skirt. "I'll drive. If we leave now we'll be there in plenty of time."

"If I drive we'll get there early. Would have lots of time to pester him."

Grabbing her purse by one handle and digging her keys from the bottom, Delia pushed out first. She said, "You'd just be bothering my dear friend Elizabeth Bruell, and we need her on our side."

Lizzie settled into the passenger seat without arguing—for once. "I didn't plan on hitting him or anything. I just wish he'd be more cooperative, more understanding of the needs of his students as whole people, not just wells for encyclopedic facts."

Delia produced a stupendous harrumph. As they neared the school, she said, "Remember about catching more flies with honey."

"That would be a pretty picture—seeing the old guy covered with honey."

"Please tell me you got my point."

Lizzie fidgeted in her seat, but said out loud, "Yes. I will be kind. I will be kind. Dear God, please make me be kind." She continued the mantra until they swerved into the parking lot by the school administration building. Delia smiled, hoping some of that kindness would stick with her through the meeting.

An hour later, they both walked out happy. Delia, because Lizzie hadn't hit anyone, hadn't been snide, or lost her temper.

Lizzie showed her delight in the results. "Aren't you thrilled, sis? He worked all that out without prodding. Maybe there is a human being in there."

"I'm thrilled he convinced Benjamin and his best friend to meet with social workers. And their parents. That part about Ben's parent's withholding lunch for three days so the kid would experience hunger probably helped."

They reached the car before Lizzie added. "It helped that the third bully, Chunky, the one who threw the brick, has left the school district."

"I think Elizabeth handled that, with a written threat from the principal." Delia drove, slowly with precision, while Lizzie gritted her teeth. Delia knew it, but ignored her. "Okay, Tyler and Ethan return to school tomorrow. I'll drive them. I wonder if the police have any more advice on dealing with this."

"I get the hint. We will talk with the police. Let me call the hospital first and see if Carry can talk with us. It sure would help if we could get a name for her friend. He probably knows where we can find that Troy guy. Or she might know."

A few minutes later she said, "No such luck. She's still unconscious. Do we go to the police station and hope to find Detective Fury in, or go home?"

"Dear sis, this boat is one block from the station. We go in. No jumping ship."

Detective Fury listened. No shouting, no threats of slapping Lizzie in handcuffs and hauling her away. Only some quiet humphs. Okay, and a few low growls. Grateful to him, and Lizzie, who reported all that had been going on in a quick, succinct manner, Delia stayed in the background.

Lizzie told about the witness to a man racing out of Wanton after the killing, and about hiding him safely. She also mentioned protecting the son and wife of one of the drug gang

He asked her to fill in a little, so she mentioned Lennie's name and address and asked if any police went there, could they go gentle. When the detective said he would send someone to interrogate Carry, she mentioned the poor woman was still unconscious. Lizzie stood her ground on how she found out who'd tortured the woman. She kept shaking her head no till the detective stopped asking.

Delia interrupted and said Tyler and Ethan were returning to school the next day. "Do you have any advice on how we can handle their fears? And what they say to other kids when they ask where they've been?"

"I'll tell you what. I want to meet this Ethan and his mom. Why don't I talk with the boys? We've dealt with bullying before. Maybe I can help." He stood. "Let's meet them at your house, probably less intimidating. I need to have more photos of our possible suspect made and go visit Lennie. Could I come early tomorrow morning before school and talk with the boys?"

"Of course," Delia said.

"Can I trust you to bring them all back from where they've been sequestered?"

She figured that didn't deserve an answer, but gave one anyway. "They're in plain sight at the Bittersweet Herb Shop, helping out."

"The whole crew? That Agatha's a saint."

"Well, maybe not all of them. Heather is probably coloring, and eating cookies."

"Smart kid."

CHAPTER 29

Detective Fury sat before the two boys, arms crossed in front of him on the kitchen table, more like a concerned father than a cop. Lizzie gave him credit for that, even if it resembled an interrogation tactic, honed on hardened criminals. He said, "Tyler, you're returning to school where some of the bullies still exist. Ethan, the kids might prod and pick on you when they see you return, making assumptions as to why you were gone. I know you both can handle this maturely."

She watched as he pulled in their trust with his attitude and his caring. The boys responded with respect. The detective hardly dealt with horrific criminals in this small county. She probably overreacted after another night of little sleep. She'd slipped in just before the detective, and sat sipping coffee with Delia, anchored in her chair like she'd been there for a while. Lizzie could see the anxiety as Delia's small butt squirmed in her seat, doing the ants-in-your-pants dance. There'd been no chance to reveal anything about her night-time foray. But the detective was advising the boys. She must concentrate.

"Okay, Tyler, you've learned self-defense," Fury said, with an inquisitive look at Lizzie before he returned to his point. "I hope you have learned self-confidence, and thus self-restraint with it."

Tyler pursed his lips and nodded as if locking those thoughts in his brain.

The detective said to Ethan. "Your dad is in the hands of some bad dudes. He won't be able to make careful decisions about you and your mom. Stay near people at all times. If he or his so-called friends approach you, yell like a banshee and beat feet, then call me."

Gently, Detective Fury grasped Tyler's arm. "You have two problems to deal with at once. First, the bullies in school, though they may now be restrained, *and* you know what behavior to look for."

The detective explained. "You've discussed bullying with your teachers, a social worker, and Miss Ort. You now know the various reasons why people bully. One is lack of self-confidence shown by a kid who continually acts tough. Another comes from a deeper problem in the attacker—this person has no respect for others and tries to intimidate."

Lizzie saw fear on Tyler's face while he waited for the second problem to be laid out.

The detective continued. "Second, the killer thinks you saw something that would incriminate him. He's not using common sense, but acting from fear. His burning down of your house is a bullying tactic. One to intimidate you by showing he can hurt your family."

Tyler shook off his hand and rose. "I can't just go back to school while my family is in danger."

Detective Fury sat up straight and stared Tyler down until the teen returned to his seat. "You can and you will, because that's the mature thing to do. Your friends, Miss Ort, Mrs. O'Leary and the police will protect your mom, and your's too, Ethan."

"Why can't I help?" Tyler shouted.

"Because you need a good education to take care of your family in the future. Both of you may have to do that."

Both teens nodded solemnly. They didn't seem to like it, but they got it. Lizzie could tell by the way they straightened their back and raised their heads tall. She radiated pride as if they'd been her own.

Delia rose from her spot, which she'd polished to a shine from wriggling. Lizzie held in her laugh. Delia said, "We have to leave now for school. I will pick you both up when it's over. You know the new rules, right?"

Then she gave Lizzie a stern glance. It said loud and clear for her to stay put—no leaving the house. Lizzie blinked agreement and ushered the detective out the front door.

"You didn't tell him anything, did you?" Delia accused as she strode into the kitchen later.

"Have a bad day at school, dear?" Lizzie countered. Assuming that fuming glance to be her answer, she added, "Sit. Let's talk."

Delia clenched the hot tea pot. Lizzie felt gratitude that it wasn't any part of her anatomy. "Good idea. Drink some tea and we'll discuss everything I did last night and you and I can determine what to do next, and what we need to tell your favorite detective."

Delia lowered her shoulders, took a deep breath, and agreed. She sat passively while Lizzie enumerated her useless night-time escapades. "First, I haunted the hospital, trying to visit Carry, calling to see if she'd gained consciousness, and patrolling the grounds looking for my shadow man. I can't believe I let him go without getting his name."

Delia slammed her mug on the table to gain Lizzie's attention. "Real slack of you? Couldn't you have threatened him, or strangled him to get him to talk?"

She mumbled a moment, then responded. "He slipped out of the car when I turned my head toward a noise nearby."

"So be it. Let's move on. I assume you didn't find him."

"No. And when I checked on Lennie to see how he was, I thought he would bite off my head in disgust. Couldn't believe I sicced the cops on him."

"How did you see Lennie? I'm sure my friend doesn't allow night visitors."

A moue escaped her lips before she outright cackled. "I didn't exactly walk in the front door. And Lennie was awake. His aches keep him half-conscious all night. He told me so."

Delia poured them both another cup of tea. "Did he tell you more?"

"Yeah. Our friendly cop brought him pictures of Troy, and Lennie gave an absolutely positive identification of the guy who ran by him that night."

"Did you tell Detective Fury what Carry's friend said, that Troy killed the dealer?"

"No. Fury had the photo because Troy was the uncle of the kid who died of an overdose. He was a suspect. But it confirms he was probably the killer."

Delia jumped up. "Isn't that it, then? Didn't Detective Fury go arrest the guy?"

"Sit. Just because he saw Troy run from the ole Wanton, and he beat Carry, doesn't prove he killed the drug dealer. Remember, the only guy that saw him do it, can't be found."

Delia fell back into the seat so fast it creaked from the strain. She dropped her head in her hands. "Now what?"

"Let's ask your detective. We'll put it number one on our list of questions." Lizzie took pity on her sister, who wasn't used to dealing with all this stuff—drugs, beatings, murder, killers. Not the normal activity for an herbalist. She ached, herself, from lack of sleep again, though she encountered nothing dangerous last night. Unless one counted the cop who hung around the Wanton shell of past industry resembling, well, a cop. She'd seen him but he hadn't seen her. Maybe that should be number two on the Fury list. Advise on reconnaissance. That should go over great.

But the shadow, the witness she had pursued, blended seamlessly into the night, if there at all, and she never found him. Or the answers she sought.

Still, she attempted to cheer Delia up. Offered her a cookie. "Here dear, you need perking up. Have one of these. They're homemade, and the sugar will do you good."

Delia did smile at that. "I made them and used stevia as the sweetener." Lizzie shrugged and savored the cookie anyway. She tried to explain where she stood in her current life with its new challenges, and how that applied to recent events. Her sister radiated concerned.

Lizzie said, "I want you to know I've figured out the connection between the deadly skills I learned and lived with most of my life, and my new resolve to serve God. I think he's telling me that I can use my skills, with maybe a bit of refinement, to help people in need. Like Tyler, and teens struggling with life questions. And drugs."

Delia swallowed to speak, though her entire face beamed, signaling her thoughts. "I'm delighted. I feared you'd be unhappy and leave."

"Oh no. Never that. I wish I'd known what you were thinking. But I'm good now. We have a killer to catch. The rest will come later."

Delia delivered the entire platter of cookies to the table. "Let's get cracking. Dave is delivering the moms back here by the time school gets out." She started her list with categories: What do we know? What do we need to find out?

The what do we know went quick. Not much there. But they made a list. Main item—we know who the killer is. She scribbled one more as she spoke, "We have a witness to Troy's presence in the vicinity."

They began to work on the clues. They added information they'd scrounged from the police. It appeared mostly in the negative. The BOLO alert garnered them nothing. No sightings, no arrests. *That* they *would* have heard.

Lizzie said, "Carry knows where Troy lives but can't talk. Delia, would you keep continual tabs on that? Beg, plead, or sneak in to ask her if she knows where he is, or an address of where he lived until the murder."

Lizzie wrote that down, placing Delia's name next to it while her sister poured tea, then placed a steaming mug in front of her.

Instantly, Lizzie jumped up. "Ahh. I know. We find out where Carry was when the ambulance came. Our shadow man said out on the lawn. I'll go see Sergeant Torkless. Get that address, and Troy's if they differ. I haven't bothered the sergeant lately." She slugged down the tea, knowing she might need the caffeine before the days end. "Call me the instant you get anything. We'll meet back here by three."

Delia sighed loud enough for Lizzie to hear. As she closed the door she heard her sister's whispered plea. *"Lizzie's barely had any sleep and is heading out again, God. Please watch her back today."*

With Delia and God protecting her back, Lizzie once again gathered the strength she'd need to confront the unknown, but she added her own entreaty. *Help me to do the right thing. God. Better yet, help me to* know *the right thing. This guy scares me.* With that, she whipped the car past town to the police station.

Great, she found Torkless in, and alone without Fury. She took that as a good sign and gave God a thumbs up. She didn't have to wheedle to get the location where they'd found Carry. As she bolted out the door she waved her thumbs up in the air again, this time startling a couple of policemen coming on shift. Fortunately, they didn't know her, and probably just wrote it off as one more crazy old lady.

Part way to the spot, she remembered about turning over a new leaf, and called her sister with the address. "I'm headed there now."

"That matches what I just found out at the hospital. It's Carry's home. I called the number the hospital gave me and talked with her roommate. She said Carry'd been living with her boyfriend on and off for months, complaining that Troy became erratic lately. The roommate wasn't home when Carry took her beating. She's off to the hospital now."

Lizzie thanked her as she eased back into traffic. "Okay. I'm still going to drive by, scope things out."

"He's not there, dear. The cops hung around for a day. Nothing."

"Still, a hunch. Can't talk and drive. I'll be there in a minute, then hopefully, back home."

A shadowed figure emerged an hour later as she drifted around the house for the third time. The edges sharpened into a distinctly taller man than before. Troy Ryther III.

Lizzie's right hand snuggled in her pocket, gripping the revolver. Ryther didn't charge toward her. He took a step, stumbled and fell onto the grass where Carry's blood had mingled with the blades, soaking the earth.

He spoke out loud but more like he talked to himself, puzzled. "I left her here. What happened? Where'd she go? Is this blood?" He wiped his nose to quell the continual drip.

Lizzie said, "You beat her severely, days ago."

He looked up and saw her. He shouted. "No!" Then sobbed. And continued to blubber, incoherently.

She wrestled between pity and anger. The throes of withdrawal shook him. Pity came from watching his pain. Yet anger that he'd killed overruled her compassion.

The cloudy damp day morphed into a sunny one, with a beam of light shining onto Troy. Highlighting the ending, she thought. This must be it. Time to call the police. She reached into her left pocket for the cell phone when her peripheral vision caught a slight movement to their right. Troy hadn't moved, but he wouldn't notice anything, living in his own world of self-guilt. Her right hand kept its steady grip on the revolver. What now?

It was the third one in the trio of attackers from behind the bar. The one named Erne. The one she knifed. He appeared fine, but then she didn't sling the knife to kill. Lethal required necessity. This guy didn't fit. Her head rose slow, her sight moving from Troy, practically prostrate on the ground, to the newer threat.

He advanced. "Ahh. I've been looking for you. I owe you one."

He looked at her left pocket as she wiggled her fingers.

She gripped the revolver tight in her right hand but kept it hidden.

He motioned to her left pocket and said, "Pull that hand out, nice and steady. And empty. No knifing me today."

She'd already seen the gun in his hand and followed his directions. Opened her fist wide to to reveal its emptiness. *Thank you God for standing me at the correct angle to this guy.* She waited for the perfect second. That's all she would need. Troy moaned. Knife guy shot.

Her aim was straight and true. His, not so good.

Her first shot sent his gun flying. The new enemy cradled his hand and backpedaled to flee. She didn't want to chase him. The second shot to his leg prevented that. He shouted. And crumbled.

That's when she speed dialed Fury.

CHAPTER 30

"You want this Ryther guy, you come get him now."

Detective Fury asked, "Lizzie, you okay?"

"Yes. Why shouldn't I be?"

She heard shouting in the background, and the irregular pitch of the detective's voice, as he spoke away from the phone.

"What's happening?"

His voice steadied as if he stopped running. "Didn't you say you had the killer?"

"Yeah, but we don't need the whole department over here. That's why I called you. You need two pairs of cuffs. You know, two guys, four hands."

The pitch of his voice changed again. "Are you in danger?"

"No. But Troy Ryther might be if he doesn't stop sniveling."

"Don't you dare touch the guy."

"I promise. I've never harmed the weak. And killer or not, this guy counts."

"And the other two hands belong to . . . .?"

She peered down at knife guy and noticed he'd stopped whining, though looking around furtively, maybe pondering escape. "Hold on a minute, detective."

She frisked knife guy and withdrew the favored knife and a small one from his boot. "You're his friend named Erne, right?"

He jerked his head downward, then over to his injured thigh. And ratcheted up the moaning.

She grimaced, more at the sound than the injury. "Prop the injured leg up on top of the other one and you might be able to save it. Keep it still. The bandage I made merely stanches the bleeding. It's not a cure. The bullet's still there."

She heard Fury shouting over the phone. "Lizzie, what's going on? What bullet?"

"Oh, the other one, you know, with the other hands that you were just asking about. His name is Erne. I shot his leg. Add an ambulance to the order. Speed would be good. Speaking of hands, mine are full." She rattled off the address, then disconnected.

Detective Fury beat the ambulance there. She didn't question how. The other policemen arrived a few seconds later and stood near the street, ready. Fury approached. Slow. Calm. Wary. "What do we have here?"

She pointed to Erne. "He needs an ambulance. His shot zinged my ear, but landed in that tree. I fired back." She pointed behind her, then added, "Mine didn't miss."

The paramedics arrived, secured Erne, and carried him away. Fury walked a few steps with instructions then returned to Lizzie and the guy sitting on the ground, now guarded by a fellow officer. The paramedics had checked him over and said he had no injuries. Fury touched his arm.

Troy Ryther III looked up. "I don't remember hitting her. Maybe I took too much stuff. All I want is to feel the numbness. That dealer shoulda been my best friend. But for him to kill my nephew. I couldn't live with that. Guess I couldn't live with killing a guy, either."

He blubbered more as the detective pulled him up as gently as possible. Then Ryther continued his rant. "Craved the drug again. Consequences didn't matter any more. And now Carry's gone." His head hung low as they walked away. Fury cuffed him as they got to the squad car.

He approached her once the killer was ensconced in the car. She held her hands up. The left hand held two knives. "I didn't touch him."

Fury bagged the knives. He didn't have to ask which pocket held her gun. It had a bullet hole in it.

"You got a bag? My fingerprints are all over it. You want me to pull it out?"

He fumbled with the bag, trying to open it, and mumbled. "Mm hmm."

His eyebrows reached for his hair line. "I'm hoping that bullet came out and not in. You *are* okay?"

Concern still marred his brow when he heard her moan.

"I feel defeated at the moment. There were no winners here. On the other hand, Tyler and Ethan's families can now begin a safe, new life. God was with me here. These men are alive, and I'm fine."

"Good to hear."

"I will get my gun back, right?"

"Ma'am, I'll put it in a locker with a note in it to process any weapons with due speed and return."

He brightened at her laugh, and continued, "Sometimes wars are fought without most weapons. You've still won this one. With the families you protected. The teens you'll help with your center. The babies born to young adults who will learn from you that drugs are not a way of life. The babies—that could have entered the world addicted—they will be clean and healthy. Those are the battles you have won, and will win."

Lizzie wrapped her arm through his as he provided escort to her car. She opened her door. "You did notice I called you and didn't do anything on my own once I found him."

His smile included his whole face, though his lips twitched. "I noticed. Welcome to town, Lizzie Ort."

"And to town I must go. Delia won't forgive me if I'm not home when Tyler and Ethan arrive. I'll wait to tell her what happened until I get there. Is there an official version I should tell her?"

"You would withhold information from your sister if I told you to?"

She stopped walking. "To be honest with you, no. But I would tell her which version she could admit knowing."

He urged her forward, laughing. "Let's get you on your way. If you want to keep this quiet you should probably change skirts before you see too many people. Some might not recognize a bullet hole, but you never know."

She eased into her car, still facing the detective. "One question. Would you find out how Troy and his friends knew I would be at the shack behind the bar the night they attempted to beat me? I wondered if the dealer with the scarred face set me up."

"No problem. We have many questions for Troy and his friend once they stop whining."

As she swung forward he noticed the blood on her left ear. "Whoa. What happened here? I thought you meant 'zinged by your ear, not through it. You should have asked the paramedic to take a look."

"The bullet barely skimmed me. I'm getting old and didn't move fast enough. I'll slap an antiseptic on it when I get home."

She closed the door and took off, driving sedately to the corner. First, get back home and tell Delia the news. Relief flowed through her veins like a drug, softening the surrounding muscles, and throughout her body.

It was over. Everyone safe.

Life could begin anew. My head feels lighter. She careened into their driveway, and stopped the car. Until now, the constant tension *was* life. And then the joy coursed through again. The ending of this scare on Tyler liberated her. And she had much to do. She hopped out of the car. Delia awaited, and the teen center plans could move full throttle now. She'd heard yesterday that she could inspect the building any time. She needed a manager, volunteers, and publicity. A full life.

Delia shrieked at the news. Then the bleeding ear caught her attention and deflated excitement.

Lizzie pulled her sister into a hug. "It's okay. The bullet whispered by me."

Delia snorted. "That weren't no whisper. More like a shout with a kick." She dragged Lizzie into the bathroom. "Sit."

While she cleaned and anointed the wound with her homemade salve, Lizzie gave her details and added the part about Erne shooting at her. Delia's hand jerked but caught the teetering tin of beeswax, coconut oil, and essential herbs.

Lizzie reached for her arm. "Delia. I am okay. This is nothing."

Delia shuddered and pulled out a bandage. Lizzie recoiled. "No way. It's a scratch. And you fixed it."

They marched into the living room and plopped onto the sofa. Lizzie said, "Now you sit and I'll tell you the rest." And she did.

"The cops are working their way through this drug cartel and I think with all the upcoming arrests, Ethan and his mom will be fine. It's time to find homes for everyone. You've already accomplished an amazing feat getting Emily and Mary jobs."

Delia had received some news. "A guy who called himself the Shadow handed me this note addressed to you. Said it came from a friend."

Lizzie ripped it open and read aloud. "I am strong enough to leave. My O'Donnell name comes from the Irish 'Domhnall' which means ruler of the world. My family in Ireland is part of that powerful history. I am returning home and taking my friend with me. He's kept me alive more than once. Now it's my turn to protect him. I heard you talking to me often, though I couldn't speak. When I awoke I asked the nurses who you were. Thank you for caring about me."

It was signed, "Carry."

Lizzie reminded Delia that Carry O'Donnell, Troy's ex-girlfriend, was helped by Troy's ex-childhood friend, the one she called 'The Shadow.'

"Why did you call him that?"

"When the three guys approached me, with Troy in the middle, this man was in the shadows, and never moved to harm me. He didn't exactly introduce himself."

Lizzie snatched her keys off the table. "That's wonderful news, But there's much yet to do. And the teen center. You can't imagine how thrilled I am at the progress we're making." She laughed, then bounced up. "I am relieved. And excited. Let me pick up the boys. I can't wait to tell them."

Delia smiled, watching her sister bubbling up with joy. "Go fetch them." She jumped up herself, then chased after Lizzie. "And watch the speed limit."

When the boys bounded into the car they gave a quick teacher report. Tyler griped about the man he called the nasty one, and they both praised their favorite, Mrs. McDonegal in math. Lizzie swiveled to them in the back seat, revealing her beaming face and grin. "It's over."

They pestered her with questions, and she finally drove Ethan home to Mildred's. Their conversation had taken longer than expected and she raced down the back roads with energy having no release except speed.

Tyler sat quiet, showing enthusiasm when his mom and Heather arrived a minute later. After a few words, he and Heather hugged and jumped up and down as a unit.

After dinner Lizzie checked that Tyler had finished his homework and invited him to visit the teen center building, to help make plans for clean up and an open house. He mumbled sure and they sped off.

Tyler didn't said a word on the drive over. She saw in the rearview mirror that his lips were squeezed so tight they could have been sewn shut. His head hung low and he massaged his temples with one hand. The other clenched the seatbelt as if he feared it might disappear.

"Hey, Ty, what's the matter?"

He raised his head, his eyes looking straight forward. "Nothing, ma'am."

"Tyler?" She'd drawn out his name, ending on a low note.

He looked at her then. His eyes wide in a white face. "You know I'll be eternally grateful for all you've done for me."

She sensed a 'but' still to come and waited.

He sighed. "But I thought you saved me to live a long and healthy life. I want to help others in some way. And the job you gave me is ideal for that. Of course, the money doesn't hurt right now."

She waited. Decided after a minute to prompt him. "But what?"

"I can't help people if I'm dead, or in a full body cast. Did you know you went through two stop signs in the few blocks we've gone. Two. And twice cars traveling legitimately through the intercession missed creaming me by seconds."

"Oh. That."

This time he waited. Looked like he tied up his tongue saying what he did, and couldn't speak if he wanted to. Kind of brave of him, she thought. Pointing out a lion's flaws. Though I'd like to think of myself as graceful as a gazelle.

But he eventually made it. A strangled sound erupted, then he said. "You can't drive like that. Too dangerous."

She shrugged. "My sense of time is excellent. I knew we could clear the intersection before they arrived."

"But they don't know that. You could have caused them to crash trying to avoid you."

"Oh. They teach you that in driving lessons?" She should have swallowed those words before she said them, but realized they came from her shame. That a boy too young to drive, found her reckless.

The snarky comment must have brought up his ire. She could see his metaphorical feathers ruffle up before he struck. "I could report you, ya know."

"You mean to my dear friend Detective Fury?"

"Ha! Anyone with a brain knows he's your enemy. You fight like verbal tigers."

She drove deftly into the youth center parking lot. "Nice turn of phrase. I'm putting you in charge of naming this center. Not too frou-frou."

He leapt out of the car and ran over to her side before her legs hit the ground. This time, he had no trouble looking her straight in the eye. "You mean it? I can really name the teen center? Wow."

He tore off, leaving her in the flying dust of the dirt parking lot. As he neared the door, he halted. Swung around. Frown lines marred his brow. "What's frou-frou?"

CHAPTER 31

With murder no longer on the agenda, Lizzie awaited a daily routine. Instead, chaos reigned this Saturday afternoon. She sat on a folding chair in the office with a window wall facing the largest recreation room. Teens scurried around, laughing, talking, and threatening each other with paint brush duels. Only once did they get away with paint on their brushes during *that* game. She may look old, but they soon learned to judge tolerance by other means.

The teen center echoed with enough voices that if someone walked in they might not know it hadn't opened yet. She didn't see Tyler. Adrenalin pumped through her for a second until she remembered the danger was gone. Still, she headed out of the office to wander around and find him. Paper work wasn't for her. As soon as there was more funding, hiring an office manager would soar to the top of her list. Ugh. Lists.

Dear Delia stood firm when asked to run the office. She'd said, "Absolutely not. I need to tend my herbs during the day, and create my salves and lotions at night. And don't forget the herbal teas. You and many others find those comforting."

It wasn't her words so much as the passion Lizzie saw in her eyes. She backed down. Thankfully, Delia kept it between the two of them. She didn't need a reputation around the teen center for getting soft.

The newest volunteer, who she saw on the sidelines earlier, ran toward Lizzie with Jenny Lyn pushing behind him. Lizzie straightened her spine and peered down her nose, chin tucked in.

They both halted instantly. She tilted her head toward Jenny Lyn. "Wait your turn dear."

"But . . ." Jenny Lyn held her tongue.

Lizzie pursed her lips and turned to the young lad. "And what is your name?"

"Josef, ma'am. A cop's lookin' for ya. The big guy knocked on the door. But we didn't unlock it because you said don't let no one in."

"Thank you, Josef." She made a mental note to work with him on his confidence. Maybe the police could provide some self-defense classes. That often helped develop personal pride and confidence.

She marched down the hall, laughing as she pictured Detective Fury's face at being locked out. Fortunately, he appeared in a good mood as she ushered him in. He seemed happy to see she'd enforced some rules before they'd even opened the doors. He moved forward slowly, his head swiveling to take in the renovated room.

"Wow! Teen power. I'll keep it in mind when my house needs painting."

"You couldn't afford them. Their rate is high. Delia's just about out of cookies."

They both chuckled and worked their way to her office. He shut the door, closing off her laughter. "Everything's okay. I wanted to talk with you about details of the case. Thought it would be a good idea to keep it private."

She gestured him to a chair and propped herself on the edge of the desk.

He began. "I wanted to thank you for sending us to Lennie. With his identification of the photo, we knew to seek out Todd once more. We were ready to grab him when he disappeared, again." He glared at her. "That night he attacked Carry O'Donnell?"

"I didn't see him do it." Lizzie shrugged her shoulders. She didn't do the ruffled hen well, so didn't try.

He held up his hands. "I know. I know. But I promised I'd give you an update. The DEA was called in and helped round up as many of the organization they could find. From the way you described your Bulbous Man, I think they got him, too."

He stretched out in the chair, the lines in his face hinting at exhaustion. "We even found Verge Innis. In a homeless shelter. He'd just gotten out of the hospital and could barely walk. That's one reason I came to see you now. We called Mary, and she will have nothing to do with him. She wants a divorce. Since she has no money, I found someone decent to help her. She's safe now, though. He'll be in jail for a long time."

Lizzie smile accompanied her heartfelt thank you. "What happened with the drug shipment? Did they find it?"

"Innis actually tried to help with that, but his info was outdated. The one you nicknamed Torpedo gave up what the DEA needed and they arrived just in time."

She sighed in relief and stretched out some kinks, herself. "Thank God." She added, "One more question, for now. Why was Jamison in the warehouse if the man with the scar was the known dealer at Wanton?"

"Damien, the one everyone described as the guy with the scar, was just the sidewalk apothecary, working under Jamison, both layers beneath the local dealer, who you helped them capture on Morton Street. Jamison came to meet Damien—probably to check on him. Apparently, he nosed around at random. Rare that he delivered drugs himself. We don't know why he carried them in this case. Damien surmised that when he came looking for him, he may have stopped one room too soon."

Lizzie rose from the desk and walked to the window, disturbed by the freedom drug dealers had to move supplies around at will. Fury probably felt the same but couldn't legally do much. At one time, she could, and would have. This time, she needed to resolve the issue from the teen center end, strengthening those susceptible to say "No" to drugs. She turned back to the detective.

He continued, "We think Troy must have been tracking him for a while. Figured the old warehouse would be a good place to confront him. Not sure. Troy has been in and out of clarity. Damien told us that when he heard the shouting he got up and checked. He made it quite clear he saw two men tear away. He knew Jamison was dead. He took off, too. Oh, and Damien said he was forced to mention you by Troy's right-hand man when they both came by looking for drugs."

"Ahh. Could he identify Troy?"

"Yes, a positive identification. It helps. Though Troy confessed, his mental state is iffy. Too bad your friend who saw it happen disappeared, but we're still on safe ground."

She grinned. "Honest, just one more question. How did you arrive so quickly when I called?"

His forehead rose, probably in disbelief that she would ever stop asking questions, but he answered, "Carry woke and sent us over to where he'd been staying. She said he admitted to Jamison's killing while he was beating her. We were on our way there when you called us. It's just around the corner."

Lizzie nodded. "I called you as soon as I knew for sure."

"Sooner would have been more cooperative."

"Point noted."

"I guess I made *my* point, then."

Perturbed for a second, she hesitated. "All the rushing around, trying to find the killer and stop him from harming Tyler and others. And he fell apart and practically turned himself in. It lacks triumph, the feeling of a job well done."

He stood to leave. "Justice comes in many forms. This one was a gift."

He studied the flurry of teens cleaning up the work gear. "It's nice to see the kids without a gaggle of Protectors surrounding them."

She sighed in enjoyment as she watched them too. The teen center coming to fruition before her eyes. "What do you mean, protectors?"

"That squad of ladies Delia had surrounding Tyler and Ethan wherever they went. The high school had so many volunteer teacher aids come in the day before your boys returned to school they didn't know where to place them all."

"God bless Delia."

"Looks like He's been watching over you, too. Thanks for your help."

He tipped his invisible hat like a cowboy and left.

CHAPTER 32

Fury walked away and for once she didn't grind her teeth. Progress. She even smiled, until it hit her. She never found Tyler. She stepped out again. Despite the locked building, she still worried about him. She found him huddled up with Ethan in a back office, paper on the desk and pencil in hand, scribbling furiously. They installed an old computer in some of the rooms for students, but he obviously wasn't used to having one.

One more item for her mental list. Find a computer tutor. It reminded her to hang a list of rules on usage, after she devised what it should contain. The kids might chop off her head if she said no games would be allowed. The center provided computers, but mostly for homework. Donations poured in, but what they could really use was a financial backer. One more item for the list.

She stood in the shadow of the hall and watched Tyler. Maybe she could have a games night. Many of the kids had tablets and laptops now, at least some of the more privileged ones. She'd have to work out a way to make the odds equal across the broad financial spectrum.

Tyler glanced up. Ethan followed the look. Both appeared excited and not unhappy she'd found them. Good. "What's happening guys?"

They both burst out with loud guffaws. Tyler took charge, saying to Ethan in an amused but firm voice. "I don't think she's asking for drugs, do you?"

Ethan snickered and shook his head as Tyler rose and pulled a chair to the desk for Lizzie to sit down.

"So why the laughter?"

Ethan pointed to his partner. "He'll explain."

Tyler gathered his papers and straightened his spine, ready to give his speech. "I'll start from the beginning. We were working on the name for the teen center. You said I could do that, right?"

Lizzie smiled. "Of course." She didn't have to say that she'd forgotten all about it. Thank heavens the boy was a responsible person and took it to heart."

"We laughed because we hoped you would consider the name, What's Happenin' for the center. It means much more than just the, what do you call it? Oh, the literal question. It also stands for good things."

Tyler ruffled the pages till he found the one he wanted. "Like a cool, awesome place. It was also a code used to ask a drug dealer if he can provide narcotics."

Lizzie jolted in her chair on that one. "Are you sure we want to remind people openly about that? Would they think we have drugs?"

Tyler said, "That's why we laughed when you walked in.We'd just been talking about using What's Happenin' for the center name. If we use that name and they come here for drugs, we can offer some of your herb concoctions, instead. Miss Agatha explained how helpful they can be."

He continued. "I had tons of ideas. Ethan helped. Like the Hope Scores Teen Center, or Teens Conquer Center. They didn't sound right. We wanted something that reflects all we'll do here, but the mood, too. The hope and success if it helps teens. Maybe The Vault. For safety?"

She didn't know what to say. Speechlessness for her a rare occurrence, yet his thought processes impressed her. He'd changed in the few weeks she'd known him. Maybe it was the detox at the hospital, or more likely the healthy food and support from trained professionals and friends. Maybe it was the more stable, though temporary home base. She'd noticed a great improvement when his mother and sister moved in with them—the whole family together, and safe. She adored this kid. He'd stopped talking. Looked at her with worry lines etching his face. She managed a swallow and a clear voice. "Tyler, I am so proud of you. You understand what I want to do here. And have some great ideas."

He beamed. "We see it as a place to help strengthen everything about a person, not just the body. It can help us learn, and be strong— you know—like inside. We don't want kids to feel locked up if we name it The Vault, just safe around friends having fun."

Ethan piped up. "And food. Don't forget the food."

Tyler rolled his eyes. "And food. But also for guidance. And you said there would be rehab support."

Ethan kept moving his head up and down in agreement. "Tell her the other choices."

"We considered Teen Zone. Tried Youth Prevails. Didn't like them. Maybe we could work with Hideout, if you don't like The Vault. I guess What's Happenin.'is out. What do you think?"

Lizzie swallowed roughly again. "Wow!"

She placed her hands down on the desk. "You've thought of everything. I'm amazed."

He lowered his head and his eyelids dropped. Shyness stopped him for a brief moment. But he continued. "We want this center to be a haven. A healthy place. For that you need food and water." He grinned. "We'll have to find some snack food and drinks."

Ethan nodded vigorously.

She laughed. "I get it. We'll put it in the budget."

Tyler rushed on. "The Vault could mean a shelter and a place to raise the young."

He looked up. "I took that to mean us teenagers. Those without safe homes are the most in need, I think."

She knew he thought of Tony, as did she. Orphaned and out on the streets, but so many children had parents who wouldn't or couldn't take care of them. She said, "The Vault really caught my attention, because it does convey the safety issue, and connotes a private place for teens."

Tyler explained. "It fits what the adult advisors and volunteers said at that meeting. Activities at the Vault could, you know, guide them through problems. Make life easier for them."

Ethan faced Lizzie. "That's like protection, right, like a vault does for important things?"

This time Lizzie broke down, the tears staying in her eyes but visible. She cleared her throat, then said, "I hope you have all that written down. If not, do it right away for our brochure. And as much as I like What's Happenin,' we probably need something more conservative. I do fear repercussions because of the hidden meanings behind the term. Use What's Happenin' as a subtitle high up, if you want. You could say something like, 'The Vault,' and then underneath, 'Where it's happenin'. And it's free.' Think seriously about that. You have a day to work on it."

They stood, too. Not sure what came next. She hugged Tyler. Then placed an arm around Ethan to include him, keeping her gaze on Tyler. "Lad, what would you think about being assistant manager?"

His eyes widened and his head lowered slowly, like in uncertain agreement.

She said. School and homework first. Then work here in the evenings."

She looked at Ethan. "I'm putting you in charge of the gaming program. Same rules apply."

They both stared at her. Then whooped up and down.

She let them experience their joy for a moment. "There's a board meeting tomorrow. Tyler, bring your ideas and thoughts on the center. Let's get that name approved. Ethan, you have a week to develop a plan to include limited gaming. We can meet next week."

She left. Walked part way down the hall. Stopped. And smiled till her facial wrinkles almost split. The whooping and shouting had begun again.

CHAPTER 33

Delia walked in, arm-in-arm with a white-haired man. She pointed out renovations and he looked around, wreathed in smiles. Lizzie watched and wondered. Where had he come from? Delia's face brightened at his every word.

Delia mentioned cookie-paid labor. Lizzie approached while he laughed. When Delia saw her she rushed right over, pulling the gentleman behind her, though he appeared quite willing to follow wherever she led. "Lizzie, Lizzie, this is the nice gentleman who inquired as to my welfare when I almost ran into him because of the deer episode. His name is Aaron Alexander Ballard."

With a puzzled frown, Lizzie extended her hand. "Nice to meet you."

The man held her hand in both of his and said, "She's told me so much about your teen center. I'm enthralled. Just what this area needs."

Her frown disappeared, but the puzzlement remained. Until he said, "I would like to discuss a fund of sorts for your cause."

She tucked one arm through Delia's and the other through Ballard's elbow, crooked for her benefit. Her new best friend. "Please, let's sit in my office. We can watch the paint brush duels safely from there—and learn more about your proposal."

Delia said, "I'd promised to call him and did this afternoon. He owns apartment buildings near us, so I thought I'd call, thinking of Mary and Emily needing homes. We had an enjoyable afternoon at tea."

Ballard settled into the metal folding chair with all the aplomb of sitting in an antique Chippendale side chair.

Delia continued, "Mr. Ballard is a long-standing contributor to the community in so many ways. He not only has apartments, or homes, available for Mary and Emily's families, but he would like to help the teen center."

A half-hour later, Lizzie beamed, shaking his hand in gratitude. His proposal of a generous fund, would provide for many amenities, and his offer of a paid qualified manager almost caused her to jump and shout, replicating the teens' exuberance.

Josef interrupted with a firm rhythmic knock on the door. She motioned him in. "Sorry, ma'am, I was asked to remind you of the meeting you called. Everyone is waiting."

She thanked him, then Mr. Ballard. "Let's get the paperwork started as soon as possible please. For now, we'll keep it quiet." They all nodded and rose

No time to relish her triumph. Not with those expectant faces outside the room. She would make the planned announcement. Two of the local businessmen worked a deal with the school over some old buses. The teens would be thrilled.

"Hey kids. We're acquiring two old buses to do shuttles for teens who are beyond walking distance. Mostly, I wanted the buses to deliver teens to their homes at night, even the ones nearby."

A couple of the teens, Ethan among them, emitted moans and groans.

"What's that all about? You want to walk? I haven't seen too much athletic drive around here. I practically have to bribe you to shoot a few hoops."

Josef, the slight, quiet, one gently shoved Ethan forward. "You explain."

Ethan wiggled his way back to the line of teens that had gathered when they heard the conversation. They'd all come nearer to Lizzie when she'd begun to talk, but none had exactly huddled at her knee in devoted admiration. With the age gap, camaraderie would take time.

They'd all made great progress in the last two weeks. Adult volunteers talked with the kids, discussed programs, and made endless notes. Many joined in to prep the center for opening. The kids had swept and scrubbed, and painted anything that would hold a new coat. Only one week till the big day. She thought they'd be thrilled about the buses.

Since Ethan groaned the loudest, she pointed to him. "Please explain your reluctance to use the buses? You live a few miles away. Why wouldn't you want a ride?"

The young guy whispered loudly in Ethan's ear, "You can't tell her. She's too old to understand."

Lizzie decided to catch him in the corner soon while she explained that all old people weren't deaf. But she held off, since he gave her the first clue to what bothered the kids. She waited to see if Ethan could find the words. Should she let him off the hook and give him a lead to get started? Just then he mumbled.

"What was that?"

He spoke louder, then turned beet red when he realized the whole room could hear. "Sometimes the girls let us put our arms over their shoulders if we have to walk home in the dark."

"Admittedly, now that our killer is behind bars, we will be safer out there, but the drug problem is still a monumental concern, right there on our own streets, as rural as they may seem to some."

They all hung their heads this time, murmuring acknowledgment.

"We'll work diligently to deal with the prescription drug problem around here. And you've all agreed to help, and have pledged to stay off drugs yourselves. That doesn't make us safe."

They started to filter away. She spoke loudly, to stop them. "I will, however, see that the lights are off in the bus, and ask the drivers to take their time, okay?"

Pumped arms in the air and gleeful shouts accompanied her announcement. She hid a grin as she walked back to the office. For complex teens, sometimes they were so easy.

Tyler trotted up behind her and asked if he could have a word.

She turned, smiling. "You have a girlfriend, too? Already? Can I throw a party or should we be discreet about it?"

"Ma'am, that's not what I wanted to talk about." He mumbled

about her driving the buses, having recently experienced another road trip with her. Tyler cleared his throat and asked with wariness. "You have designated drivers for the buses?"

"Not yet." Seeing his frown, she decided to relieve his concern, and added, "Tyler, I promise I won't ever drive the shuttle buses—at least until I get my driver's license."

The moan didn't escape her hearing, but delight in her new life goal helped her ignore it. She opened the office door and scanned the room, the papers carelessly strewn on the desk. Alarmed, alert. No one there. Old habits die hard. This time she had caused the mess. Once she realized that, the room appeared more cheerful.

She still needed a manager but for now, she had the help she needed. *Thank you God. You're a good partner. And yeah, I will take the darn driving test.*

Did you enjoy *The Way Out?*

**Please leave a review at
Amazon.com , Goodreads.com, or your favorite review site.**

**Want to know when I release new books? Free information on handwriting analysis and herbs? Or a free short story?
Join my mailing list at
www.judymehl.com**

*Also find Judith Mehl's Kat Everitt mystery series at
www.judymehl.com*

www.ingramcontent.com/pod-product-compliance
Lightning Source LLC
Chambersburg PA
CBHW070921180626
46817CB00003B/1154

* 9 780986 276675 *